COP: A Novel

DANIEL B. SILVER

authorHOUSE®

AuthorHouse™ LLC
1663 Liberty Drive
Bloomington, IN 47403
www.authorhouse.com
Phone: 1-800-839-8640

This is a work of fiction. All of the characters, names, incidents, organizations, and dialogue in this novel are either the products of the author's imagination or are used fictitiously.

Published by AuthorHouse 06/05/2014

ISBN: 978-1-4969-1448-4 (sc)
ISBN: 978-1-4969-1447-7 (e)

"For Bryan, Nick and Isaac"

CHAPTER 1

When I pass by, all the people say, "Just another guy on the lost highway."
—Hank Williams, "Lost Highway"

There are a few distinct and differing options available to a government employee who wears a star, a shield, or a badge on his or her chest when dealing with a drunken waste of space that has just let loose upon the officer's skin a vile amalgamation of mucous, saliva and—in some extreme cases—blood.

Today, this situation presents itself while the officer is seated in a marked patrol vehicle: a Crown Victoria with a black and white paint job delineated between the front and rear seats by a combination of clear plastic and wire mesh.

By the way: for purposes of this demonstration, *you* are the officer in question.

In many modern patrol vehicles, the wire mesh portion of the noted delineator is sparse enough to allow the aforementioned "loogie" to pass through it. Said loogie is often propelled by a warm burst of metabolizing alcohol-scented breath toward the back of one's cropped

1

---

head, down the back of one's neck, past the wool uniform shirt's collar, and into the humid microclimate that exists between the officer's naked back, your naked back, the plain cotton undershirt, and the department issued ballistic vest.

And I'll pause briefly to note that when I first ran aground of this scenario, this officer's back, my back, was recently, permanently marked with a traditional intra-dermal design involving a large eagle, two cannons, three nautical stars and a banner bearing the text: *"Words without thoughts never to heaven go."* The tattoo hadn't fully healed yet, which meant that the revolting matter running across it had a fighting chance of making its way into my bloodstream. This—as you may have already guessed—pissed me off. I really didn't need anyone else's ailments. I had enough of my own.

Anyhow, *your* options are as follows:

1. Tell your partner—the similarly attired person seated next to you, who is fortunate enough to be driving the patrol vehicle and not the front passenger because that puts said partner in front of the plastic portion of said divider, which effectively protects him or her from what is currently being propelled at the back of your head—to accelerate. Pick up the vehicle's onboard radio microphone, or just use the mic attached to your shoulder, to broadcast that the custody is currently spitting on you. Then, have your partner stop the vehicle, both of you get out, remove the prisoner, and place a *spitter*—a

thin hood that looks like a really loose nylon stocking—over the lovely arrestee's head.

This tactic is reliant upon your department to actually stock and train you ad nauseam how to use spitters. Because a permeable, breathable nylon bag with a drawstring can somehow lead to in-custody deaths, which in turn lead to expensive lawsuits, which in turn really piss off the mayor—who is due to announce his candidacy for reelection in the coming days—of your major metropolitan city. But, for this scenario, you have a spitter and you use it. If you don't have one, you stop your vehicle, get out, and let the prisoner hack to his heart's content while your and your partner standby for a patrol wagon to respond. Once the wagon is on scene, you, your partner and the Wagon Master—I love that term—transfer the suspect to the rear holding area of the van. This area is not anywhere near the Wagon Master's/driver's seat. The custody can now spit all he or she wants and only make a mess for the next unlucky prisoner. You see, most major metropolitan police departments don't employ janitors to clean those things; it's reliant upon the Wagon Master, who is usually not the most motivated or brilliant member of the force. Sad but true.

Anyway, problem solved. You go back to the station/the company/the precinct/the what-the-hell-ever, clean up and book the prisoner for being drunk in public and battering an officer . . . via loogie. You then prepare a strongly worded memorandum to the departmental administration questioning the thought process that led to half of the divider in your vehicle being permeable in the first place. Said memorandum is read, reviewed and stamped—provided it is of sufficient relevance to be sent to the next level up—by your sergeant, the lieutenant, the captain of your station, the Division Commander, the Deputy Chief of Patrol Operations and—so I've heard—the Chief of Police him or herself. Your memorandum is then classified as *APPROVED* or *DENIED* and sent back down the chain of command where, one day, you find it waiting for you in your mailbox with a bunch of stamps and initials all over it.

Jack shit then changes.

2. Tell your partner, who is still in the driver's seat and watching the situation unfolding next to him with simultaneous interest and disgust to, "Just fucking drive, dude!" Turn the brim of your department issued baseball cap, which is not supposed to be worn with your wool uniform— but screw it; what are they going to do, fire you?— to the rear. You do this to hopefully deflect the onslaught of nastiness flying at you from behind. Then ride out the storm. Try not to think about the mass of mucous slowly sliding down your

back. Also, try not to lean back into the seat so as to further squish the disgusting amalgam against your skin and grind it into your ballistic vest, which is a bitch to clean.

Once at the station, you and your partner jump out of the vehicle, do a quick glance around for a random unemployed jack-off with a video camera that may be hiding in the bushes, and drag the vomit-covered, kicking, spitting, biting, writhing, enraged and *polluted* asshole out of the back of the car by his head. Momentarily try to figure out how he slipped his handcuffs to the front. Throw him on the ground. Wait until you can hear him making that horrible rasping noise in the back of his throat to gather up extra slime to expel on you; wait for it a second more for good measure.

Then boot that motherfucker in his bloated, distended belly with sufficient force as to make him choke on his own spit and be unable to function because of it.

You do this just once. Just so he feels it and puts his jets into reverse. Just to ground the hot wire that is his anger. Just to say, without *saying* anything: "I am an agent of the people of this city, county and state. I am an enforcer of the criminal laws governing such. I am also a person, like you. I will not tolerate your disregard for basic human decency. I will not allow you to conduct yourself in such a disgraceful and disgusting

5

manner any longer. You have failed so completely, so impressively, that you have moved me to see that it stops here. This is my line in the sand. This is my ultimatum."

That's what you'll be thinking, but it'll probably just come out sounding like what I said, which was an impassioned, "ALRIGHT, COCKSUCKER! SPIT ON ME AGAIN! SPIT ON ME AGAIN; I FUCKING DARE YOU!"

Now, after witnessing this little meltdown, your partner will probably tell you to, "Take it easy, man!" But *he* doesn't have a snail-trail of looch from the base of his neck rapidly heading toward the crack of his ass. So, it's pretty easy for him to say, isn't it?

You'll shoot your partner a sideways look, display a little sneer and then drag the asshole into the booking cell by his left foot—a process that will undoubtedly, inadvertently remove his left shoe—and book him for the charges described above. Forgo the memorandum. Just go get cleaned up.

And, if you're me, you'll stand there in the locker room with both hands braced against the sides of the whisker-flaked, toothpaste-crusted, dirty porcelain sink staring into the mirror at your crooked, past-broken nose and the beads of sweat on your forehead. You'll wonder if you look sick and reflexively check your skin for signs of jaundice. Maybe you'll take a leak and perseverate over its hue. You'll look down at the scars on your right hand and the illustrated skin on your arms. You'll lose yourself in the distorted reflection of your face in the tarnished silver symbol of authority on your breast and wonder: *How did I ever wind up here?*

You'll exhale deeply.

And for some reason, you'll think: *I really need to write this stuff down.* Hence the memoirs of Officer Dougie Cohen, SFPD, star number 5445: a nice number if I was compulsive, like that detective on TV.

But it's the *im*pulses that have always been my problem.

Anyhow, those are your options: the viable ones. Sure, you could shoot the guy and bury him in the desert, but that's not really very feasible; he's just a drunk idiot after all. Or, you could totally ignore the situation and hope it goes away, but he *is* a drunken idiot and you are employed to do a job wherein you are supposed to interact with these people so others don't have to. That's why they give you the badge/star/shield/whatever, the gun, the uncomfortable wool uniform, the ballistic vest, and the coffee-stained Crown Vic with the equally coffee-stained, aging, onboard laptop computer.

If this situation presents itself on the first day of your probationary period—the first year of patrol that comes right after your field training; the time when everybody is on their extra-special-best behavior so as to avoid giving the potentially soon to be "released" or "terminated" officer fuel for another mayor and city controller-maddening lawsuit—then you are lucky. Choose option number one and you are an officer of the peace: a consummate professional, one with sufficient moral fiber and patience to reach to the upper echelons of command. You may even—provided you are of the race, sex, or sexual preference de jour—become chief one day. You may also herald the destruction of effective police work, but you probably don't really give a damn about it anyways. Another potential outcome of the first course of action: the whole experience will hit you in the face like a cold, calloused smack of reality and you'll wind up prematurely going back to corporate finance or whatever other "real job" you defected from in the first place.

However, if you choose option two, you will become a cop.

Small towns require the services of law enforcing pseudo-androids, the kinds of officers who don't mind telling teenagers that smoking is bad for them and lecturing sixth grade students about the evils of marijuana. These same men and women are also ever vigilant to correct truancy, ticket moms in a hurry to get the kids to soccer practice, and patrol the borders of the controversial new skateboard park, like sharks waiting for the tuna to dare swim beyond the protected confines of the net. I'm not saying there isn't a place for men and women like this; I just couldn't ever relate to them and their place certainly isn't in a big city.

As a teen, I grew up in a medium sized town—Ventura, California, the next county north of Los Angeles—and I hated the police officers because I had insolent hair, rode a skateboard, and was into punk rock. When you are a participant in that scene, it's required that you don't like the police. Seriously, it's in the handbook.

Then I moved to The City. I started to learn a little about the shitty side of life. I got a job as an orderly in a busy county hospital that primarily serviced an economically depressed population. I quickly came to realize that my radical-left views about law and order were pretty much just simpleminded socialist/anarchist/nihilist/Communist rhetoric and didn't fit in with reality of life in urban America. I learned that going to protests and shouting sound bites and slogans into the face of a man or a woman with a riot helmet on didn't do anything to help the world; it just made my whiney ass feel somewhat empowered.

Who I was going to call upon were I ever in serious trouble? It certainly wasn't the unwashed throng of bleeding hearts around me.

I realized that big cities needed, our society needed, cops.

And one day, I thought that maybe *I* might be good at policing. I'd always been such a vocal critic of "fascist" and/or "racist" and/or "mustachioed" policemen; wouldn't I, such a sensitive and understanding young man with such deep roots in leftist politics and counterculture, be perfect for the job?

Of course I would. I was a vegetarian for eight years. I had a black friend in middle school. The second girl I ever had sex with was Mexican. She later attended Mills College, and you couldn't even get accepted there unless you'd burned an American flag in the middle of some major thoroughfare.

I was all about challenging assumptions. I was all for understanding the points of view of other people from different social and economic backgrounds—provided they fit in with my accepted dogma.

Wasn't I enlightened?

And one day, I thought: *Maybe I could wear the uniform? Perhaps I could be the kind of officer that I've always imagined one should be?*

If that wasn't narcissistic enough, I thought that I could somehow change policing for the better.

Dougie Cohen: boy genius.

But, I was never much of a fighter. I grew up in a pretty sheltered environment. I didn't even start exercising regularly until I was about eighteen, when I realized that grown men weren't supposed to look like female runway models. I'd never shot a gun before or punched anybody. In high school, I was in rock bands and wrote poetry about how depressing life was and such. I drew doodles on my binder of my school in flames. I would likely have been deemed "high risk" or "emotionally unstable."

I cried a lot.

Until I began working in an ER that was filled with blood and guts, getting tattooed and hitting the gym on a regular basis—my first steps in the direction of non-wussitude—I was on the fast track to growing up into an irreversible pussy. I had nightmares all the time. I was scared of other people. I was socially awkward. I was a caring listener of a boyfriend.

I'd bend over backwards to any girl who let me touch her ass. Cheat on me six times?

Sure.

Smash my cherished belongings in a rage about God-knows-what and who-gives-a-shit-anyways?

Fine.

Just let me sleep with you once every six months; then nail yourself to the cross after doing so for the next six. When I bring up the idea of sex prior to the six month deadline, feel free to shame me into believing that I only think with my penis. That'll work. Grind me into the dirt with your vintage shoes and weep immaculately applied makeup onto my grave. Apparently, so history demonstrated, I was game for all of that . . . for a while.

One day—after I ended another pointless, loveless, boring relationship—I went to work. I soon found myself drawing blood from a detoxing junkie with nonexistent veins, holding basins for vomiting drunks and cleaning the watery feces from the bed of an old GOMER *(Get Out of My Emergency Room!)*. I thought: *I need a new gig.*

I always had a secret love of those eighties cop/"buddy" movies.

A few months after that *eureka*-moment, and about three weeks after I started dating a girl named Tessa—a new respiratory technician at St. Mary's hospital in Oakland, where I had been employed since I was nineteen—I filled out an application to take the San Francisco Police Department's written test.

Tessa was different than all the other girls, of which there were a few; stop me if I'm bragging. She actually seemed as if she wanted to keep me around for something other than to fulfill a role as a walking, talking fashion accessory. She laughed at my stupid jokes and liked the same music that I did. She wasn't grossed out by my work related stories because she dealt with the same stuff. She thought my recent interest in Irish culture and politics, because my mom was mostly Irish by blood and I was trying to "find myself" or whatever was "cute." Despite the professional career, she still had insolent hair and wore studs on her leather jackets. She sported skin-tight jeans over Doc Martin boots. She had robins tattooed on either side of her neck that held a banner in their beaks, which read across her throat: *"My words fly up. My thoughts remain below."*

And when I told her that I was applying for the police department as we sat in a little moonlit park in Pacific Heights lazily rocking on the swing set, she said, between slugs of Jameson out of the bottle, "Cool, Dougie-O, cool."

When she talked like that, it made me melt.

CHAPTER 2

*"A good traveler has no fixed plans, and is
not intent on arriving."*
—*Lao Tzu*

"Mr. Cohen," Sergeant Castagnola stated, "go ahead."

"Yes, I was just thinking that it—" I began to reply before being reminded by the good sergeant that I had, once again, failed to properly introduce myself before speaking to a superior. As a cadet, one was always obligated to introduce oneself in such an instance. This was, roughly, occasion forty-nine of three-hundred and fifty-eight in which I failed comply with the appropriate directive. I was never in the military and took a while getting used to the chain of command.

"Who are you?" Sgt. Castagnola prompted.

"Err, sorry. Crap. Cadet Officer Cohen, Sir . . . sorry. I was just thinking that it seems odd how we're taught all these external signs that a person is about to become combative; one of those is overt verbal hostility."

"That's true," Sgt. Castagnola answered. "What about my previous statement is it that you feel conflicts with that? I'm in no way telling you not to protect yourselves."

Daniel B. Silver

"It's just that it sounds—to me, I mean—like you're saying we aren't supposed to react to peoples' hatred even though it's a warning sign of a possible attack or resistance." Occasion fifty of three-hundred and fifty-eight continued, "I mean, I guess you didn't really say that. I just kind of inferred it as a subtext in what you were saying and, forgive me for speaking frankly, but I can't help but wonder how somebody is supposed to be fair and impartial when someone else is screaming in their face that they are a *this* and a *that*." You weren't supposed to swear in the academy. Nor, were you supposed to swear on the job. Though I had earlier uttered it, I did not consider *crap* to be a cuss-word. At this point in my training, nobody bothered to correct me for using it. I thought it probably safe.

I could see Sgt. Castagnola start to get *that* look on his face; it was the one that he often displayed when I was asking questions beyond the scope of the lecture.

I added, "Cadet Officer Cohen, I'll make it work though. You can count on me." I think my classmates were probably relieved that I shut up and let the lecturer proceed.

"Good, Mr. Cohen. Glad to hear it. It's always a *pleasure* to hear your perspective." Sgt. Castagnola nodded in a somewhat dismissive manner and continued with his lesson. I wasn't sure if the positive reinforcement was in reference to my placating agreement with him, or because I finally remembered to name myself before I spoke.

Toward the beginning of the academy, I started to realize that policing may have been a tad more complicated than I'd previously thought.

My only preparation for the twenty-nine weeks of marching, sweating, nearly crapping my pants, and learning what the police academy beheld: a few words from my background investigator—who is kind of like one's spirit guide during the hiring process—and a one page typed letter, which I opened on June 15th, 2001. The letter was no small surprise. Tessa and I had been dating for ten months already and I had fallen for her, hard. The text of this note was as follows:

> Congratulations, Applicant!
> You have been selected to join the San Francisco Police Department's 199th Cadet Class. The class will start promptly on July 1st, 2001, at 0700 hours. Men are required to report in a suit and tie and women should be in appropriate, formal business attire. Our department follows a paramilitary model. You should be prepared for a highly structured, highly disciplined environment with an established chain of command. Attached is a map to the academy and a list of uniform items which you will need to have by the second day, July 2nd. You do not need to bring these uniform items with you on day one. Further instructions

will be provided as required. Report with
this letter in hand and welcome to the
SFPD.

Sincerely,

Captain Jonathan Riordan #343

Commanding Officer

Training Division

The night that I received the letter, I penned my resignation to St. Mary's Hospital. I resisted the temptation to simply scribble *"Dear hospital in charge guy, me done!"* on a cocktail napkin, despite strong leanings to the contrary. Later that same evening, Tessa and I went to go see a classic English punk band, The Deadbeats UK—not to be confused with The Deadbeats US, a new wave band from around the same era—on their reunion tour.

While standing in line for our *will call* tickets outside the Fillmore auditorium, Tessa and I got approached by a young female junkie in her early twenties. She could probably have been attractive if she bothered to get off the *scag* and hit the shower, but her poor complexion indicated that she was on the fast track to being completely haggard.

"Spare change?" the girl asked.

I ignored her, but Tessa said, "No, sorry."

"I bet you are, bitch," the junkie chick muttered as she walked by.

"Excuse me!?!" Tessa exclaimed.

Oh boy. Here we go, I thought.

Tessa continued, "Excuse *me*, bitch," she called out while leaving her place in line and posturing aggressively. "Why don't you sell your fucking pussy like the rest of us did? Or maybe you can call daddy and have him send you some money from your trust fund?"

The look of utter surprise on the girl's face told me that she wasn't interested in fighting my angry, ex-stripper girlfriend. "Whatever . . . sorry," the junkie said and scurried away.

Tessa bounded back toward me. I caught her in my arms. She had been drinking and her inhibitions were obviously decreased.

"That was awesome! I totally destroyed her," Tessa bubbled.

"No more beers for you," I replied.

The doors to the auditorium opened shortly thereafter and we entered. Tessa left my side to go use the bathroom and came back with two pints of Scottish ale, already ignoring my previous statement. The band came onstage looking like older, fatter versions of themselves. Tessa and I moved toward the front of the room through the crowd of young and old men and women with tight jeans, bullet belts and leather jackets. Mohawks and multi-colored liberty spikes did abound.

Per my Standard Attire Procedure TM, I wore a Fred Perry polo shirt, black jeans, a three-row studded belt and burgundy Doc Martin shoes. A young, "traditional"-looking skinhead with a Trojan Records patch on the back of his bomber jacket—the symbol of a famous reggae label from Jamaica, indicating that he wasn't a neo-Nazi—nodded at me approvingly as Tessa and I pushed by.

"Oi," I said, greeting him in the accepted language of punk rock.

Once at our desired place, a few rows back from the front and at the edge of what would undoubtedly soon be the mosh pit, the band launched into one of its hits: a song called "Fuck Old Bill". For some reason, I knew that "Old Bill" was once common British slang for members of the London Metropolitan Police. Tessa had already finished her beer by the time the lights dimmed and the opening chords of the classic anthem crashed through the ratty Marshall amplifiers.

"Fuck Old Bill and the goddamn law," the lead singer began to yell into the microphone, still sounding like he did twenty years prior—only plus ten thousand cigarettes. "Piss on his mates in city hall. I'll do what I want, what I think is fair . . ."

Tessa turned to face me and sang along with the words. She grabbed me by the crotch and pulled me close to her, surrounded by the chaos of *pogo*-dancing fans. Tessa reached for my free hand, the one not holding the remainder of my beer, and guided it under her little, plaid skirt. She wasn't wearing any underwear. "I'll fuck Old Bill anywhere," she mouthed along with the singer's next line. I reluctantly pulled my hand back in an effort to keep my face from flushing.

"DID YOU PLAN THIS?" I called over the music. I smiled at her and took a quick glance around the auditorium at the mass of would-be revolutionaries and anarchists. It suddenly struck me that I was about to enter the police academy. For an instant, I could almost imagine what the life of a double agent must have been like—or the feeling the guy who owned the Pakistani restaurant in the Pentagon's food court must have had on a daily basis.

Without warning, Tessa led me by the hand toward the women's room.

"YOU DON'T WANT TO WATCH THE REST OF THE SET?" I called to her as we snaked back through the crowd. She didn't answer.

Tessa yanked me through the crowd and soon pushed me through the entrance to the women's room, into one of the unoccupied stalls. She locked the door, pulled down my pants and turned away from me. Tessa lifted up her skirt, exposing that which needs no introduction and is always a welcome sight on such a sultry, attractive girl.

"Just do me quick and we'll be done in time to catch plenty more songs."

The girl didn't mince words. I didn't need to be told twice and had been hard since she molested my hand on the dance floor. We got right to business.

"Consider this a congratulatory gift for your new job," she gasped, bracing herself against the tile with one hand as she held onto her skirt with the other. She looked back at me with a lusty, toothy grin on her face.

"You fucking rock. I think I love you," I replied. I knew I'd probably still be *doing* her in a bathroom stall at the show if there wasn't an occasion to blame it on, though. The girl could party.

Back then, I still was not sure if I started the application and testing process due to a genuine interest in police work, or if it was a desperate attempt to flee my previous career. One major motivating factor, for sure: my heartfelt desire to be able to say "NO" to the dregs of society rather than be expected to empathize with them and placate them in an extra-nice and healing manner . . . even when what Drunkie, Junkie or Fatty needed was a swift kick in the ass.

The written exam was easy enough. It was comprised of basic math—which I, by some divine intervention, somehow remembered how to do—English, reading comprehension and some logic puzzles. Prior to starting the test, the police chief said a few words of encouragement. I remembered that he was dressed rather informally and not adorned with the various polished brass accoutrements that I was used to seeing on high-ranking members of the department during television appearances. He sported a polo shirt with a gold star embroidered on it. Opposite to that on the right side of his chest, was written: *"Chief Yu."* He seemed down to earth and genuine when he wished us luck.

"Good morning, everybody," Chief Yu stated. "It is my honor to welcome you to the written exam, and I wish each and every one of you the best of luck in the hiring process. I hope that you'll forgive us in advance for how long everything takes, but we have a lot of steps to get through. The moral of the story is to not give up. Do your best. If you aren't selected, don't take it personally. Try again.

"It doesn't seem that long ago that I was sitting where all of you now are. I was nervous and unsure if this was really what I wanted to do. But, really, don't worry about that right now. This is a lengthy process and there's plenty of time for you to change your mind later. Take it one step at a time and, again, good luck. Thank you."

A few awkward efforts of light applause, which sounded quite dull, like a bag of pancakes thrown from a second story landing onto the linoleum floor, rang out through the cavernous hall. In a few moments, we were bubbling in our names and contact information on the answer sheet. This seemed to take ages as the thousand or so people in attendance all had to be walked through the process by a proctor. Eventually, the test began when the proctor said, "You may start."

Jump forward fifty-three minutes: I put my pencil down on the table and looked around the enormous room at the other wannabe policemen, most of whom were wiping beads of sweat off of their furled brows. The sight was sufficient enough to motivate me to reopen my test booklet and peruse it for the section of the test that I must have, in my excited state, failed to complete. I could find no such section though. I was done . . . first . . . out of everybody.

It was uncomfortable.

This had long been a problem of mine and—I began to suspect—my superpower. Rather than be graced with the ability to fly, the capacity to scale walls like an arachnid, elemental powers to control the weather, or the faculty to excrete clitoris-stimulating pheromones via my kiss, I was born with the supernatural aptitude to complete standardized tests in an expedient manner. Now, I realize that this may come across as pompous, but I didn't say that I always complete tests *accurately*, just rapidly.

Trust me, there's a big difference.

And, there I was: standing up, scooting my chair back across the polished tile floor of the civic auditorium, which made a sound of sufficient decibel level as to draw comparisons with the Blue Angels, Canadian Snowbirds or other such aerobatic, supersonic jet collective. Smiling sheepishly, I picked up my motorcycle helmet and gloves—I didn't own a car—my test, my smoking and red hot pencil and walked the required items to the large female civil servant seated in the rear of the auditorium. I improvised a little and placed my test booklet, answer sheet and pencil in separate places in front of her; their proper locations had not yet been delineated by any other candidates.

"Done already?" the skeptical woman seated behind the table asked. She bent her chin to her chest and tipped her eyeglasses down her nose with a chubby pinky finger.

"Yeah," I whispered back. I swept my arm across the table, presenting my test materials. I asked, "Is this good, how I have this stuff here?"

"Fine," she replied, chancing what was either a subtle grin or an upside down frown in the process.

"Is there anything else I need to do . . . or . . . am I done?" I whispered.

"If you're done with the test, you're done for the day and they'll be in touch with you in a few weeks," she stated, dismissing me with a wave of her hand. "You'll get your results then.

I received the notice for my physical fitness test in the given timeframe. On a pre-designated Saturday, I was summoned to the police academy for—what I later learned was—an obstacle course, a sit-up test, a stationary bicycle ride, a bicep strength test and a trigger pull station. Upon arrival, I took a place in line with about three-hundred candidates. The other folks in line with me milled about with similar expressions on their faces as those poor standby passengers in line at an airline ticket counter, bags to be checked in tow, with ten minutes until boarding. We stood in one single file line, stretching out the front door of the building into the foggy morning air.

While waiting, I heard people speaking softly and in hushed tones about a dreaded *wall*, which was—if I were to infer its size from the wavering tone of the whispers around me—roughly fifty-three feet of over-vertical, polished steel, coated in a greasy film and surrounded by a moat filled with malnourished crocodiles. I began to grow uneasy as I had heard that the standard Police Physical Test Obstacle Course, or *PPTOC*, only involved surmounting six feet of wooden or cyclone fence, not the monstrosity being ruminated upon by the men and women around me—men and women who were of very mixed physical conditioning. I sincerely hoped that the grading was done on a curve. Were that the case, I was assured a passing grade.

Eventually, we were ushered into the auditorium where a hulking, middle-aged sergeant from the academy's *PT-DT* (physical training; defensive tactics) staff explained the obstacle course to us: "This course starts from a seated position on this chair," the sergeant stated as he gestured toward a single folding chair, which was positioned deliberately in a square, marked by tape, on the polished hardwood floor of the academy's auditorium. He added, "Upon hearing the whistle blow, you will exit the chair and run down this path." He began to jog in the required direction as he spoke. "Your first obstacle will be this low wall."

Wait a minute, I thought. *That's the wall?*

It wasn't a wall. It was a three foot sawhorse with a section of carpet, apparently to increase grip, on the top. Obviously, the powers of myth and legend were not dead.

"Get over the wall however you can. Vault it . . . jump it . . . whatever you feel is best for you but, be warned, we've had people blow knees and ankles on this thing. You have plenty of time to get over it. Just be careful."

Wow, I thought.

The explanation progressed. "Next, you'll go under this high barrier (a stick between two poles, like that used for playing beginner limbo) and over this low one (advanced limbo). If you knock either of the barriers down you'll get a ten second time penalty. Now, weave through these cones and come to the sled push."

I had been wondering what the sled was for. More to the point, I'd been wondering what the seven feet by seven feet of L-shaped wood construct, which had a stack

of Olympic-sized weights on the lower portion, was for.
I learned: it was a sled . . . for pushing.

Fair enough.

"Now, guys and gals, I know you're gonna be excited
but—and this is critical—SLOW DOWN before you
get to the sled. There's carpet on the bottom so it
doesn't scratch the floor and helps it slide, but the sled
is weighted. It requires some effort to move it. If you
go running full blast into it, you're gonna be hurting.
We've had people jam shoulders and break their noses
on this thing. What I would do is slow down. Then, I'd
turn around and put my back to it. Then I'd just walk the
thing backwards over this line on the floor." The sergeant
pointed to the green line of tape, six feet from the sled.
He continued: "Whatever you choose to do, make sure
you PROTECT . . . YOUR . . . FACE before impact."
For emphasis, he brought his elbows up in front of his
face like a close boxing guard. "Exit the event to THE
LEFT. If you don't go to the left, you'll have to go back
around and do it again. That'll take time. So, I'll say that
again: exit to THE LEFT and get on over to the dummy
drag." Prior to explaining the next station, he reviewed,
"Once you get over here, after exiting the sled push in
what direction . . . ?"

"To the left," various voices answered in unison.

"Good, you've got it; to the left. Anyhow, you'll
drag this here dummy—however you can grip it, by the
way—and you'll go from this line out and around this
cone. Then back. The course is then over." Good news
followed: "If you finish the course within forty seconds,

you have enough points to pass the entire test. Are there any questions?"

There weren't.

We were ushered outside the auditorium, and waited for our respective turns on the course. Over the next hour, I studied and reviewed just about all the cadet class graduation photographs I could stomach. They adorned the academy's hallways. As my turn on the course approached, I was thankful to be given a chance to run around a bit. I'd never been good at standing in line for long periods.

When the line finally withered down to me, a proctor escorted me inside the auditorium. I took a position in the corner of the room to watch the guy just ahead of me take his run, my final orientation. I thought that this was a pretty smart idea. It also was quite motivating, in that I wanted to do better than the previous sorry sack, who, moments before, struggled over the three foot barrier, couldn't pick up the dummy—let alone move it—and exited the sled push event to the RIGHT.

Dumbass. Wasn't he listening to the instructions? I thought.

I sat down in the "start" chair when prompted. The hulking sergeant approached and positioned himself in front of me with a stopwatch in hand.

"Are you ready, son?" he queried.

"Uh . . . sure, ready as I'll ever—"

"Go!"

Fucker, I wasn't expecting that, I thought as I shot out of the chair.

I ran; I jumped; I ducked; I dodged; I weaved and, within moments, I closed in on the weighted sled at a speed I hadn't hit since . . . well, since I drove up to the academy, but that was via a motor vehicle. Predictably and like an asshole, I failed to heed the cautious warning provided to me just over an hour prior. I ran full speed toward the large wooden sled with reckless abandon. I felt like a locomotive that was about to demolish the frail plywood structure in front of me, leaving only a smoking pile of sputtering flame where it had once been. I felt like I was having the formative event in my life wherein my strange, mutant powers finally surfaced. I would then have to go into hiding and live the life of a Banner-esque vagabond, lest I became the subject of nefarious experiments by a secretive government agency. My speed would be the subject of campfire stories; my final time on the course, the stuff of academy legend. I felt invincible, marvelous, and superhuman.

Instead, I nearly knocked myself unconscious.

Through obvious divine intervention, the lights in my head did not totally fade to black. They simply dimmed, considerably, for a precious couple of seconds. I regained a nominal amount of coherent thought and was able to recall that I had not budged the sled one inch.

How much weight is on that thing? I pondered.

Becoming one with The Force and/or other existential power of similar theme, I managed to slowly push the sled past the demarcation, via no small amount of groaning and straining. Clearly, my lower body strength was an area that could stomach improvement. I then trudged to the dummy drag on rubbery legs, but not before being stopped by a test monitor mid-effort as he goaded me in the proper direction in which to exit the previous event: to THE LEFT.

Despite the previously noted pitfalls, I managed to complete the obstacle course in less than forty seconds and, therefore, had sufficient points to completely slack off for the rest of the exam. Yet, in what can only be described as being out of character for me, I didn't slack.

If I may offer a momentary diversion: There was once a "professional" football league called "The XFC". The XFC—for those of you who are graced with the ability to forget stupid phenomena of popular culture—was a football league invented by the founder of "professional" wrestling, which those of us who have basic cable suffer through on Sunday nights when we are too lazy to find the remote. The league was supposed to be a sexier and more theatrical sporting event than its established pigskin-playing counterparts. It was an ambitious and expensive idea—if not terribly naïve—that floundered within a few months leaving the players out of work.

During the stationary bike sprint, I was seated directly next to a very large man who, as he furiously pedaled, loudly, enthusiastically yelled, "Come on! Yeah! Get some! Go! Go!" This man was sweating profusely and had a glorious *mullet* hairstyle, circa 1988. He was clad in a magenta tank top and teal parachute pants. All in all: the kind of guy who had probably crushed an empty beer can on his forehead once or twice, and had been considered distinctly more popular for doing so.

I cheated a look to my right in order to study the delightful, tragic specimen. It seemed that this individual was talking to himself, not another candidate. It was self-motivation. I found the outbursts quite silly and distracting, but I soldiered on, trying to keep my amusement to myself. The guy was huge and probably wouldn't have cared for open mockery. After dismounting the stationary bike, he began telling everybody within earshot that he was previously a XFC player. His proverbial deck of cards all fell into place.

Though I knew he had me beat on just about every event during the physical test—excluding the sit-ups, perhaps—I was confident that the presence of this man in the applicant pool meant that I was one body closer to a job.

The next step of the hiring process was a person to person interview with a civilian representative of the city and a member of the *force*. "The Oral" was widely regarded as the most effective manner to cull the herd of prospective cadets. For the interview, I wore a vintage suit, which I believe made me stand out. I wish I could say that it was my idea; it was Tessa's, my aide to all things fashion. She picked out the suit about a month prior with the interview process in mind. Though she worked until the wee hours of the morning, she awoke early to help me with my tie.

"You look good, baby," she said as she cinched the knot around my neck.

"Thanks, it's only because you're here. I'm not sure I could button my shirt right now with the way my hands are shaking, much less tie a knot."

"Nervous?"

"Yeah, I just don't know what to expect. That, and I've never been interviewed by a cop before and that's kind of stressing me out."

"You'll do fine. Just be yourself." She straightened my collar and saw the look on my face. "On second thought, be a little bit *not* yourself. Don't make any jokes. They might not think you're as funny as you seem to."

"Alright. Very reassuring," I said, laughing. I picked my keys off the table.

Tessa pulled me close by the lapels of my circa nineteen-fifty tweed coat. "I love you, my soon-to-be officer. God, that's so hot. I have always wanted to seduce a cop," she said right before sticking her tongue in my mouth. If she was trying to motivate me to leave, she wasn't doing a very good job.

I cut the kiss short, lest my thoughts deviate from the coming task. "I love you too. Go back to bed. I'll tell you all about it when I get back."

I fought traffic, lane-splitting the whole way for an hour, and arrived at the moderately priced hotel where the department was holding the interviews. My motorcycle made parking easy, keeping me from being tardy. An hour and a half later, after listening to a prerecorded audio tape of a commonly encountered police scenario and answering scripted questions based on my memory of the tape, my interview was complete. I left feeling that I might actually have passed. As it turned out, I was right.

Our mailman brought me the next rung to ascend: a background information packet. The background packet was a blank template for the resume of my near-entire life. It included spaces for the names, locations and contact information of everyone that I had ever lived with, slept with, worked for, gone to war for, been honorably or dishonorably discharged by, or earned/failed to earn a diploma from. It also had questions regarding any criminal activity that I had or hadn't been involved in, a space for grade point average information, instructions to attach my "DD-214" form—if I had prior military service, which I didn't; I ignored that part—a series of medical questions, and a space to describe any of my tattoos—specifically their content and anatomical locations.

This space was roughly big enough for me to write the following sentence: *My upper body is predominately covered in tattoos.*

I had hoped that this portion of the background packet, as it was given such a small writing space, didn't deal with too important a topic. I later learned the above written sentence was the pull-tab to a can of worms: a small but quite humiliating can as it dealt with images and text permanently inscribed on my flesh.

After a few weeks of phone calls and digging in the cardboard box that comprised my file cabinet, I finished filling out the dreaded thing and waited anxiously to turn the packet over to my background investigator at our scheduled meeting.

I reported for my background interview as ordered, a few weeks after being issued my background packet. I brought the completed forms with me for the investigator to use as a *cheat-sheet* of sorts into my life. The interview was structured much like any other job interview. I did my best to portray myself as a disciplined and eager young man to the armed gentleman seated behind the ancient desk in front of me. My investigator, Officer Manning, asked me a number of questions as he went over the paperwork I had provided to him. He scrutinized any blank spaces, as I expected an investigator should. I was relieved that he seemed to move right past the tattoo portion without as much as a raised eyebrow.

I was so pleased that I didn't even mind talking about one of the sections I failed to complete.

"Why doesn't this Stephan (a former roommate who rarely paid any rent and was invited to move in by another roommate, but only stayed for a few months before getting a girl pregnant and moving to San Diego to stay with her family . . . you really didn't need to know all that, I know. Sorry) have a phone number?" Officer Manning probed.

"Uh, well, that's because we really haven't talked since he moved out of town. You see, we never were really that close. I don't have any way to contact him anymo—"

"Remember the job you're applying for," Officer Manning deadpanned. He had a point.

"I'll remedy the situation as soon as possible, Officer."

"I'd recommend that. It's the people you don't talk to anymore that are the ones we are most interested in speaking with."

"I promise I didn't kill him." He didn't even flinch.

Tough room, I thought.

My failed attempt at a joke aside, I thought the interview went fairly well. Officer Manning provided me with appointment dates for my psychiatric, medical and polygraph exams. I don't know if he saw the cold sweat begin to form on my upper lip when he mentioned the word *polygraph*, but I certainly felt it. I bid him adieu, snatched up the piece of paper containing the schedule of appointments, and got out as quickly as possible. Being the subject of a police investigation was making me nervous.

I was relieved to see that my polygraph test was only a few days away. *Finally*, I figured, the ball was starting to roll. I really had no desire to wait the standard month and change for the polygraph interview, a section that I was somewhat anxious about, and apparently I didn't have to; I was going to get the damn thing over with. In hindsight, I suppose that I didn't have much to hide, but I thought at the time that my teenage criminal exploits would be automatic disqualifiers for employment. Being belatedly arrested was another significant worry.

Dear God,
When I was a teenager between the ages of fifteen and seventeen, I didn't

know anybody who was over the age of twenty-one, at least anybody who was a good enough friend that I wouldn't mind propositioning him or her to buy me alcohol. Consequently, my small group of friends and I were often forced to shoplift all bottles of cheap and lightly-carbonated wine, "forty-ouncers" of malt liquor, and the occasional donut. We needed these items to substantiate evenings of pointless conversation in the foothills of Southern California because there wasn't anything else to do. I wasn't as nutritionally aware back then, forgive me. I also suffered from a condition, related to anorexia, colloquially known as vegetarianism. I now know that this dietary plan is more or less blasphemy; I have renounced it. By the way, as long as we are talking about it, your other creatures are delicious. I like the cows the best. Oh, also, I often used to skateboard on private property and smoked pot like three times. Again, I'm very sorry.

Sincerely,

Dougie Cohen

The sad collection of misdemeanors referenced in the above letter was the limit of my criminal past. Admitting that now is downright embarrassing. These days, if you grow up in a big city and you're not on your third robbery arrest by the time you sprout pubes, you just aren't going to succeed at anything. In fact, you might actually have to get a job. And who the hell wants one of those?

Some friends had been giving me differing strategies for "beating" the polygraph since I had first applied for the department. As I never thought I'd travel so far in the hiring process, I never really bothered to listen. I do remember one key bit of advice that seemed to come up multiple times.

That advice: "Do not, under any circumstances, tell the truth."

I thought this sentiment to be impressively simpleminded. I was aware of the research that showed sociopaths—who are devoid of a conscience and therefore don't recognize that their actions are wrong and, consequently, have no exceptional nervous system response to hiding their transgressions—breeze through such tests. But I was, in all realms non-digital and non-populated by the screaming minions of hell as found in your average *first-person shooter* type computer game, not a sociopath. I was a kid from Southern California who still felt guilty for those three times he smoked pot and shoplifted beer and donuts, though, not necessarily in that chronological order.

At least I was punctual.

On an ensuing Saturday night, I sat in an eerily quiet and sparsely lit office complex sixty miles to the south of San Francisco. I waited to be attached to a complicated, bizarre instrument and to be grilled about my transgressions. I was wearing a suit and tie. Not knowing what to expect, I figured it was better to be overdressed rather than underdressed.

Tessa, out of the goodness of her heart and because she loved road trips, drove me down to San Jose for the polygraph appointment. Along the way, she did her best to get me psyched up and decrease my obvious stress level. Once we arrived, Tessa waited in the car and I made my way to the appropriate office in the small complex. I lightly knocked on the door—in case there was another poor man bearing his darkest secrets to the investigator—so as not to interrupt. Hearing no immediate answer, I took a nearby chair and sat in the silence trying my best to remember that I hadn't really done anything wrong in my life, just illegal.

Whatever helps you sleep at night, right?

I wasn't beyond redemption, was I? Sure I wasn't; I was just a silly teenager and had made a few mistakes: all part of growing up. And all that was years ago. I'd walked the path of the straight and narrow for many moons since and paid my debt to society by being a hard working ER tech in a busy county hospital. I'd helped save lives by the hundreds. I was a good man, and, because of that, I was going to ace the exam.

I was ready. I was in the zone ... I had also, incidentally, mistaken the date of my polygraph appointment from 2-20-01 to 1-20-01. As it turned out, I was exactly one month early.

I remember thinking: *I thought it was weird to schedule this type of thing on a Saturday* right before I slapped my hands to my face and ran them back over my cropped head in frustration.

One month later, I went to my actual polygraph appointment. One could just barely make out a small, yellow bruise on my forehead. This bruise was a side effect of my head's repeated contact with the dashboard of Tessa's little piece-of-crap car during the hour long ride back home from the previous, botched polygraph excursion.

As I recalled my lame mistake out loud during the next drive down, Tessa voiced her upbeat perspective.

"At least we know where to go and how long it will take," she bubbled.

"I swear: I think you might actually dance to the quartet that was playing when the Titanic was sinking— were you a passenger and not already dead, which would make you unable to dance . . . obviously. And if that quartet was The Specials or The Selecter or some other band that you might actually be caught dead dancing to. I think both those bands had more than four members though. A quartet is four people, right?"

"Still nervous, babe?" she asked in response to my meandering tangent.

"How could you tell?"

We arrived, and I walked up to the appropriate office. I met the retired FBI agent who was to interview me. He introduced himself as "Agent Lee." He was a kind Asian man, who had an aura of confidence about him. Though he likely would have found it amusing, I didn't bother sharing the story of my first trip to his office.

After a solid handshake, Agent Lee hooked me up to an ancient looking instrument and administered the test. As soon as the first wire band was positioned around my chest, I crumbled and ignored all the previous advice given to me: I told the truth. Amazingly, I passed without the use of breathing exercises, narcotics or slight of hand.

"All you ever stole was alcoholic beverages, mostly beer and donuts?" the retired agent asked as he manipulated a knob on the machine in front of him.

"Yep, I would have bought it but we didn't have any friends who were over twenty-one. So, you can see the logistical issue there."

"That's funny," he stated. "Where is your family ancestrally from?" Agent Lee asked, probably as a question to get a baseline reading of a truthful response for comparison.

"We're American mutts, half-Irish with some other boring Caucasian-ness thrown in there for good measure." I answered, before noting, "Just so we're clear, I *buy* beer now, with money . . . promise."

"Erin go bragh! I don't doubt it," he said. I still don't know if he meant that as an insult or not. Agent Lee picked up the long piece of graph paper that had recorded the tracings of the various sensors affixed to my body. He smiled, apparently satisfied, and I let out a deep sigh of relief. "Well, looks like that's it. You're done. Everything looks fine." He smiled and extended his hand.

Phew.

The psychiatric interview was next, immediately followed a medical examination, which was just a basic physical by a doctor including a body fat analysis. Both offices were in the same building. I immediately knew, upon meeting the psychiatrist who was to interview me, that I had this part of the process nailed. The doctor was an attractive and well dressed homosexual, a demographic that frequently adored me—I can only assume that this is because I was/am in fact adorable—and this gentleman was no different; he had nothing for me if not coy glances and pearly, white teeth. My strategy was simple: gay it up.

In accordance with this approach, I flirted with the good doctor to the best of my ability, and, consequently, I was not diagnosed with any kind of mental illness, any disorder which would preclude the government from giving me a loaded firearm. I believe the interview went something like this:

> Dr. Gayguy: "So, do you, generally, desire to have the power to harm others and get away with it?"
> Me: "Only Jennifer Lopez. Did you see that dress she wore to the Academy Awards? My God, it was like a one of those busses in Manila collided with a car full of clowns and the combination of the two of them went barreling through a laundry line."
> Dr. Gayguy: "Tell me about it! That was hideous. Whoever made that deserves to be shot. Hey, do you drink coffee? Because I know a place . . ."

Needless to say, I was a hit, and I didn't have to fellate the guy . . . or even go out with him. I knew there was a reason I took drama in high school. My experience with the psych interview made me smile. Back then, I used to smile all the time.

Maybe if I hadn't have joked my way through an opportunity to speak with a licensed, professional psychiatrist, I'd smile more now.

CHAPTER 3

"I either get super euphoric or darkly depressive, misery being my default position. My soul flies erratically on the wings of what I would imagine is a feeble bi-polarism."
—David Bowie

I was still working night shifts at the hospital and was sound asleep at about 0900 hours, when my phone, which I had forgotten to unplug when I'd gotten into bed two hours prior, began to ring. And ring. And ring.

Rad, was my first conscious thought of the day.

I picked the receiver up and brought it to the one ear that wasn't buried in my pillow. It may help explain the following interaction to note that I'd never been a morning person.

"Hmmmmph," I greeted, cheerily.

"Mr. Cohen, this is Officer Manning: your background investigator."

Oh really? I'd forgotten. I'm a complete moron.

Luckily, I didn't say what I was thinking. Instead, I said, "Good afternoon (it wasn't the afternoon), Sir." I

41

winced and rubbed the sleep out of my left eye. "What can I do for you? Is there a problem?"

"This is an emergency. I need to see you NOW."

"Sounds great."

"The deal is: we need to clear something up before I can move forward with my investigation." He sounded pissed. I guess he heard about the beer and donuts I stole. That or he finally talked to one of my exes, no doubt learning that I was a "big, fat jerk" or something equally mature. Either of these explanations seemed plausible at the time.

"When I gotta be there? My suit is at the cleaners."

"Just get out of bed, throw on whatever you have, and come down here . . . right away."

It seemed serious; he knew I was asleep and still didn't give a shit. Not that I was really enjoying the process. "I'll be right there," I said.

Prior to the phone call, I had been having one of my reoccurring nightmares. In the dream, I was hiking in the Rocky Mountains near Long's Peak, which is a really tall mountain near Estes Park, Colorado. As a child, my family had its reunions at a ranch located nearby. Back then, as I hated horseback riding, hiking was regular substitution.

During the dreamland hike, I crested a ridgeline and snaked my way down a single-track trail to the canyon below. Throughout the descent, my surroundings were eerily silent; the crunch of dirt underfoot and light breeze blowing through pine needles provided the only sounds of notice. Crisp air dried the sweat on my brow and also plastered my damp T-shirt against my chest; it felt refreshing.

Ah, Colorado, you can't beat the scenery, I thought.

After what seemed to be about five minutes, I made it to the base of the canyon, to the side of a small stream below. Because I didn't have any water, I decided to take a chance with dysentery and satiate my thirst the old fashion way.

I knelt down and took a drink of the cool snowmelt runoff, ignoring the rustling of surrounding vegetation, which I attributed to the draft. At first, the water tasted sweet and seemed to leave a slight hint of vanilla on my palate. I took a big gulp and then went right back for more as a warm feeling, like a small sip of high-proof bourbon, spread down my esophagus to my belly.

Best water ever, I thought.

The rustling of reeds and leaves intensified with the wind. I ignored it and continue to drink because the stream's water was, at the time, the best thing I'd ever tasted. In fact, the liquid was so sublime that I didn't even seem to care that the sky darkened around me as cloud cover quickly hid the late day sun.

Two noises like tree trunks being dropped on a field of reeds emanated from my rear, but, again, I didn't respond to the sounds. I didn't even move. I just kept taking in more and more of the delicious tonic until I heard an angry growl and felt hot breath on the back on my neck.

The first swipe of the massive, brown paw took the left side of my face off, along with a portion of the same side's ear. A stinging, hot stream of blood ran down the side of the exposed muscle and fat of my wound, what used to be my cheek, and into my eye. Instinctively, I tried to stand. After pulling my head back from the stream, I saw the reflection of a gargantuan grizzly. The hair on the bear's face was matted and dreaded, caked with blood and dirt. He had deep, charcoal-like eyes that smoldered with wild intensity and malice.

I tried to roll onto my back to kick the animal away but the bear effortlessly held me in place with his immense weight. I struggled to breathe under the pressure, but just gasped, feeling utterly helpless, waiting for the impending, inevitable doom. And, right as I was about to black out, he clamped his jaws down on my exposed, pale neck. The pain was terrible. I started to scream.

Then the phone started to ring and the bear faded away as the trickle of consciousness brought me back from the apparent brink of death by mauling.

Rad.

When I heard Officer Manning's voice, all I could think of was what would have happened if he hadn't called.

I arrived at the "Emergency Background Meeting" unshaven, half-awake, and probably smelling slightly of the booze that hadn't a sufficient chance to completely metabolize. This isn't to suggest that I was a huge drinker, but two beers followed by a little over an hour of sleep yielded a predictable physical state and condition of breath. Luckily, I hadn't topped off the brews with a sleeping pill to ensure that I actually got a full night's sleep. I had been trying to wean myself off the drugs—I was worried about the prospect of a urine test—with mixed results, but, until Officer Manning called, I was at least sleeping. I was happy about that part. It was quite a bittersweet feeling, considering what my mind was conjuring up during slumber.

I was a little nervous, a little buzzed, and a little pissed to be in the fluorescent glow of morning office life when I should have been unconscious.

Just my luck: a DUI stemming from a job interview, I thought.

Prior to entering the office, I exhaled against the back of my hand and began to take a whiff before realizing that I couldn't correct any possible malodor.

Fuck it, I thought, and knocked on Officer Manning's door. A female voice yelled a response: "Come in."

This is a good time in the story to note that Officer Manning's office was not just *his* office. It was a room containing several desks, which belonged to a myriad of different background investigators, many of whom were present and, upon my entry, eyeing me with marked interest as if they knew what was coming and were anxiously awaiting my reaction. Were I a Catholic, I would have crossed myself right then.

Seeing me, Officer Manning stood up from behind his desk, pushing his rolling chair back against the pale yellow wall to his rear.

"You're late," he said.

"Sorry," I replied. I didn't bother to ask how I could be late to an unscheduled meeting. This was probably a wise decision. "It won't happen again."

"Come in and take a seat," Officer Manning instructed.

I cautiously sat down at Officer Manning's desk, still aware of the various eyes studying me as I moved. I couldn't help but notice a Polaroid camera placed tactically on top of the desk.

Officer Manning sat down. "Okay, the reason you are here is because there's a concern regarding your tattoos. Of particular concern are the German-looking eagles (they're Celtic, thank you) on your chest. Some members of my team are concerned that you may be a skinhead. How are you going to convince me that you aren't?"

Wow.

Let me present to you an essay that I wrote in high school about skinheads:

Skinheads: The Rise And Fall Of A Youth Culture
By Douglass Cohen, Grade 11
Social Studies
10-07-93

The "skinhead" movement and subculture started in the mid to late nineteen-sixties. It was a working class reaction to the "mod" subculture, which had a large emphasis on high fashion. Keeping up with fashion trends and owning expensive clothes was generally not realistic for the youth of working class England, and many young people consequently felt alienated by the mods, though they shared similar interests. Simultaneously, the stylish Jamaican hipsters of the poor immigrant neighborhoods in London imported popular, new Jamaican music into the underground nightclubs in the area. The fans of this music started to label themselves "rude boys" in reaction to the prevailing hippy culture so prevalent at the time.

The skinhead movement was associated with the mods, in that Italian scooters were the desired form of transportation, and the rude boys, where a good amount of the skinhead fashion and music was taken from. The cropped hair came about as it was a haircut that was radical enough that others would take notice (hippies were everywhere and had long hair), but not so extreme as to upset one's parents or disqualify one from general employment.

The punk rock scene and its new style of rock music didn't emerge until the late seventies. Up until then, skinhead music had always been from black Jamaicans. During the punk era, skinheads could often be seen at punk shows and soon began to form "street-punk" bands, a raw and basic style of punk rock. It wasn't until the early eighties that increasingly prevalent racial tensions in England created a new kind of racist skinhead culture and bands to go with it. Organizations such as the KKK saw this form of music as a sexy new way to attract new and disaffected youth. It wasn't long before the young racists of the world claimed the skinhead look as their own, tainting the name to this day. But non-racist skinheads do exist still and the recent resurgence in ska and Italian scooters bodes well for the skinhead movement to disassociate it self from the racists who tainted it long ago.

By the way, Social Studies is my favorite class.

Grammar aside and if it isn't evident by now, I used to be a fan of Italian scooters, punk rock, and other English subcultures and styles from years past over the course of my mid to late teen years. I was such an enthusiast that I wrote several, hastily prepared and poorly proof-read social studies assignments in honor of my interests, which secured me a series of solid or somewhat mediocre grades.

After my punk phase, I got into the mod scene and its fashion from the late sixties: skinny ties, fitted pants, close-cut suits, et cetera. After punk rock, I started listening to English ska music from the seventies, which led me to earlier Jamaican music. Historically, I'd always had very short hair as I thought I looked pretty good that way. And I had this buddy, Kyle, who was also into scooters; we hung out all the time. He started dressing like a mod, and I figured I might as well try something a little different than he was doing. So, I guess you could say I used to be kinda skinhead-y or skinhead-ish for a phase.

The first time Tessa stayed the night at my house, she dug through my closet—uninvited, mind you—and found a lot of my old clothes. Having been a participant in similar social circles, she recognized the button down shirts, suspenders and short-legged jeans that comprised the skinhead uniform.

"Oh boy, what's this stuff?" she asked. "Is there something you need to tell me?"

"Don't worry. I wasn't a Nazi. I just had a scooter friend who was a mod. I thought I'd rock the skinhead look to be different," I told her.

"Yeah, I was kidding. I figured as much because I know your full, Jew-ass name; I'm not a moron." That sarcasm of hers enamored me to her even more than her understanding of youthful rebellion. "But, if you want to put this stuff on and *pretend* you're a Nazi so we can reenact that sex scene with Russell Crowe in *Romper Stomper,* I wouldn't stop you." She even liked Australian, independent flicks. The girl was red hot cool.

All this considered and if you hadn't already noticed, as Tessa did, I was born with a Jewish last name. Despite my reasonably extensive knowledge of underground music and fashion, I was not about to bother explaining most of the above to Officer Manning, mostly because I didn't really think he would give a shit. One can have perfectly valid, innocent reasons for naming one's child *Adolph,* but none of them will ever make sense to most of the population. I did, however, plan on playing up the "Jew angle"—even though it was from my dad's side of the family meaning I wasn't actually a Jew, merely half a Jew—as much as possible.

Most importantly, I was quite offended by the implication that I was a goddamn Nazi of all things.

"I'm *NOT* a racist or any kind of bigot," I stated. "How, in any way, would you have that impression?"

"Because of your tattoos," Officer Manning said. "Those and your haircut. Some of the experts around here are worried. And, frankly, so am I."

"I grew up listening to underground music, singing in bands, and riding a skateboard or a scooter. There wasn't any specific reason I decided to get . . . wait a minute; experts on tattoos, skinheads, or what, exactly?"

How do you get that job? I digressed, internally.

Officer Manning didn't answer.

I continued: "You really shouldn't be worried. I moved to The City because it's so open-minded. I moved here because you can be gay, straight, black, white, brown or red—whatever. I can have tattoos here, none of which include a swastika or anything like that, by the way, and shave my head and still be a candidate for the police department. What do I need to do now?"

Officer Manning picked up the camera and said, "I need you to take your shirt off."

Rad.

Officer Manning escorted me to the corner of the room, where I sheepishly shed my poorly tucked shirt. Upon my doing so, the four other background investigators currently working around us promptly stopped whatever they were doing and stared at my half-naked body. I did my best to maintain proper posture. My grandmother would have been proud.

"Extend your arms out to your sides," Officer Manning said.

"Okay." I did as instructed.

Officer Manning snapped a photo. "Turn to the side."

Again I complied and he took another shot.

"Face away from me," he ordered.

"Sure." I began to realize that any prospective criminal career I may have had planned for the future was, from this day forward, no longer feasible.

When Super-Embarrassing Picture Time was a wrap, Officer Manning led me to the opposite corner of the room where I sat in an uncomfortable wooden chair at a desk. He placed a box of pens and a yellow legal pad in front of me. Inching closer to my left ear, so close that I could feel his breath, he said in a hushed tone, "I need you to write the dates, times, places, and reasons that you got each and every tattoo on your body—right now. This could be the difference between you being hired and eliminated from the process. Those pictures I just took are going to be attached to the packet I present to the hiring board."

This is going well, I thought.

I'd always applauded my parents for their writing skills and eloquent prose, which some would argue I inherited a bit of. It was these writing skills that got me through eight long, handwritten pages of counter-accusations and dramatic, if not slightly embellished, family history, which I later presented to Officer Manning.

I wrote somber notes about ancestors who died in Hitler's train cars, internment camps, gas chambers and firing squads, of which I imagined there were a few, but I didn't know their names or many other details. I also wrote about getting attacked by mobs of racist, white trash idiots from my home town because I didn't subscribe to their moronic beliefs. In reality, the beating up part never really happened, but we often exchanged hard looks and mutual insults. Also, one of those dudes spit on my backpack once because I called him a "wannabe Nazi moron." I swore revenge, were I to ever catch him also wearing a backpack.

I closed with an angry diatribe about being judged by the way I looked and how ironic that was considering the source. In short, I pretty much bullshitted my way through the document and, I must brag, a flight of creative brilliance. There may have been a few grammatical errors but those were intentional—to convey a sense of urgency—I assure you.

Upon completion, I said an abrupt, "Let me know," to Officer Manning. I left, reasonably sure that I'd never hear from him again.

Weeks later, after I got that surprise letter from Captain J. Riordan #343, I found myself wearing a powder and navy blue uniform—comparable to that of a Maytag repairman—in the company of forty-nine similarly dressed men.

I was ordered to walk on the right side of the hallway at all times and maintain military bearing. I knocked three times on the door to the staff office when I had any official business or questions, repeating as instructed: "Cadet Cohen wishes to speak to (insert rank and name here)." I showered in the nude, which was something I never quite got used to, with a boisterous lot of classmates, many of whom did not last more than a few weeks in the program.

I ran endless laps around a baseball field—used primarily for off-leash dog walking despite signs indicating punitive action if the leash rule was ignored—while wearing a gun-belt and carrying a baton, at about 0615 hours in the San Francisco morning. During these workouts, which immediately followed my morning coffee, I had to actively concentrate so as not to crap my pants during four-hundred meter sprints and mile long "Indian runs" in formation. Were my buttocks to fail, it would have been pretty humiliating considering the short-shorts my fellow trainees and I were required to wear during workouts. I know this is gross, but it's the truth. Running first thing in the AM was oft met with a collective groan from my fellow cadets for a reason: It blew.

I frequently and without hesitation complied with the following orders:

"Make a hole."

"While stepping forward, cross-draw the baton to a high ready position . . . move!"

"Drop and give me fifty."

"Right face."

"Forward march."

Welcome to the academy, Cadet.

CHAPTER 4

Our house it has a crowd. There's always something happening and it's usually quite loud.

—Madness, "Our House"

Growing up in a medium sized town in "SoCal"—as it's known up in "NorCal"—was a practice in blissful ignorance. There were two kinds of people where I grew up: white and Mexican. Mexico, as far as mainstream Ventura culture was concerned, encompassed every bit of land south of the US border. There was one exception to this rule, Costa Rica. Costa Rica was described as its own universe, where the surf was reportedly, and so I was repeatedly told, *"Amazing."*

Most white people in Ventura spoke disparagingly of Mexicans because they were "taking over" or were substandard operators of automobiles. I thought such statements sounded ignorant and plain dumb. I rather liked our Latin cousins because of the affordable and tasty food they brought with them. I also respected that Mexican immigrants seemed to do all the jobs that Americans often wouldn't, such as cleaning the bathrooms in my schools—ineffective though that effort may have been.

In my public high school, of roughly two-thousand teenagers, we only had about ten black kids. One of them was my close friend, but I never really thought of him as black. I just thought of him as "Paul" . . . that being his name and all. And as Paul didn't speak Spanish, as he didn't drive a car with all manner of cheap, sparkly, aftermarket crap and/or murals of Aztec warriors adorning it, I thought Paul was just like me. Considering there were only two options available by my logic at the time, Paul was apparently white.

To complicate the perceived bicultural racial demographic of my hometown further, I'll note that the first girl I ever made an earnest effort at seeing naked, Brenda, was Filipino. I didn't figure this out until years later. During the time we were "dating" (I don't know if that's really the appropriate term for our relationship, as we were only fifteen and didn't really go out on actual dates), I didn't even know where the Philippines were; I just figured that Brenda was from a different part of Mexico. It wasn't until moving to The City that I realized the true nature of Brenda's ancestry.

I lay this foundation to further illustrate the following issue: I was relatively new to Asian culture, Asian people and Asian names prior to moving to San Francisco. As a young man, I knew of white people, Mexicans, and one Filipina. I had one token black friend. Via working in a busy county hospital's emergency room for five years, my education on the matter had improved dramatically.

But I still thought some cultural differences and quirks were funny, which probably was not so much a facet of my ignorance. It was likely an uncorrectable flaw in my personality.

Accordingly, on the first day of the academy, when I met the Asian cadet named *Charles Kok*, I snickered. I knew that such an action wasn't the most politically correct thing to do, or, for that matter, the wisest thing to do when meeting somebody—who you potentially may one day rely on to save your ass—but it happened. And I wasn't alone my appreciation of his unique name.

When I was first introduced to Charles, he pronounced his name in the most damning of ways: Cock. How anybody with such a name would ever inspire fear in the hearts of criminals was beyond me, but I was an easily replaceable stranger in a strange land. I thought it best not to comment on the matter.

I could tell that our primary instructor, Officer Gregory Hurwitz, was also slightly taken aback by Cock. This became apparent during the first morning roll call as we all stood in platoon formation, which we had just learned.

"Tuvera?" Officer Hurwitz called out.

"Sir!" Cadet Tuvera replied.

"Chang?" Officer Hurwitz continued.

"Sir!" Cadet Chang said.

"Co . . ." Officer Hurwitz paused; we could see his eyes widen ever-so-slightly. "Ca . . . Cock?" he finally spat out.

I just about died. A burst of laughter erupted from my belly.

"Here!" Cadet Cock replied, incorrectly.

Officer Hurwitz then graciously took time out of his day to show me how to do proper, police academy-standard pushups; fifty of them, if I recall correctly.

Day two featured the first day of physical training, also known as "pee-tee" or PT. On that same day, my fellow cadets and I reported to class in our cadet uniforms. Officer Hurwitz instructed us to wear our hats at all times when outdoors, and to immediately remove them when indoors. In the morning, we were issued our gun-belts, portable radios, CPR masks, and handcuffs. We were also given our canisters of pepper spray placebo, batons, riot helmets, plastic training guns and ballistic vests. After being allotted ten minutes to secure these items in our newly assigned lockers, we were told to immediately return to the locker room and change into our PT gear, which consisted of navy blue T-shirts, matching shorts, and running shoes of our choice. Our gun-belts had to be worn over the PT uniform as well, for added style and torture.

Having never been a high school athlete, I was completely unfamiliar with the locker room environment. Furthermore, I hadn't been to prison, frequented a mainstream gym or indulged in a trip to a gay bathhouse. The idea of showering with a large group of men was a little uncomfortable. And, honestly, I was slightly intimidated by it.

This had nothing to do with the size of my penis, thank you.

Daniel B. Silver

Despite my apprehensions, the process of changing and showering went relatively smoothly. At the risk of raising questions about my sexuality, I'll dare to note that my class' time in the locker room was often quite fun, as we were away from the scrutiny of our instructors. As days grew to weeks, the locker room became a refuge from the academy's staff and the place where my fellow cadets and I felt free to bitch, moan, swear, fart and whip the crap out of each other with rolled, wet towels. This boisterous environment, often accented with fair amount of screaming and giggling—a result of the whippings or the prodigiously cold water that flowed from the showerheads—frequently generated a sufficient cacophony as to get the entire class in a moderate amount trouble.

The herald of such trouble was usually Officer Hurwitz. He would march into the class, order us to attention and then give us all a stern lecture about proper academy etiquette. These lectures generally ended with some form of reasoning and/or pleading for us to behave ourselves like adults. From these repeated, impassioned performances, I inferred that my class was often difficult to control, at least from a behavioral standpoint. These reprimands aside, class-clowning thrived in the academy despite the pushups, which were often demanded of me to deter such insolence. Luckily, I was sometimes able to make the academy staff laugh, Officer Hurwitz in particular, and this served to lessen the pushup burden.

With every topic of academy instruction, we cadets were given a test. As per my uncanny ability to complete standardized tests quickly, I was often the first cadet to close my test booklet, put my answer form on the test monitor's desk, and move down the hall to the lunchroom. The lunchroom was the designated post-exam waiting space. As a college degree or superhuman ability similar to that of my own was not a prerequisite to entering the department, I had grown accustomed to some of my classmates taking a considerable amount of time to complete their tests.

We were usually given a generous timeframe to complete our exams, which many would take full advantage of in an effort to make sure they had answered every question to the best of their knowledge . . . or, in some cases, to sweat and curse their way to complete and utter failure. Regardless of the reasons for the lack of expedience on the part of the other men around me, I was often left sitting in the lunchroom, twiddling my thumbs, and wishing I smoked cigarettes so as to pass the time. Luckily, Officer Hurwitz quickly discovered this little quirk about me and allowed me to venture off campus to get coffee, something that I both require and cherish, in and effort to help me fill some of the downtime that I had.

It was during this downtime that, every so often, bored members of the staff would engage me in conversation and slowly—so I suspected—began to trust that I was not the type of person who would:

A. Be offended by what they had to say in regard to my performance or the performance of my classmates.

B. Fail.

C. Sue them or the department, should I fail or be offended.

On one particular occasion, I had finished my test, gotten coffee, and drank it as the other members of my class trickled in to the join me in the lunchroom. I could usually count on seeing the same core group of people within the first ten minutes after I had completed my test, the other efficient test takers. This day was no different. The post-workout, post-test caffeine dose was a potent diuretic and sent me scrambling down the right side of the hallway to the restroom. Though I had to pass the staff's office, which was always a gamble, I was relieved to have another valid excuse to leave the lunchroom. One could only look at a vending machine for so long, which was the only option available to me other than debating multiple choice exam questions with anxiety stricken classmates.

On the return trip from the locker room, I passed the staff's office and did my best to look straight ahead when passing. I did not wish to capture the attention of one of the instructors and be issued some menial task. Ignoring them and moving quickly *usually* worked, but, as fate would have, not always.

"Cohen, get me coke in here." I was snapped back into reality by Officer Hurwitz's voice, seized like the Millennium Falcon in the Death Star's tractor beam.

"Get you a Coke, Sir?" I clarified. In his defense I may have mumbled.

"Yes . . . NOW."

"Yes, Sir," I said, figuring I could handle this job without remarkable incident.

I didn't bother to ask Officer Hurwitz for coinage; the vending machine accepted paper bills and figured he'd pay me back after the item was delivered to him. It was, after all, against established academy policy for staff members to purchase items for the cadets or vice versa. Fraternization was strictly forbidden among our respective castes.

I walked back into the lunchroom and swaggered up to the soda machine. I felt like I had finally been accepted into the fold of the veteran policemen who comprised the staff. I had been asked to do a favor, not just a random task; I had been trusted with obtaining refreshment for one of my instructors and it felt good.

I did my best to flatten out the crumpled bill in my pocket and inserted it into the vending machine. The machine seemed to chew it for a while before spitting it back out at me. I tried again, taking extra time to straighten all of the bill's corners. It was, again, rejected. I then used the corner of the machine itself to saw the bill back and forth trying to iron out the wrinkles with friction. I fed the bill in once more. No go.

Fuck, I thought, and reached for another bill.

I produced a new bill and did my best to make it as pristine as possible. I secretly kicked myself for buying coffee with the good bills and leaving the crap for the one task that could make or break me with the man who had near total control over my academy experience. Finally, the machine accepted the dollar and I pressed the appropriate button, which cued the sixteen ounce bottle of sweet effervescence to drop into my waiting hand. I smiled, removed the bottle from the open area of the vending machine and heard someone yell, "COHEN!"

I turned, toward the source of the noise and saw Officer Hurwitz standing there. I grimaced. "Sir, is there a problem?" I asked, holding the bottle of cola in my left hand, not my *gun hand* or "strong" hand—in my case, my right hand—as we were also taught on the first day.

"What is the goddamn holdup? What the hell are you doing!?!" he demanded, doing his best R. Lee Ermey impression, only from Brooklyn and Jewish.

"Getting you a *Coke*, Sir," I replied, giving the bottle a little shake and displaying a sheepish smile.

His face went cold. "Get out here," he commanded. He then pointed at Cock. "You," he said, "get your ass in the office!"

It all made sense now.

Cock, coke, shit.

Officer Hurwitz addressed me once more. "And you, outside, now," he added.

I followed with soda in hand and head hung low. I snuck a sideways glace at some of my classmates— Chang, Tuvera and Murphy—who had similar thought processes as I. I could tell these men already knew what had happened and, conversely, thought it was supremely hysterical.

Dicks.

I followed Officer Hurwitz into the hall outside the office.

"Cohen," he said and motioned to the ground at his feet, causing me to relinquish the soda, remove my baton from its holster, hold it out in front of me in a diagonal position and drop to the ground below, "one hundred. Count 'em out."

I began to rep military pushups, cheater pushups, which I thought were easy until rep number fifty or so. All the while I counted, "Onesir, twosir, threeesir, foursir, fivesir . . ." all the way up to my target number, straining and faltering for the last forty reps while rocking back onto locked elbows for brief periods of rest. Once completed, I said, out of breath, "Cadet Cohen requests permission to recover!"

"Recover," he answered. I stood in front of him, holding my baton at across my waist with taxed arms. His eyes and voice softened. "Cohen, you're a funny guy and I appreciate that—it'll help you survive in this job—but you're a cadet; you aren't a cop yet, and you need to play the game. I know you understood what I was talking about when I told you to 'get Coke' and it was a funny gag you had planned there but, really, you need to keep stuff like that under wraps until you graduate and get out into the field. After that, you can be the biggest jokester in town. Got me?"

"Yes . . . Sir," I said between breaths. It was heartening to know that he wasn't completely fed up with my antics.

"Good, as long as we're here, there's something else I want to talk to you about."

"What's that, Sir?" I asked. This could have gone either way.

"Dougie," he said, placing his left hand on my shoulder, "you're smart and you are destined for great things in this department. In fact, I think I'm going to be saluting you some day but you need to realize something."

"What?"

"You need to understand that you're just a white, Jewish guy, like me. You aren't a black lesbian, a gay Latin guy or part of the 'old guard,' San Francisco native, Irish cops who've been in the department for generations. You don't matter. You aren't connected. You and I are the cannon fodder and scapegoats for this place, the ones who have no political padding from the bullshit that flows downhill toward us. We don't count for much here; we don't have special cards to play; we're only as good as our wits and work ethic. It's going to be a challenge for you to thrive in this environment with the way you operate, but don't let this place get you down. Don't let it take away who you are."

"I won't, Sir."

"Be yourself, don't kiss any ass that you don't need to, and keep your head up. You'll get noticed eventually; it may take a little longer because you don't fill the right quota but it'll happen. And, if it doesn't: fuck this place. It's just a job. You get me?" He looked right into my eyes.

"I understand. I know I'm just a warm body to fill a spot on the roster, to the bosses at least, but I'm gonna try to kick ass when I get out of here. If I can't, then *oh well*. I appreciate the good words though, Sir," I replied.

I didn't have the heart to tell him that I was more Irish that Jewish, but I got the point he was trying to make. I didn't know anybody. I had no "juice."

"Good man. That's it, as you were," Officer Hurwitz stated, reassuming the role of drill instructor.

"By the way, I'm sorry but I thought that guy's name was 'Cock.' Since when the fuck is he 'Coke' now? Who's even named Coke? That's like being named Nike or Butterfinger . . . pardon my French." I braced myself for the onslaught that I expected would follow.

"Oh, Mr. Cohen," he said while shaking his head and starting to laugh. "You really did all those pushups for nothing? Welcome to the goddamn police department." I could tell that he was going to march right back in the staff office, close the door and have a good chuckle as he told the tale to the other instructors. I thought I'd try and get the last words in.

"I like pushups; it's okay. Want that soda? It's free," I said, gesturing to the bottle lying on the ground.

"Not after you dropped it, I don't," he wisely said.

"Damn." I snapped to attention, gave him a crisp salute, which he returned, and walked back to the lunch room to ask Cadet Cock why the fuck he changed his name.

After twenty-nine weeks of experiences very similar to the one spoken of above, which were made enjoyable by my above average athleticism, above average academic proficiency, and above average sarcasm—thereby labeling me a "gifted but potentially troubled" (I snuck a look at my personnel file in week four) cadet—I was standing on a stage in a high school auditorium getting a silver star pinned to my left breast by the new, current chief of police, Chief Shannihan. I had a real gun in my holster, which I loaded at the conclusion of the ceremony. My parents and Tessa were present in the audience. The three of them cried; Tessa because she probably realized she couldn't keep weed in the house anymore, my mother because she hated the very idea of me being a cop and worried for my safety, and my father because he was proud of me.

I had twenty four hours to celebrate before I started field training and began my first day as a patrol officer in the San Francisco Police Department.

CHAPTER 5

"I like you. You're all right. Actually,
I like you better meeting you than if somebody
had just given me your record."

—Joey Ramone

Pop Quiz:

Two vehicles run a stop sign. You, the new officer in the first day of the first phase of FTO (the slang for both Field Training Program, of which there are three phases, and field training officer, the guy or gal teaching and grading you), must now chose one of these vehicles to effect a traffic stop of. If you observe a violation such as this and fail to take action, at the very minimum telling your FTO what you saw, you will face a consequence of some sort. This will probably be a bad grade at the end of the day in the "Self Initiated Field Activity" section of your Cadet's Daily Evaluation Record, the hallowed and feared form used to track and grade a new officer's performance in the training program. I'll elaborate:

- Vehicle #1 is a 1991 Toyota Camry. This vehicle has one undersized spare tire as a substitute for the tire that was previously on the driver's side, rear. This vehicle is being driven by an Asian female, possibly Chinese, in her late forties. She appears, from your vantage point, clean and modestly dressed. Her hair is pulled back in a ponytail and she wears corrective glasses. This is all the information you have about this woman.

- Vehicle #2 is the same vehicle as described above but its occupants differ in demographic. Inside the Camry, occupying all four seats, are a group of teenage black males. These subjects are all wearing black beanie caps and are reclined in their seats to a sufficient degree as to make seeing anything but their eyes and headwear nearly impossible. The local hip-hop radio station is playing from the crappy stereo inside the passenger compartment but you can only barely hear the music as, well, it's a 1991 Toyota Camry with a stock stereo. This is all the information you have about these subjects.

Question: Which car will you stop? Assuming that the violations occur at the exact same time and that your position to conduct either stop is the same?

Answer: You, a phase one trainee, have just graduated the police academy and have been instructed that race, manner of dress, sex and/or economic status have no bearing on your enforcement choices. This department policy was drilled into your head throughout your stay at the academy, particularly in the last four weeks of cultural sensitivity training. As you are totally unable to take any of the noted factors into consideration, you either ask your FTO what car you should pull over or your head explodes. Your FTO tells you to pull over a car at random or picks one based on his or her preference for enforcement action. If your FTO is simply interested in writing a ticket for the noted violation, he or she will choose one of these vehicles based on the luck of the draw. If your FTO is interested in whether or not the vehicle is stolen as it is a Toyota Camry—built between 1988 and 1991 and, therefore, possesses a flaw in the ignition design, which enables one able to start it with practically any item that vaguely resembles a key—he or she will instruct you to choose Vehicle #2. Also, if your FTO is interested in finding a gun, narcotics, or making a warrant arrest, again, he/she will choose the same car.

The chances are great that your FTO is not a racist or a bigot. Your FTO may be black, him or herself. But your FTO—as he or she has a minimum of three years on patrol—has learned that unassuming Asian females don't often steal old Japanese cars. Nor do they often shoot people, transport narcotics or bench warrant on criminal cases. Unassuming Asian females in their middle years, who have no overt signs of narcotic addiction, do commit crimes—horrible crimes, in fact—but not usually the type that you will detect over the course of a simple traffic stop. Four black male juveniles, who are dressed like thugs, often do commit overt and easily discoverable crimes. So do a group of white, Asian, Middle-Eastern, Polynesian and/or whoever-I-left-out teenage males, who dress like thugs and pack themselves in a car that's easily stolen.

In fact, four young females that are dressed like thugettes and of the same various cultural demographics also commit easily discoverable crimes. However, I don't recommend stopping a vehicle containing thuggish female teenagers—regardless of what kind of car it is—as they are, quite simply, complete pains in the ass.

Work as a cop in a big city and you'll learn that racial profiling is ridiculous and superfluous; you'll learn that "race" is an outdated concept. Culture, income, religion: these are far more informative and relevant factors for predicting behavior and formulating prejudices.

Race is for description and identification. Your SFPD options: black, white, Latin and other.

But, discounting any of those factors, and no matter where one polices, your criminal element will be easy to spot. They are the ones with the pounding subwoofers, the ridiculous vehicle accessories (read: spinning rims), the oversized clothing and the custom, ornamental dental inserts. They are also the ones with the rusted, trashed and filthy automobiles that are filled with random belongings, the conspicuously new bicycles—despite clothing that would seem to indicate the bicycle's rider lacks sufficient funds to possess such an item—the missing teeth, leathery skin, the always wide-open eyes, the penchant for leather and metal trinkets and the month-old bleached hair. They are the walking zombies of skid row and the greasy men in overcoats loitering near the children's playground, or binge-drinking frat-boys waiting for a girl in a bar to abandon her drink.

There are only a few flavors of American street-criminal: *thug, tweaker, crackhead, sleaze* and *crazy*. They run the gamut of all races, creeds and colors, depending on the city and state.

Learn to identify them and you, Officer, will never get bored.

CHAPTER 6

"Guys, I don't mean to burst your bubbles or make the job seem insignificant in any way but the people you are going to be arresting as patrolmen are not the evil, albino scientists of the world. They aren't the guys who lurk in dimly lit rooms filled with Bunsen burners and huge computer screens. There's an old cop adage that says, 'We don't catch the smart ones.' In a lot of ways, that's true."

—Paraphrased from a statement by
Sergeant Russell Gordon, SFPD

Day one of field training was upon me and I was riding my motorcycle up 6th Street, the diseased phallus of San Francisco's notorious Tenderloin District, toward Tenderloin Station.

For those of you who don't know, the Tenderloin is an area in San Francisco that is located just blocks from some of the areas that are most crowded with tourists, shoppers, hotels and San Francisco landmarks. The Tenderloin is also a complete and utter shit-hole: drug dealing and prostitution are rampant, violent crimes happen daily, probationers and parolees are dumped into the various halfway houses located therein and fleabag hotels can be found on every block. Every new mayor promises to clean up the Tenderloin because it is the municipal equivalent of festering abscess on the face of the supermodel that downtown San Francisco wishes it were.

Every mayor has also completely and utterly failed. The great United States Air Force is the only governmental agency with sufficient *resources* to accomplish such a task.

I arrived at the station and used the magnetic card that I got a week earlier during cadet orientation—in which I brought my load of uniforms and equipment to my temporary locker—to open the garage door. I coasted the motorcycle down the steep driveway, into the small basement garage and found an out of the way place to park. After doing so, I walked to the stairwell door and punched in the entry code on the door's keypad, which I'd written down on a small piece of paper during orientation.

The code worked and I ascended the stairs, slowly and quietly like I was sneaking in the building. About halfway up, I remembered to display my gleaming and polished SFPD star on my outermost garment. I did this, obviously, to identify myself as a cop. I didn't wish to wind up tackled and arrested for sneaking my tattooed and out of place looking self into a police station; to do so seemed like a poor "first day in training" activity. But, as my star was so damn shiny, it also identified me as a new cadet and, therefore, as someone who was only slightly more welcome than some random, tattooed, twenty-four year old kid that *had* actually snuck in.

A temporary locker room had been assembled for the cadets inside the station's surprisingly large gym. The area was a rectangular construct of large, dark, metal cabinets with a curtained gap for a doorway. These cabinets were even larger than the lockers in the permanent locker room, the one for officers and sergeants. I soon gathered that the discrepancy in locker sizes had provoked ire among some of the established members of the station.

It was not until later in my career that I learned every station had a group of cops that unleashed Blitzkrieg-style invasions of vacant lockers and then immediately filled them up with all manner of God-knows-what. I could only imagine that the act was a concerted effort to hide belongings from The Wife, who was currently suing for past due child support, or to satisfy some sort of obsessive and Freudian need to fill dark, vacant spaces. All that aside, new cadets didn't usually have far to travel to provoke controversy. At least this provocation was relatively slight and beyond our control.

As I'd arrived about one and a half hours early—never can be too careful—I took great pain getting dressed and making sure my uniform looked clean, pressed and polished in the right places. I wasn't alone; two other cadets, who I'd rather not have engaged in any conversation with at the time, soon arrived and began to change next to me. That bummed me out. It's not that they were bad people; I just thought that they were destined for struggle during training due to overconfidence. Though intelligent enough, they were slightly bullish and a little lacking in the common sense arena, which could present a sour spot in the first impression that I was hoping to convey.

As a police cadet, one starts out being only as good as the rest of the class. And, as in many other arenas, one spoiled curd can ruin the whole tub of cheese.

For the day, I'd chosen to play the quiet and eager new recruit, bright eyed and ready to learn. In most ways, I was just that and the necessary acting was minimal. I felt that those two classmates, Frank Porchese and Tony Sipiano, were a little too *unique* for the first day, a good day not to make any waves. So I kept my distance.

I should note that by *"unique,"* I really mean: "total goombas."

In an effort to blend in as proficiently as possible, I opted to wear a long-sleeved uniform shirt to avoid the inevitable stares at my tattooed arms. It wasn't that my arms were anything impressive but, historically, people liked to stare at the images thereon. I'd grown used to it. Like being a celebrity, if one really hated the attention so much one wouldn't have gone down that road in the first place.

The process of getting dressed took much longer than I thought, as I needed to make sure I had my nametag, vest, whistle, two matching pens, my notebook, all required items on my gun-belt including my gun and radio, my 26" baton, the eight-point service cap and a small bag to hold any required forms that I would accrue throughout the day. Additionally, I polished my star, the brass accents and rivets on my gun-belt, and my new boots.

Terse dialogue and awkward silence between Frank, Tony and I served to elongate the process significantly. They were confident and jovial and wanted to grab-ass like in the academy; I just wanted to get the first day over with.

Run silent, run deep.

After checking and rechecking that my "gig line"—the line formed by the shirt's buttons, belt buckle and fly of the pants—was straight, that my shoes hadn't picked up any new scuffs and that my .40 caliber automatic pistol was clean and loaded, I walked out of the locker enclave into the gym proper. The walls of the gym were covered in mirrors on two sides, huge mirrors that reached from the floor to the high ceilings offering life sized, real time reflections as one passed. I didn't really see how these mirrors would help exercise but I did see how the mirrors helped increase insecurity or vanity, which I imagined were likely the primary motivating factors for most people to exercise in the first place.

I surmised that having such mirrors helped the *idea* of exercise, not so much the act itself.

Upon walking out into the gym, I saw my uniformed reflection for the first time. Of course, I had seen what I looked like in my dress uniform during graduation but wearing the basic wool patrol outfit—"The Wool," as it was known—felt different. I wasn't dressed up for Halloween; I was about to *"Enter; stage-left!"* at the cue of the stage manager.

With a momentary pause and a deep breath, I walked out into the main working area of the station and into a new life.

For about five awkward minutes, I milled about the station trying to stay out of the way and not look too nervous. I shook some hands and received some indifferent and, sometimes, downright cold stares. About five minutes before lineup, my FTO, Officer Dean Ramos, approached me. He glanced down at my nametag and a spark of recognition crossed his face. Dean was my height, about 5'08", appeared to be in his early thirties and had a non-regulation mustache that jutted across his upper lip and then plunged down the sides of his mouth toward the floor. He had blonde hair and he looked like I thought a cop should. He had a depth to his gaze that betrayed his experience, something that I wouldn't attain for some time. I didn't know it then, but Dean and I also had similar senses of humor.

Before I thought to, which made me wince, he extended his right hand.

"Hi, I'm Dean," he said, introducing himself.

"Hello, Sir. Dougie Cohen," I replied, shaking his hand in a manner that I thought a cop should.

"Wow. Some handshake you got there. You can drop the 'sir' stuff, by the way," Dean said.

"Yes. Yes, Sir. Uh, forget that last part," I said, marking the first failed attempt at humor on my new career.

"So, got everything?" he asked.

"I think so."

"Is your gun clean?" he prodded.

"Yep, just cleaned it," I replied, glad I had, actually, just cleaned it.

"Is it loaded?"

"Yes, it is."

"Good, lemme see it."

In response, I removed my pistol out of the triple retention holster—so called because it took three different actions to draw the gun to decrease the possibility that a suspect would be able to disarm the officer—from its home on my right hip and handed it to Officer Ramos. I heard Officer Hurwitz's voice yell in my head: *"Don't EVER give your gun up!"* I winced again.

Dean pulled the weapon's slide back and checked that a round was chambered, which it was. He then hit the magazine release button and ejected the magazine into his free hand, glancing at the rounds contained in it. Satisfied, he slapped the magazine back in and handed the gun back to me.

"Okay, he said," a buzzer sounded, "lineup."

Lineup/roll call/muster/whatever went quickly. The swing-watch's grizzled lieutenant read us the day's teletypes, containing descriptions and summaries of suspects, crimes and vehicles. I eagerly wrote down all information given, still not really sure what I was and was not supposed to make note of. Dean and I, and the rest of the ten officers present, were told our sector assignment— the area we were responsible for patrolling and handling all reportable incidents in—and our radio call sign. After coming to attention, and giving the lieutenant a salute at the sergeant's order, we were dismissed.

Dean and I ran our first call for service right after the briefing; a taxi driver had gotten involved in a pay dispute with a customer and reportedly threatened the guy with a crowbar. The cab driver left the scene prior to our arrival. I took a report from the 911 caller, the taxi's former passenger, and Dean called the cab company to have the driver return to the scene, which he did. I was obviously new to the job but did my best to appear confident as I fumbled through interviewing the disputants. We didn't wind up arresting anybody when all was said and done. I was relieved; it was one more new thing that I wouldn't have to flail my way through.

After we abated the dispute, Dean and I went back to the station where he undertook the monumental task of explaining the various purposes of the hundreds of forms that I had to acquaint myself with, which were in various locations around the station. About an hour and a half later, we headed back out on patrol and ran a few more calls; I acted in a mostly observational manner as this was an orientation week, a period of pure instruction— devoid of grading—to take it all in.

When not running calls, we slowly cruised the tiny Tenderloin district observing the teaming mass of humanity around us.

Every so often, Dean would direct my attention to something like a possible drug deal about to go down, a guy walking away from us with a guilty look on his face or a shady looking car, one that had been in the area for an unreasonable amount of time, a prospective customer, robber or shooter. My inexperienced and untrained eyes usually didn't observe what Dean had, when he had. I could feel Dean's frustration regarding my inexperience and, over the course of a few hours, I began to understand that my perception of the world around me would need significant alteration and drastic change if I was going to learn how to successfully police.

As I pondered the huge task ahead of me, Dean said something wonderful: "Let's get coffee."

Dean drove our car to one of the two Starbucks franchises at Powell and O'Farrell Streets, located directly across the intersection from each other. Coincidently, the coffee houses in question were situated next to sushi bars that were also across the street from each other. I thought that was pretty hilarious.

Sushi bars and coffee shops: the *real* San Francisco landmarks.

We got our drinks and sat down at one of the tables. For a while, we sipped at our cups in awkward silence. Over the course of the evening, I had inferred from Dean's affect that he wasn't overly enthusiastic about training a new cadet. I decided to investigate the matter, in the spirit of the job.

"Uh, Dean, do you enjoy training cadets? Or, is this maybe something that you're stuck with?" I asked. I could see the wheels turning in his head as he searched for the appropriate answer. A few beats later he came up with it.

"I haven't trained anybody for a while," he said, flatly.

"Why is that?" I asked, trying to keep the ball rolling.

"Because I usually work plainclothes," he said. "To tell you the truth, it was a surprise that they gave me a cadet. I didn't even know I was still a FTO because Tenderloin hasn't gotten a class of cadets in years. My partner got one of you guys as well and we can't work our normal gigs because of it, which kinda sucks. Also, neither of us remembers how to do the FTO paperwork. It's not your fault, though. In fact, I shouldn't even be telling you this. But, then again, we shouldn't be sitting in a coffee shop on your first day either."

"Sorry," I said. Seizing the opportunity to discuss an area of interest, I continued. "What is it like working plainclothes?" I asked. "That's what I want to do, totally. I mean, don't get me wrong, I'm here to learn every thing I can and I don't want to get ahead of myself but the plainclothes work seems really cool." I was slightly worried that this statement would make me come across as "salty," which is not good at all when still a rookie.

"Plainclothes is fun. Working plainclothes frees you from the responsibility of answering the radio for calls and that allows you time to get a little more involved in investigations. And it's easier to work with informants who wouldn't want to be seen talking to a uniformed cop," Dean stated.

"Do you have any informants?" I asked. Dean opened his mouth to answer but his cellular phone rang. He picked it out of his pocket and put it to his ear.

"What's up? You got something?" he said to the caller on the other end of the line. I could just barely make out a female sounding voice coming from Dean's phone. Dean's conversation was choppy, to the point and—for some reason—whispered. "Yeah . . . okay . . . half an hour . . . see you there." He hung up and looked at me, resuming his normal tone of voice. "Yep," he said. "And, lucky you, you're gonna meet her." He smirked.

Dean and I pulled up in front of a nondescript looking bar, which was next to a fire station, a little less than a half an hour after we finished our coffees. The bar's name: *Queen Mary's*. I had a feeling that it wasn't an English pub, considering its near proximity to a gaggle of impossibly tall and narrow-hipped hookers that simply stood, smiled and waved at us as our marked patrol vehicle approached. It was apparent, even to me, that these "girls" were used to the presence of police and even more used to the fact that no red-blooded, American, male cop—at least, one that was in his right mind—actively sought interaction with a big group of bitchy, El Salvadoran transvestites.

I asked Dean if he had ever arrested one of the trannies before.

"That's what the vice guys are for, Officer Cohen," Dean responded.

Dean pulled our car right in front of the bar and then told dispatch over our vehicle's onboard radio that we were meeting with a citizen in a "business" located at Polk and Sutter Streets. It wasn't that Dean wanted the world to know where we were. "Giving frequent updates as to what you are doing is good policy in police work. That way, when your coworkers hear you screaming for help they automatically know where to start driving," Dean instructed. He turned his head toward me as he put the vehicle in park, "After you," Dean said, pointing toward the bar. He wasn't joking.

"Um, Sir, it's my first day. Is it a good idea for me to go into a place like this?" I asked. I'd long heard the rumors of old-time cops drinking on duty, getting their whiskey in opaque, paper or Styrofoam cups. Such activity was now, understandably so, a big no-no. Maybe, MAYBE, one could get away with being sauced while on duty by having an indoor administrative job and thirty-plus years of service to his or her credit. The department would likely turn a blind eye to such a case as there is only so much damage that one can do while sitting at a desk, armed only with pencils and a telephone. But, on a cadet's first day in the field, walking into a bar when not on a call, especially a transvestite bar in the "Whore Triangle," could look pretty bad.

So, I wondered, was this the type of situation that would give me good cause to speak up, in the interest of self-preservation? Was it a good idea for me to follow my FTO into Lord-knows-where?

Hence the previous question.

"How couldn't it be?" Dean answered. He then exited the car and closed the door. For a moment I was alone in the vehicle, a police car, wearing a police uniform in the beautiful city of San Francisco.

Cool.

I was also about to walk into a tranny bar with my FTO.

Not cool, I thought before muttering, "Just please don't follow that sentence with, 'What could possibly go wrong?'"

I opened the car's door, exited and did my best to close it quietly—probably due to the close, personal interest I had in not alerting the neighboring firemen as to what I was currently doing.

Instinctively, I looked back and forth down the sidewalk and prayed that nobody was watching. I followed Dean to the bar's entrance. Dean held the door for me, forcing me to walk in first. I caught a glance of Dean's smile as I passed him and could tell that he was quite amused by the obvious look of terror on my face. However, I did my best to portray a confident and professional air as I walked in, letting my eyes adjust to the change in lighting.

To my surprise, *Queen Mary's* (patrons aside) looked like any other slightly upscale, dimly-lit bar in San Francisco. It had a long bar on the left side of the room that was constructed of dark wood and accented with brass fittings. A row of mirrors was mounted behind the dimly-illuminated bottles of booze. The walls were painted a deep blue and a row of high tables and chairs were scattered about on the right. The lighting was tasteful, maintained by either the antique chandelier that hung from the ceiling or the brass wall sconces that dispersed ambient light upwards. I could imagine men wearing corduroy jackets, smoking pipes and sipping brandy in this environment. So, that said, it was interesting to see a mixture of normal looking men speaking to heavily made-up and elaborately dressed "women" in hushed tones. Dean crept up behind me.

"Watch their demeanors change when they notice us," he whispered in reference to the aforementioned couples. As if on cue, the prospective clients, who were keeping the *girls* company, tore their gazes away from their dates, glanced up at us and then abruptly either leaned back in their chairs—feigning disinterest and/or indifference—or got up to get another drink. The more feminine aspects of the various parties just shot scathing glances toward us and then began drumming their long fingernails on the tables in front of them.

I really hoped that one of the men would jump up and scream, *"YOU HAVE A WHAT DOWN THERE!?!"*

It didn't happen.

"Surprise," I whispered back to Dean, "the police are here."

Dean approached the bar and waved to the bartender, a middle aged transvestite who had obviously grown tired of the painstaking regimen of shaving, exercise, waxing and makeup application necessary to maintain the illusion. The bartender approached, smiling. Dean waved me closer.

"Mary, meet Officer Dougie Cohen," Dean said.

Did you need to use my whole name? I thought.

"Hi, darling. Welcome," Mary stated, presenting a hand to me, palm down. Instinctively, I took her hand like any other lady's and gave it a quick touch and a slight nod of my head.

"Oh, such a gentleman," Mary said to Dean. "Where'd you get this one and why are you wearing that gorgeous uniform?"

"I'm training him; it's his first day," Dean said to Mary. "They pulled me away from plainclothes duty because of him. They told me the kid needed a new dad," Dean joked.

"You can be my daddy any time," Mary replied.

"Thanks for the offer," Dean deadpanned. "I'm all booked up, though."

"Can I get you guys anything?" the bartender asked.

"I'll have a club soda," Dean said. He added, "He's fine," in reference to me.

"He certainly is," Mary said and turned away to fetch the drink.

"No offense," Dean stated to me, "but you don't need to be seen with a possible cocktail in front of you on your first day, right?"

"I understand; I'm gonna go hit the head," I said and sheepishly walked toward the rear of the bar, trying my best not to make eye contact with anybody.

"Have fun!" Dean yelled after me.

I approached the bathroom; to my surprise it didn't smell terrible. It smelled quite pleasant actually—for a bathroom in a bar. I began to enter the seemingly empty restroom and then realized why the place had a pleasant odor: perfume. I slowed as I briefly pondered why I would be smelling perfume in the *men's* room. Quickly putting two and two together, I realized that this would have to be a surgical strike and hurried to a urinal.

As I began to unzip my uniform pants—always a pain because of the gun-belt—I listened for anybody in the stalls behind me. The silence indicated that I was in the clear. I let my bladder relax and began to pee. About five seconds passed. I glanced up and noticed the mirror directly above me; the mirror with the slight downward angle as to focus all reflection on my genitalia. Horrified, I pushed as hard as I could in an effort to empty my bladder as quickly as possible. As I neared completion, I began to hear footsteps and voices approaching the bathroom.

Fuck, I thought, *hurry the fuck up! What were you thinking taking a leak in the men's room of A GODDAMN TRANNY BAR while wearing a police uniform? Asshole.*

My penis was back in my pants before the last drop had even hit the porcelain. I zipped up like pulling the ripcord on a parachute and backed away from the urinal. Just then, one of the more masculine patrons of the bar entered the bathroom in the company of his effeminate, eau de toilette soaked date. I quickly made my way to the sink, washed up and then nearly ran out of the bathroom just in case any residual cock reflection was left for them to see. I continued to race-walk to the end of the bar, back to Dean's side.

"Why the hell did you let me do that? I thought you were supposed to make sure I didn't do stupid shit?" I gasped as the panic slowly eased.

"Easy, boy; easy—because it was funny," Dean replied, laughing. He pointed down the bar toward the bathroom from which I'd just emerged. I looked toward it and saw the couple that had nearly gotten an eyeful of *Dougie Cohen Jr.* exit the bathroom, laughing and waving toward me. I frowned and sheepishly waved back.

"You set me up," I said to Dean, betrayed.

"So much for the honeymoon," he replied and wiped tears of laughter from his face. I thought my head was going to burst into flames.

"Good work," I had to admit.

Mary approached holding a small glass filled with bubbling and clear liquid and cocktail napkin. She set the items down in front of Dean. Dean picked up the drink, took one sip and, as he did so, removed the napkin from the counter and put it in his pocket. He took another sip and placed the glass back town on the bar—along with a twenty dollar tip.

"Thanks," Dean said to Mary.

"Anytime, handsome," Mary replied. She added, to me, "Don't be a stranger."

"I get the feeling he might," Dean said, motioning in my direction.

"Wouldn't blame him," Mary said. "That bathroom trick was just mean. The poor dear looks like somebody just walked over his grave."

When we were back in the car, Dean produced the cocktail napkin that he had secreted in his pocket and began to study it. I could see that there were a few bits of information inscribed on it, by hand. After reading the text—which contained a name, description and address— Dean began to use our vehicle's onboard computer to conduct further investigation into the activity and subject that Mary had, apparently, alerted him to. As he ran vehicle registration, warrant and criminal history inquiries, he spoke to me.

"Mary is a confidential and reliable informant, also known as a 'CRI.' A CRI is a person who has proven themselves so reliable that a warrant can be written based on their knowledge and actions. You probably won't be developing any informants anytime soon but it's good to know this stuff anyways. I have a few snitches that I need to meet with now and then to let them know I still value their efforts. That's why we went here today; plus, I wanted to do that bathroom gag but that was more of a secondary motive. A 'CI' is an unproven informant, like some guy who walks up to you and doesn't want to give you his name but says that some other guy across the street has a gun or something. The CRI has been formally registered with the department—after providing good information on a number of occasions—and is now on the payroll. Their identities are a closely guarded secret and the suspect's defense attorney has pretty much no privilege to know who they are, only the presiding judge of the criminal case," Dean explained.

"Do they get a monthly salary?" I asked.

"No, it's on a case by case basis. The average is a hundred for a gun case, seventy-five bucks for a dealer and one hundred-fifty for both; but there's no set pay scale."

"So, what's written on the napkin there?"

"Hopefully, it's your first arrest." Dean's smile returned.

The next work night, at about 2300 hours, Dean and I walked up to the front gate of a derelict hotel with a really grandiose name: The Aristocrat. I didn't bother to tell Dean the joke I knew that shared a punch line with the hotel's title. Dean and I were working a foot patrol and wearing our eight point service caps, as was required when one walked a beat. Dean's cap looked worn and cool, in stark contrast to the blue radar dish perched atop my head.

"When you wear that thing, with your pale skin and shaved head," Dean said, "you look kind of like you have cancer."

"Great, thanks."

Dick.

The seemingly innocuously named hotel was, in keeping with the week's current theme, the headquarters for the transvestite and transsexual hooker crowd and the cast of freaks who loved them. I'd like to add the caveat that not all of the men who have sex with transvestites or transsexuals are freaks, but in this specific case, at this specific location, they were.

Dean had briefed me as to what we were doing during the walk over and told me that, on the previous day, Mary had tipped him off to a methamphetamine dealer who Dean had arrested many times in the past.

"You got tipped off to somebody who you already know?" I clarified.

"Yes," he answered.

"Weird."

"Yep, you done talking now? Can I go on with the story?"

"Sorry."

What Dean learned from Mary was where the dealer was *currently* residing. Prior to the meeting, this information had been a mystery. Somehow, Mary had tracked the man down. A few computer queries later, Dean learned that Mr. James Runningsteed—he was reportedly of Native American descent but looked like any other white tweaker—still had an active, warrantless search clause as a condition of court-ordered probation. Dean decided to take me along and conduct a *knock and talk* to check up on Mr. Runningsteed's business activities.

As we were going into a fleabag hotel full of parolees, probationers and drug addicts, Dean thought it best to have his normal plainclothes partner, Chris, who had also been knocked back down to uniform duties to train one of my more gifted classmates, Jay, assist us. On their first night of patrol, Chris and Jay got into a harrowing car chase turned foot chase and then turned knockdown, drag-out fight. This incident resulted in a killer arrest, as the guy they pursued and fought had, in his possession, a backpack full of crack cocaine and a loaded handgun. That morning in the cadets' locker area, Jay told me all about it and I was really jealous. My first arrest had been a shoplifter—already taken into custody by the security at a major corporate music store—right after we had left Queen Mary's. Such an arrest was the police equivalent of shot-gunning a nonalcoholic beer.

Needless to say, I was ready for something slightly cooler to happen.

Jay and Chris, who were also walking a beat, joined us in front of the hotel and Dean pressed the buzzer for entry. An Indian guy glanced out the front window toward us, grimaced and then walked back out of our sight. A few moments later, the gate buzzed and Dean pushed it open.

"One of you needs to put your handcuffs around the gate so it stays unlocked," Chris instructed. Jay reacted first and cuffed the gate accordingly. The four of us moved into the lobby—if you could call it that—of the hotel. Dean approached the manager's office, which was separated from the public by a thick layer of bulletproof (or, at least, knife or body fluid-proof) plastic.

"Can I see the guest registry?" Dean asked. Without any reply, the clerk retrieved a stack of cards from the drawer in front of him and then slid them trough the metal tray at the base of the window. Dean scrolled through the cards until he found the one with the name *"Bob Runningwater"* written on it. "Is this guy in his room?" Dean asked, holding the card up to the window.

"I think so," the clerk replied with a heavy Indian accent and slid the key to room sixteen into the tray. Dean swapped the card for it and turned to Chris, throwing him the key.

"We'll give it five seconds," Dean said to Jay and I. "If he doesn't open up by then, Chris is gonna open the door up with the key and we'll go piling in there. These rooms are only like ten feet by ten feet, and don't have toilets, so there's no reason why it should take him any longer than that to open up. If it does take him any longer than that, he's either scrambling to find a hiding place for his shit, grabbing a weapon, feigning sleep or dead. He's not exactly a health nut, so that last possibility wouldn't surprise me all that much."

"What's he calling himself this time?" Chris asked. Apparently he had a history with our suspect as well.

"Bob Runningwater," Dean said.

"A master of disguise!" Chris exclaimed, causing spontaneous laughter among our group.

"Okay, let's go," Dean said, swirling his pointer finger in a circle next to his head in the universal sign for "fall in." We followed him up the stairs to the first floor. As we ascended, I began to hear a cacophony of techno music, moans, showers and doors slamming, no doubt in response to our presence.

A surprisingly attractive tranny came walking out of the shower, a towel wrapped around her ample, augmented bust—some Third World hack did a surprisingly good job—and one around her hair. I looked away, feigning disinterest but, I'll admit, the curiosity was there, confusing though it was.

Remember, there's a dick down there, I repeated in my head.

He/she sauntered past me, glanced at my name tag and stated, in a sultry, accented voice, "Ello, Oowoffisa Cowe-en."

"Ma'am," I replied and continued walking.

"That ain't no *Ma'am*, Cohen," Chris corrected.

"Now you tell me," Dean interjected, glancing back at us with a smile. "Where were you with that one last

Saturday?" Again, we all laughed. We were quite the jovial crew.

When we arrived at room sixteen, Chris readied the room's key near the lock. Jay and I took positions on either side of the door like we were taught in the academy. Dean pressed his ear against the door, listening for movement or voices inside. He then nodded to Chris and mouthed the words, "He's in there."

Dean looked at Chris, Jay and I, giving us all a readying look. Dean lightly knocked.

"WHAT!?!" a voice yelled from inside.

"Eeez me, mang," Dean said, using a very unconvincing accent.

"Hold on. Fuckin'—ayy," the voice stated. I heard a brief commotion from inside, like the occupant therein had tripped on his way to answer the door. Soon, the door flew open, giving us all a look at the greasy, shirtless, Keith Moon look-alike inside. "Oh, what the fuck?" he said, observing the four uniformed officers standing in the hallway.

We barged into his room while ordering him to turn around and put his hands behind his back. Jay and I were pumped and yelling out stern commands as instructed in the academy.

To our chagrin, Mr. Runningsteed completely ignored Jay and I and, instead, continued to regard Dean and Chris with great concern. "How did you find me and why the fuck are you wearing that blue shit? Did you guys get demoted?" he asked in an exasperated manner, obviously confused about Chris and Dean in uniform.

As our orders continued to fall on deaf ears, Jay and I finally decided to grab Runningsteed's arms and put handcuffs on him, minus the academy taught fanfare of:

A. Assume a bladed stance.
B. Position your body to a forty-five degree angle to the suspect's rear.
C. Place your inside hand to the suspect's upper arm, near the triceps.
D. Put your outside hand on the suspect's elbow.
E. Then move your inside hand to the wrist.
F. Remove your cuffs.
G. Place the ratcheting band on the meaty portion of the wrist.
H. Apply light pressure.
I. Ratchet the cuffs to the proper degree of tightness.
J. Lock the handcuffs.
K. Kiss the guy, etc.

As it turned out, just putting the guy's arms together and throwing the cuffs on worked quite well.

Note to self, I thought.

Dean and Chris addressed the two of us. "Go find it," they said, simultaneously.

"Find what?" Jay and I replied in unison.

"The dope," Chris said.

"Dopes," Dean added.

Barum-bum-bum, I thought. I'm sure the scowl on my face was poorly hidden.

Jay and I gingerly began searching through Runningsteed's piles and piles of malodorous and slimy belongings. Sexual lubricants, condoms and dildos littered the room along with CDs, broken electronics and cigarette butts. Everything seemed to be in a specific place but still, somehow, the room remained a total disaster. I soon learned this was a common trait among tweakers: endless organization minus sanitation.

Twenty minutes later, after opening every single container and searching every pocket of every item of clothing in the room, Jay and I were stumped.

"You still haven't searched *him*," Chris said to us both.

Jay and I then began to search Runningsteed's fitted, slimy, black jeans. I noted that our suspect seemed to have an odd trait when handcuffed that caused him to lean forward and frown every time our search neared the area of his pelvis. Were I as experienced then, I would have recognized this as a "tell," a sign that criminals give when they are trying to keep their arresting officer(s) from finding something illegal or damning, much like what professional poker players are constantly, simultaneously looking for and trying to hide.

But, back then, I just figured that he was ticklish.

After what can only be described as the longest search to ever be conducted on a pair of pants, Jay and I gave up.

"I got nothing," I said

"Sir, I don't think there's anything in here," Jay said, confidently.

Dean and Chris exchanged a knowing glance. Chris then ushered Jay and I aside, grabbed Runningsteed's handcuff chain and pushed down on it, abruptly.

"Ah, fuckin' take it easy," Runningsteed complained, as the metal band of the handcuff dug into his radius.

"STAND UP STRAIGHT, James; you master of deception, you," Chris ordered. Runningsteed complied, but it wasn't like he had any other option.

Dean walked up to Runningsteed's front, unbuttoned the top button of his jeans, reached in and pulled out a small cloth bag that had previously been safety pinned to crotch area of our suspect's pants. Dean held this item up, displaying it to Jay and me. Dean then removed one of several, plastic, golf ball size bags of off-white crystals from the little crotch-cozy.

"This is meth," Dean said, giving the plastic baggie a little victory shake. "Dougie, call for a unit to take him back to the company, please. You can do *that*, right?"

"John-forty-two-david," I said into my radio, "can we get a four-o-seven?" At least I had that part down.

CHAPTER 7

"I want to see you shoot the way you shout."
—Theodore Roosevelt

I've got a friend who works for a police agency, which shall remain nameless, in the East Bay of the greater San Francisco Bay Area. It is a notoriously liberal city that is home to a notoriously liberal university. This friend, Alan, is one of the more mellow cops I've ever met despite the fact that he's twice my age and probably twice as tough.

Alan told me a story once. He was on patrol, by himself—as they all are in his agency—and getting a cup of coffee. He struck up conversation with a citizen who wished to express her dismay in regard to a physical altercation between a uniformed police officer and a suspect, which she had witnessed. We'll call this woman: *Jane Publique*.

I think the conversation went something like this:

Jane: "Excuse me, Officer. I'm very concerned."

Alan: "Okay, what's got you feeling that way?" [Stirs cream into coffee.]

Jane: "I saw one of your coworkers the other day. He was rolling around on the ground with some poor soul, and the officer punched the gentleman in the face! Can you believe it?"

Alan: "Well, yes, sometimes such actions are necessary when one is *fighting* with another person who means him or her harm."

Jane: [Exasperated] "Don't they teach you guys aikido or something?"

Now, I'm not sure about the rest of the conversation but, from what I understand, that last line about aikido is a direct quote. For those of you who don't understand the humor in that statement, I'll provide the following history lesson that took me about five minutes of internet research to compile.

Aikido was founded by a Japanese man named Morihei Ueshiba, who is now commonly referred to as the "O-Sensei" (translated to mean "great teacher") by the followers of his martial art. As a young man, Ueshiba became proficient in traditional Japanese jiu-jitsu, sword fighting and spear fighting. He spent some time in the Japanese military after barely meeting the minimum height requirement. Though he went on to be a successful soldier, Ueshiba was a spiritual man and became a devout pacifist in his later years.

In 1925, Ueshiba was challenged to a match against a fencing instructor who was armed with a wooden sword. Reportedly, Ueshiba "defeated" him by constantly dodging various attacks until his challenger relented. Ueshiba apparently realized that he was on to something and came to believe that, through similar techniques, one could resolve any physical altercation without any force being used. Ueshiba dedicated his life to the invention of an art that used these techniques, the furtherance of pacifism and his take on Budo, which translated means: *"The Way of the Warrior."* Eventually, modern aikido, a martial art based on dodging, redirection, a few stunted strikes and some upper body joint locks, was born.

The O-Sensei had this to say about Budo: *"Budo is not felling the opponent by our force; nor is it a tool to lead the world into destruction with arms. True Budo is to accept the spirit of the universe, keep the peace of the world, correctly produce, protect, and cultivate all things in nature."*

Many of the joint locks used in aikido, which are also more or less the same joint locks derived from the ancient art of Japanese jiu-jitsu, are taught nationwide in police academies. Knowledge of these techniques is very helpful when dealing with a drunken asshole in a bar that is being less than cooperative but *not* swinging at you. The same techniques are also very good at motivating handcuffed suspects to move. These techniques, absent decades of training, are not very helpful to the average police academy graduate currently rolling around on the ground with a convicted felon—one who isn't very happy about the prospect of being placed in handcuffs and taken to jail for an unknown amount of time. Usually, to get such a person in handcuffs, an application of force is going have to be used. To prevent the same suspect from taking the officer's gun and murdering him or her with it, again, force will be required. Force is also something that is, for the most part, absent from modern aikido instruction.

Still not convinced that a right cross, a leg-sweep takedown, a knee to the stomach, a slap to the back of the head, a strike across the thigh with a baton or a whack on the shin with a four cell flashlight are proper maneuvers for your city's peace officers to be using? Let me pose this question to you then: how old were you when you saw your first action movie? I'm guessing pretty young.

I'm also guessing that, in said action movie, you saw Bruce Willis, Sylvester Stallone or Arnold Schwarzenegger hit somebody with their fists or an object. I'm also guessing that later in the week, when playing with friends, you emulated Bruce, Sly or Arnie's actions. That was your first lesson in defensive tactics, the moment when you decided what a "real" fight looked like, skewed though it may have been. With that lesson in mind, what would you do if you were grappling in the middle of the street with a parolee who would rather see you dead than go back to prison?

Would you take such an opportunity to accept the spirit of the universe, keep the peace of the world, correctly produce, protect and cultivate all things in nature?

I doubt it.

I'm not, in any way, mocking the accomplishments of the O-Sensei, downplaying his wisdom or implying that nothing in aikido is relevant or useful for policing. However, police work is violent. There's no getting around it. The citizens of the United States give their law enforcement officers firearms because it is commonly accepted that guns are a necessary tool of the job. Toward

101

the end of his life, the O-Sensei probably wouldn't even touch a gun let alone fire one.

The O-Sensei was a good man, a visionary, and a spiritual leader. But the O-Sensei wasn't expected to put handcuffs on people at the end of a struggle. Cops can't be pacifists; cops are paid to shoulder the burden of dealing with violence, sometimes through violence, so that the civilian population does not have to. It says so, right in section 835 of the California Penal Code in a few run-on sentences:

> *"Any peace officer who has reasonable cause to believe that the person to be arrested has committed a public offense may use reasonable force to effect the arrest, to prevent escape or to overcome resistance. A peace officer who makes or attempts to make an arrest need not retreat or desist from his/her efforts by reason of the resistance or threatened resistance of the person being arrested; nor shall such officer be deemed an aggressor or lose his/her right to self-defense by the use of reasonable force to effect the arrest or to prevent escape or to overcome resistance."*

To my knowledge, the O-Sensei never arrested anybody. Keep that in mind the next time you see a man or woman in a wool uniform fighting with a suspect. Also, if the cop looks like he or she is losing the fight, please help. I promise it won't make you an honorary member of the Gestapo.

If you still have questions about how violent or dangerous police work can be; if you still think that those stories you heard about a veteran officer who never drew his gun in thirty years of service are the standard; if you insist that talking can solve any conflict: allow me to present an example.

Allow me to illustrate how Dougie Cohen lost a few important marbles.

CHAPTER 8

"Today . . . is Christmas! There will be a magic show at zero-nine-thirty! Chaplain Charlie will tell you about how the free world will conquer Communism with the aid of God and a few marines! God has a hard-on for marines because we kill everything we see! He plays His games; we play ours! To show our appreciation for so much power, we keep heaven packed with fresh souls! God was here before the Marine Corps! So you can give your heart to Jesus, but your ass belongs to the Corps! Do you ladies understand?"

—R. Lee Ermey in
Stanley Kubrick's Full Metal Jacket

One and a half months past graduation from the academy, I transitioned to the second phase of field training. Tom Eastman, my ex-marine FTO, had a vastly different personality than Dean and had an equally different teaching style. I had first learned of his reputation toward the end of my time with Dean, when coworkers would question me as to who was going to be training me next. The interactions usually went something like this:

Random Coworker: "So, who's gonna be your FTO next phase?"

Me: "Tom Eastman, Sir."

Random Coworker—"Whoopee; have fun [walks away snickering]. You're fucked."

These repeated and ominous interactions were, to say the least, troubling. I had grown used to Dean's easygoing demeanor and related to his dry sense of humor. Despite my lack of experience, I thought Dean and I would be a good team, the kind of team that could star in a series of cop/buddy movies together, such as my favorite such film of all time, *Running Scared*. I figured that Dean could be Billy Crystal and I would be Gregory Hines, just considerably paler.

Dean did his best to prepare me for the transition to Tom's teaching style.

"Look," Dean said, "you're a smart kid and you're doing well but I think I've done you a disservice by becoming too much your friend and not enough of an instructor. Tom has a very different style than I do and you need to be on your A-game with him or he's gonna dock you. He fails a lot of cadets and he's kinda used as a hit-man for the Field Training Office when recruits have discipline problems—or if they need to be driven to quit or need a little 'grounding.' I suspect you would fall into the latter category."

"Grounding, why? Do people think I'm salty, or something?"

"Yeah, kinda. I think that it's because you laugh too much," he admitted. "Don't worry, you'll do good. Just remember that he might not find your jokes as amusing as I do."

"Great," I said. "So much for riding this out via charm and personality."

Working with Tom was different. I felt like a bumbling fool during our first week together, like I had learned nothing from Dean and could do nothing right. But, despite his reputation as a ball-breaker, I never got the impression that Tom treated me unfairly. After a week or so, he even spoke to me.

And it, almost, was all downhill from there.

I quickly figured out what Tom's expectations were as an instructor: fuck up once and he would sit me down and give me a prolonged but educational lecture regarding my infraction. Though I thought the lectures were repetitive, they got the point across and usually corrected the problem—usually. If, by some chance, I repeated the same mistake then I would be yelled at. Fair enough.

I woke up on a Tuesday evening at about 1900 hours, two hours before 2100 lineup, feeling uneasy. Tessa had already left for work, hours prior. I wasn't sure why I felt this way but figured it was just a side effect of my normal insomnia intensified by frequent interruptions to my circadian rhythm; that and the whiskey I'd consumed before bed, a necessary diversion after the previous night's shift with Tom.

I made a cup of nuclear coffee and sat down on my stationary bike, pedaling, sipping my liquid inspiration, and watching CNN. The early evening news was reporting its standard regimen of death, tragedy and politics. I didn't know why I felt so off-kilter; my mood should have been predominately neutral; I was simultaneously looking forward to work and not looking forward to being highly scrutinized for ten hours.

After five pretend miles, I got off the bike, hit the head, made something to eat and was on my way to the shower when the aforementioned general feeling of uneasiness turned into one of moderate anxiety, as if I was waiting for a phone call from a missing loved one. Determined to push this uneasiness out of my mind, I headed downstairs to my apartment complex's gym and donned my heavy bag gloves. My dad taught me bag drills and the basics of boxing when I was about nine or ten. On occasions such as this, when I was feeling so anxious, I liked to recall a bit of that training.

I popped in a familiar CD, *Combat Rock* by The Clash, and started jabbing out a cadence on the seventy pounds of vinyl, sand and duct tape suspended from the joist above me. I worked combos in between five and eight blows. I bobbed and weaved around the bag, trying my best to remain in constant motion until sweat began to coat my gloves and, in turn, leave a Rorschach test of perspiration and saliva on the floor and striking surface. I hit and moved; I struck and danced until I felt satiated, until I felt the morning jolt of caffeine dripping off the tip of my nose—until steam rose from my bare shoulders into the air around me. I worked until I was panting and my mind was distracted from the ominous feeling that had been racing through my head, the thought that had surfaced after about thirty seconds on the heavy bag: *I think something shitty is going to happen tonight.*

The few other people from my apartment complex who had filtered into the gym regarded me rather oddly. I ignored them, took another shower and jammed over to work.

Tom and I were assigned to walk a beat that night. Our staffing was such, due to the presence of my fellow cadets and me, that the lieutenant was able to fill not only one but two foot patrol teams. Officers Sarah Sarkissian and Paul Grady were assigned to walk the neighboring beat. As the Tenderloin district was only so big and as Paul and Tom were partners, when not training cadets, the four of us teamed up.

For the first two and a half hours of the shift, we handled a few low-priority disputes, took a stolen car report and "took on" some suspected dealers at the intersection of Turk and Taylor Streets. At 2338 hours, dispatch asked us to handle an emergency call.

"John-forty-two-david," the dispatcher said, "I've got an A-priority domestic fight in progress at 536 Hyde, apartment number 602. The 911 caller is reporting hearing a commotion with a woman screaming in the apartment above. Can you handle?"

Tom nodded at me, expectantly.

"Yeah, check. John-forty-two-david is responding," I transmitted back.

Sarah, who was very friendly and obviously trying her best to prevent me from flailing in front of Tom, pointed at her chest and mouthed, "Don't forget us."

"Can you put the forty-three-david on that run as well?" I added.

"Ten-four," stated the dispatcher.

Tom, Sarah, Paul and I walked the block or so from our current location to the given address. A few minutes later, we arrived at the multilevel apartment complex's front gate. Tom rang the manager's room for entry.

"Who is it?" asked a groggy, male voice through the street-level speaker. I made a subconscious note to answer such a question by stating, "Candy-gram," if and when I was done with training.

"SFPD," said Tom. With that, the front gate made the angry, buzzing sound that denoted it was time to enter. Tom pushed it open and walked in. Sarah and Paul followed suit.

I pulled out one of two pairs of handcuffs from their place on my belt and put one cuff around the metal gate. Once this task was completed, I ascended the granite steps to the, also buzzing, front door that Sarah was holding open for me. I quickly scanned the room for an object to keep this door from closing and locking, as my other handcuffs didn't have anything to wrap around on the door's solid surface. I pulled a tenant's yet to be retrieved phonebook toward me with my boot and wedged it between the door and frame.

109

As both the door and gate were now propped open to ease the flow of backup, should assistance be needed, I joined my fellow officers at the base of the elevator and watched as Paul repeatedly pressed the appropriate button in an effort to call the elevator to the ground floor. After about ten presses, in rapid succession, it was apparent that the elevator was not currently in order. Tom addressed us.

"Looks like *stair* time," Tom said.

"Great," Paul and Sarah groaned, simultaneously. The four of us then began to ascend the six flights of stairs to apartment 602.

"Cohen, you better get your ass up there first," Tom warned.

"No problem, Sir," I said and began taking the stairs in double.

I began to hear yelling and banging as we approached the third floor landing; nothing noteworthy, just the typical sounds of an argument, late at night, in an apartment with hardwood floors. These sounds intensified as we finally arrived on the sixth floor—I was first as ordered—and our party was alerted to the proper apartment by an abrupt crash behind the door of apartment 602.

I approached the door. The lingering malaise in my gut got worse.

FUN FACT:

It varies on the source of your statistics, but domestic disturbances and traffic stops are the situations wherein most cops are seriously hurt or killed.

In a traffic stop, the culprit of the violence is usually a wanted man or a person trying to conceal the illegal drugs, dead prostitutes or guns that they have secreted in their vehicle. The officer makes the stop and gunfire ensues at some point either before or after the initial contact with the suspect. It's either that, or a drunk driver slams into the patrol car after being drawn in by the flash of the emergency lights.

In the domestic disturbance, the officer walks into an unfamiliar, possibly fortified environment that is rich with potential or real weapons. Also, the victims of domestic violence are known to turn on the officers— who they called to protect them from their drunken, angry spouses—upon witnessing their attacker being led to jail.

The lesser spoken of reality of domestic disputes is that, frequently, people who let their emotions get sufficiently out of whack as to necessitate a 911 call are, in my experience, not the brightest shining stars of the populace. I'm not belittling true domestic violence, but few domestic disturbance calls ever amount to that; most are simply two intoxicated morons screaming at each other because, "That bitch took my three dollars!" or something equally ridiculous.

And it seems as though they are always, always drunk or high.

Paul and Tom stood behind me in the narrow hallway that led to the apartment door, which was commonly referred to as the "fatal funnel" due to the very real threat of one bullet killing four people who are stupidly lined up in a single file column on the other side of the entryway. Because of this, both Paul and Tom positioned themselves with their sides facing the door, backs to the wall. Sarah and I did as well. I knocked and began to announce our cause, intent and authority. In other words: "Police! Open the door!"

"Poli—" is all I managed to say before the door flew open, inwards. Instinctively, Sarah and I took a step back. Before me was a large, corn-fed looking white male, in his early twenties. He was shaking his head back and forth. I could see his hands were empty.

"Man," he said, making a thumbs-up motion with his right hand and gesturing it behind him, into the apartment, "this is out of control. You've gotta get in there," he finished.

"Come out into the hallway, sir," I ordered.

Also walking out of the apartment, behind the big guy, was a somewhat pretty white girl with bleached hair and an above average amount of blemishes on her face. *Tweaker*, I immediately thought as:

1. Methamphetamine addicts seem to always develop terrible acne.
2. We were in the goddamn Tenderloin, wherein almost everybody was a doper or drunk or out of their mind . . . or a combination thereof. So it was a safe bet.

Both the white guy and, who I initially thought was, his girlfriend walked out into the hall with us. Paul and

COP: A Novel

Tom began to interact with them first. I figured that these two subjects were likely the disputants in question.

"What's going on?" Tom asked, before I thought to.

Fuck, I thought, *I'm gonna get docked for that.*

I didn't hear the question's answer due to another loud crash from inside the apartment. This crash was of sufficient volume as to send both Sarah's and my head spinning toward the source.

Looking through the open door, I saw a sinewy white male, who appeared to be in his twenties, stumble out of the studio apartment's kitchen. He was clad only in boxer shorts and holding his left hand to his head, as if in some sort of pain. He abruptly stopped and swayed, not seeming to notice Sarah or me. As Paul and Tom were actively dealing with the two other subjects, Sarah and I cautiously entered the apartment walking toward the near-naked man.

"Hey, are you okay?" I heard Sarah ask, off to my right.

The guy didn't answer, which concerned me.

"HEY, ARE YOU OKAY?" Sarah asked again, in a more authoritative tone.

In reply, the silent figure slowly drew his gaze across us. Observing the two uniformed officers in front of him, his expression went from one of apparent discomfort to a complete blank. I then noticed his eyes dart to the side of the room and back. His chest rose in deep inspiration.

At that instant, I knew that the oddball before me was about to flip out. I could tell that Sarah had similar feelings by her change in posture. Like the final falling coins in the payoff from a slot machine of misfortune, the

113

feeling of uneasiness began to trickle away as my adrenal response kicked in.

"Let's cuff him," she said in a hushed tone and I nodded in agreement.

We both took one step toward the man who would, very soon, change my life. In a few hours, I learned his name: Jameson Ratchet.

For a moment, Ratchet watched Sarah and I approach him and then dove, face first, toward the area of the room that he glanced at moments earlier. Neither Sarah nor I could see what he was diving towards, as the foot of the bed blocked the area from view. But, whatever it was, I was pretty sure it wasn't good.

Two thoughts about what Ratchet was doing came to mind:

1. He was trying to retrieve an amount of narcotics in order to throw them out of the window or stuff them down his throat. This was the preferred option as he would probably start choking, be unable to fight and I could show off my prior skills from years in the ER by giving him the Heimlich maneuver, saving his life and simultaneously retrieving the dope. *Harrah!* I'm the big hero; though he's off to jail, he thanks me for his new lease on life and I get a good score from Tom at the end of the day.

2. He was going for a gun and planning on killing Sarah, me and then, maybe, himself—if Tom and Paul didn't kill him first. Heroism in such a case can be slightly more complicated.

I leaned toward option number two but wasn't sure. I knew that I wouldn't actually find out until it was too late. I raced toward Ratchet and dove toward his back.

Just before landing on Ratchet and flattening his body against the floor, I observed that both of his hands were inside a green messenger bag that was on the ground, against the wall. At the same moment that my uniformed and accoutrement adorned body began to crash down on his, Ratchet pulled his hands and the bag under his body. To make sure that he didn't pull whatever it was out of the bag, I looped my arms around Ratchet's body and grabbed him in a bear hug, securing his arms under mine as best as I could.

The backs of my forearms felt a hard, metal object through the nylon. Ratchet began to scream and yell.

"I'll fucking kill you all!" Ratchet thrashed under me, trying to pull his arms free. If there was any question before, I was now convinced that the guy was not trying to discard drugs.

Wide eyed, I turned my head toward Sarah, who had come up to our left sides. "This isn't good," I said as Sarah announced over the air that we had an emergency.

"John-forty-three-david, CODE THIRTY-THREE!" she called out into her radio.

Tom, get in here, I thought. Little did I know that he and Paul were now busy subduing Ratchet's girlfriend who had, upon hearing the commotion inside her apartment involving the police and her beloved, pile-of-crap boyfriend, put two and two together and gone completely nuts.

Convinced that Ratchet had a gun—which I'll note is a *bad* thing for those of you unfamiliar with the technology—I took a quick mental inventory of the various force options available to me.

The San Francisco Police Department's guidelines for the use of force by its officers, in ascending order of gravity, are as follows:

1. Verbal persuasion; "Hey, dude, get your hands out of your pockets."

2. Physical control; "Fine, I'll take your hands out of your pockets for you."

3. Oleoresin capsicum aerosol spray; "Fine, you're gonna be an ass and bury your hands in your pockets? That's cool. Take this! Ha! Oh sorry, Dave. I didn't realize that you were still wrestling with the guy. I assure you that the burning will stop after a while . . . so, do you want a napkin or something?"

4. The department issued baton; "Get your hands out of your pockets or I'm gonna go back to the car, fiddle around for the keys, unlock it and get my stick because I always forget to bring it with me. Then, when I get back, you're in trouble."

5. A lateral vascular restraint technique, also known as a carotid choke; "Dave, choke his ass out but don't you dare occlude any portion of his wind pipe—such an easy thing to do when that guy that you're fighting is thrashing like a gator—as that may expose us to undue civil liability."

6. The department issued firearm; "Sir, I told the guy to take his hands out of his pockets and he did. Unfortunately, he also removed the gun that was formerly in his pocket and started shooting at me with it. So I pulled my gun out and returned fire, striking him seven times, so I've been told, in the chest. What's that? He's going to be fine and make a full recovery? Oh, great. What a relief that is . . . fucker."

Though I had a number of tools on my belt, I had no ability to retrieve my can of pepper spray—an item that is, in most situations, useless anyways—my baton or my gun because my hands were currently occupied. So, I made an attack decision, which I believed to be my only option at the time, other than letting Ratchet go and playing quick draw with him: I head-butted Ratchet on the back of skull really, really hard. I'm still not sure why the technique came to mind so readily. I imagine that I saw it in a movie, but I can't remember what it was.

"You hit me!" he blurted out, slightly dazed.

You were expecting something else? I thought and then said, "Yeah, I hit you. And I'll do it again. Stop resisting!"

Heartened by the crazed man's response to the first strike, I served a few more blows to the back of Ratchet's head, targeting the base of his skull. I remembered from my medical training that this area of the skull was particularly vulnerable. Yet, I had never head-butted anybody before and the volume and violence of the act surprised me. As I didn't have the aid of any illegal stimulants affecting my sympathetic nervous system and keeping me from passing out, I feared that I might just wind up hurting myself more than the possible armed man below.

However, as I was not fielding any other suggestions, the blows continued.

The struggle went on and our two bodies soon became wedged against the radiator, in the corner of the room. Thankfully, the radiator wasn't hot. I could hear Sarah repeating the distress call as she buried her arms under us, trying to remove Ratchet's hands from whatever it was that he was holding.

Out of the corner of my eye, I saw Tom come running into the room. Tom momentarily stopped and observed the scene. He then, decisively, grabbed Ratchet's legs and pulled the two of us—as I was attached to Ratchet's back with every ounce of strength I could muster in my excited state—away from the wall.

As we slid across the hardwood, Ratchet rotated under me to his left side, just slightly, just enough for me to catch a glimpse of the automatic pistol in his hand. For an instant, everything slowed down as my adrenal gland dumped its contents into circulation.

Oh shit, I thought as reality came back up to speed.

"HE'S GOT A FUCKING GUN!" I yelled in a manner that I hoped would convey urgency and not panic. I later learned that his statement was somehow broadcast over the air and to the army of cops who, if they weren't already, were now racing to our aid, speeding through the maze of streets downtown.

God, I hope that gun isn't mine, I thought, irrationally. I was fairly sure that being disarmed while in field training was a good way to fail.

As the gravity of the situation seeped into my brain, I drank in a myriad of stimuli that caused my pupils to dilate, my heart to quicken, my blood to pump and my brow to perspire. Any lingering aches, pains and discomfort that I may have had throughout the day faded completely away.

"I'll do it; I'm gonna pull the trigger," Ratchet moaned.

"No!" I belted out, crashing my forehead back down on Ratchet's skull. Intermission was over. I was back in the fight.

Tom assumed a position to hold down Ratchet's legs. Sarah, again, came up on my left and I could feel her hands probing under Ratchet's body for the weapon.

"John-forty-two-david," Tom calmly broadcast, "our subject has a possible gun underneath him. We're trying to get it free."

Paul left Ratchet's flailing girlfriend chained to the stairwell's railing in the hallway. He ran into the room and took the open position on my right.

I tried to brief those around me of the situation: "He's got a gun; I saw it. I'm holding his arms so he can't get it out. He keeps trying to, though."

"Alright," Paul said, looking pissed. Paul promptly punched Ratchet's face with his closed, gloved left fist about four times. Though his head bounced off the floor from the impact, Ratchet continued to scream and thrash in an obvious effort to obtain a clear shot at one of us . . . now probably at Paul first.

Seeing that it had little effect, Paul stopped punching Ratchet and removed his pepper spray. Paul gave Ratchet a two second liquid burst, which seemed to take forever, into Ratchet's eyes. As the aerosolized capsicum suspension hit the air, I began to cough.

I started to head-butt Ratchet again, foolishly ignoring the fact that he was now coated in a chemical irritant, a substance that was easily transferable to others. The tangy sharpness of the capsicum essence summarily made my eyes tear up and my nose run upon contact.

Great, this is going really well, I thought.

"I'll kill you! I'll fucking KILL YOU ALL!" Ratchet screamed as I saw, through tunneling vision, Paul, Sarah and Tom scrambling to pry the gun out of Ratchet's hands.

"Not before we fuck you up!" I grunted through clenched teeth; I'd never before had opportunity to say something with such venomous conviction. I was, officially, getting angry.

My left hand had a death grip on Ratchet's right, the same hand that was holding the gun. Consequently, I was also effectively pinning Ratchet's left arm. Figuring this would be sufficient—in light of the presence of the other officers attempting to control him as well—I pulled my right hand up toward Ratchet's neck. Since the discovery of the gun, I thought it very likely that, at some rapidly approaching moment, one of the other armed officers in the room would remove his sidearm and blow a large hole in Ratchet's head.

Peculiarly, this moment never came. All the same, this didn't stop me from plugging my ears as best as I could via a sharp inhalation against furled nostrils. I knew that a gun going off right next to my head would have my ears ringing for days.

I reached up and began to slide my right arm around Ratchet's chin, intent on choking him into unconsciousness. I'd never done this on a live and resisting person before and I was completely unaware of the one substantial problem associated with the technique. This danger wasn't mentioned in the academy.

As my hand traveled across Ratchet's neck, I began to flex my upper arm and forearm toward each other, attempting to constrict the carotid arteries that lay between. Without any obvious hesitation, Ratchet shot his head downwards and seized the meaty muscle below my right thumb in between his teeth, biting down with savage force. I had always heard that, pound for pound, the jaw had the strongest muscles in the body.

If I wasn't convinced before, I certainly was at that point.

"Let go of my hand, cocksucker!" I ordered as I crashed my rapidly swelling forehead into the base of his skull. To my chagrin, every time I landed my head upon his, the pressure on my thumb increased. I pulled, pushed and tried to make a fist, thereby enabling me to extract my hand from Ratchet's incisors—to no avail.

Stupid, stupid, stupid, I thought.

I could see Ratchet's face and jaw straining as he clamped down on my hand. He bit with such force that I believed it was only a matter of time until he completely amputated the muscle.

"Okay, asshole. Go ahead, bite it off. Bite it off and get ready for a bullet in your FUCKING HEAD!" I figured some tough talk might expedite the process. Plus, I *was* planning on killing the guy.

Subsequently, I thought the sentiment was rather appropriate.

I waited and waited, feeling tremendous pressure but little pain because of the surge of endorphins and adrenaline racing through my brain. Despite trying to mentally prepare myself for the possibility, the traumatic amputation never came. I was simply stuck.

"He's biting my hand," I said, sounding rather embarrassed despite the pain. Paul heard me but his hands were busy trying to get control of the gun and he was unable to come to my aid.

"Get it out," he said, obviously unaware of the difficulty that I'd insofar had in that venture. But Paul had a point; I needed to do something.

I quickly surveyed my options: my left hand was busy keeping us from being shot and my right hand was obviously otherwise indisposed. Strikes via fist and head had been done to death with little obvious effect, as had a shower of pepper spray. Short of a miracle, an amount of improvisation would be necessary.

And as I was now palpably enraged, it wasn't going to be pretty.

Any lingering thoughts I'd had of trying to remain calm and deal with the situation in a concise and effective manner were washed away in an instant, not unlike the blood that drips down the screen in the opening of a James Bond flick. Before that moment, I was more or less a sarcastic jokester with a heart of gold. I was a world-loving liberal, and a kind, gentle soul who liked to help people but was in a really bad situation. As the screen in my mind turned red, I felt predatory and wrathful. It was a new experience. I remembered a training video from the academy. In one segment, a cop who had been ambushed in his car and shot all to hell was interviewed about the experience.

First, he said that he thought: *Oh shit!* Then he thought: *Oh God!* Then, finally: *You're dead, asshole.*

I knew what I had to do.

In front of me, big as anything, was the right ear of my would-be murderer. And I decided that as much of Ratchet's ear belonged to me as the tissue he was so intent on removing from my hand. It was not a pound of flesh, but I was sure The Bard would still be amused.

I put the soft, fuzzy skin and cartilage of the lower half of Ratchet's ear into my dry, panting mouth and I bit down, hard.

Ratchet began to utter stifled grunts at first but soon transitioned into a wail as his mouth began to slowly open. I jabbed my right pointer finger into Ratchet's eye socket, pressing the moist orb back with my short, lacerating fingernail. Ratchet screamed, freeing my hand as my incisors came together and blood hit my tongue. I pulled my wounded hand out, opened my mouth, raised my head back and spit a section of Ratchet's bloody ear back at him.

"Fuck you," I said and began leveling elbow strikes to the side of Ratchet's turned head, relishing the sound his skull made as it bounced between my forearm and the floor below.

Finally, Tom, Paul and Sarah were able to get Ratchet's gun out of his grasp and Tom ripped it away, still cool as one can be considering the circumstances. I made a mental note to try and be like that—*if* I didn't just write myself out of the FTO program for biting a suspect's ear off.

Backup poured through the door in droves. The struggle continued but, absent the gun, the overwhelming force provided by the many officers in the room soon saw Ratchet in cuffs. Even handcuffed behind his back, he still made futile attempts to remove any holstered gun was in reach, a wild thing fighting captivity until the end.

The threat may have been gone but the malice behind my eyes clouded my judgment. Once more I choked Ratchet, if for nothing else than for revenge. I squeezed and squeezed, longer than I thought it should take for him to finally go unconscious. Paul placed a firm hand on my shoulder and leaned into it.

"Dougie, it's done; it's over," Paul said, "let him go."

"Yes, Sir," I answered, sheepishly.

And when I relaxed my arms and climbed off the suspect's back, he fell down limp on the ground below me, gasping for air like a marlin in its death throes on the white deck of a powerboat. I spat on him and kicked him in the stomach before blue-clad arms ushered me out of the room.

Some of my coworkers drove me to the hospital, where I first got to see myself in a mirror. My shirt was fully un-tucked and my pants were cocked sideways.

So much for that gig line, I thought.

My forehead was an angry red and smeared blood, my own, covered my right hand. Ratchet's blood had collected in the corners of my mouth and front of my chin. It had begun to form a gritty, coppery crust. My lip was split and I couldn't stop tonguing the wound, sucking the blood back in, absentmindedly.

During the car ride to the ER, I listened to the traffic on my radio. I heard the on-duty captain, various lieutenants, a slew of sergeants and a myriad of officers trying to pick up the incident's pieces and bring order to chaos. I heard orders being given to detain any and all witnesses, interview all neighbors and then a stressed call to get the suspect, Ratchet, an ambulance.

It seemed that somebody had noticed the damage to Ratchet's ear and that he was still only semiconscious— no doubt a side effect of exhaustion from the fight, decreased perfusion of oxygen to his brain and the myriad of stimulants in his system beginning to wearing off.

Suspects with this trifecta were the ones that tended to die in police custody: crazed dopers who blew their hearts up with a combination of exertion and drugs. Somehow those deaths usually seemed to be ruled the fault of the police in civil courts—as if a series of baton jabs to a man's back could magically stop his heart— hence the urgent call for medical assistance.

I sat in the back of the patrol car on the hard, plastic seat, and thought about the prospect of Ratchet's heart stopping. I hoped that, if it occurred, I was part of the physiology for such an event. I grinned.

At the hospital, after I had seen my reflection, a nurse told me to sit on a gurney and remove my uniform.

"I'm going to ask that these officers take control of your gun," the triage nurse said.

"I'm fine," I replied, not liking the idea.

"It's cool, man. We got it," said Jason, one of the kind officers who drove me to the ER. I trusted him and hearing his voice grounded me.

I did as instructed, unfastened my heavy belt and handed it over stating, "As long as Tom won't be pissed."

"Relax, bro. You did good."

A short while later, Sergeant Banner—a middle aged, Filipino, stocky Army veteran with a flattop haircut— visited me in the ER as I sat, hoping that a nurse or a tech would irrigate the wound to my hand at some point in the near future.

"Good job, Mr. Cohen," Sgt. Banner said. "How are you feeling, son?"

"Good, Sir," I replied. "Good times."

"That man nearly killed you," he stated. "Don't try to act tough when you don't need to. It doesn't suit you," Before I could counter he said, "Let me tell you what's gonna happen. First of all, take that goddamn gown off and put your uniform back on. You're a cop for Christ-goddamn-sakes; look like one. I don't care what the rules are in the hospital. Second, a captain and a few detectives are going to come ask you some questions. Third, when you get back to the station, you need to write a statement and give it to Tom because he's doing the report. Fourth, the gun was a loaded forty-five caliber automatic with a round in the chamber, you lucky, vicious little bastard. Fifth, when you exit this building, be prepared for the cameras and press."

"Yes, Sir," I said and reached for my undershirt. "I should probably tell you now that I bit him." An incredulous look came across Sgt. Banner's face.

"You bit who?" he asked.

"The suspect; the white guy; I bit him . . . but he bit me first."

"So, what you're telling me is that I get to inform the captain that you just tried to eat a suspect? That's how his ear got like that, isn't it?" He paused for a moment and added, "You are out of your mind, young man. But at least you're still alive for me to tell you that."

"Motherfucker tried to eat me first!"

Sgt. Banner sighed and walked out of the room, shaking his head. As he exited, he called back, "I'll let the investigating officer know he needs to write a warrant to make sure the suspect doesn't have any communicable diseases."

I didn't respond.

I called Tessa from the nurse's station in the emergency room and gave her the rundown of what had happened. She was silent on the other end of the phone, up to a point.

"What was that?" Tessa asked. "You *bit* the guy."

"Yeah, I bit his ear. I didn't really have much of a choice at the time."

"That's disgusting. Why would you do that?" Tessa asked. "Fuck, how did that taste?"

"It tasted like blood; it was gross. As I said, the guy had a gun and was trying to shoot me . . . so—"

"Well, are you going to go on the HIV cocktail?"

"I don't know. That's one of the reasons why I called. I was thinking about it."

"You should. You don't know what that guy has."

"Alright, babe, I'll tell them I want it." I exhaled deeply, "Looks like it's gonna be condoms again for a while."

"We'll talk about that when you get home, Dougie." She paused and said in a somewhat obligatory manner, clearly distracted by the disturbing story I had just told her, "I love you. I'm glad you're alright."

"I love you too," I said, adding emphasis to the words. I felt somehow worse now. "I'll be home late."

"Okay," she said and hung up.

I walked back to my bed thinking that I shouldn't have told her anything.

About two hours later, I was released from the ER with a diagnosis of a mild concussion (self-inflicted), chemically irritated eyes and a nasty human bite to my right hand. Prior to leaving, I wound up cleaning the wound myself as nobody ever came to do it for me. I was given a prescription for antibiotics and took my first round of anti-HIV, anti-viral meds, which I was supposed to take every morning for the next six months.

I walked outside, kind of curious about the media fanfare previously advertised by Sgt. Banner but found nothing but the cold, San Francisco night air; it felt good on my face, which was still hot from the pepper spray.

Some cop gets bit, a suspect goes crazy, and nobody gets shot: not news.

The light breeze seemed to help carry the violence away from my mind and helped me forget the cold conversation that I'd just had with Tessa. Along with a state of clarity, a feeling of melancholy set in.

In the days, weeks and months after the incident, Ratchet was always in my thoughts. Ratchet tested negative for HIV, but I'd need to get tested for six months to know for sure that I was in the clear. In the back of my mind, I'd see the specter of his face, constantly reminding me that he still might have killed me. I'd think about his stupid, white trash name and the ninety day jail sentence that he received from the local judicial system. As it turned out, Ratchet was a fugitive from Arkansas; he was wanted for shooting at a cop, which made it much less complicated for our courts to give him a sweet deal, one that he wouldn't protest, and then let the legal system in Arkansas deal with him after extradition.

In my most honest moments, I sat in earnest sorrow because Ratchet would walk the streets again one day.

Because I let him live.

Ratchet would hurt somebody else because I didn't do what needed to be done. Maybe I could have outdrawn him and put two bucks worth of copper and lead into his back. Maybe I could have quickly produced my knife and jammed it into his airway.

Maybe.

I remembered the coppery taste of his blood in my mouth, his skin between my teeth, and I studied the bite mark that was permanently stamped on my right hand. I thought about that day because it was the day I learned something about my desperate will to survive and discovered the aphotic place in my heart that had no issue with doing evil to my fellow man in its facilitation.

And part of me even liked it.

But that was the irony: trading a mouthful of flesh for peace of mind and general health; immediate survival versus slow circles around the drain.

Three months passed and I was almost finished with FTO. Tom, Sarah, Paul and I stood on a stage and received Medals of Meritorious Conduct and Bravery—"MCBs" per department slang—for our actions in apartment 602. I had a plastic smile on my face for the cameras, civic politicians and command staff present. I should have been proud. I should have been happy, but I just felt miles and miles away. Tessa was there, seated in the small auditorium with my parents. She recognized the look in my eyes. She knew that I was just thinking about one thing: what I would have done in the same situation if I had to do it all over again. She saw that when I laughed, I laughed from the irony, not from joy.

She knew what I was thinking because I thought it or said it every night when I took my "just in case" anti-viral medication, and every time I broke down in her arms and wept out my frustration—frustration over having to treat sex like a shuttle launch because of the unknown danger of disease transmission. Frustration because of how terrible the anti-virals made me feel. Frustration because one day, seventy-two hours before the award ceremony, my doctor told me that he had "good news and bad news."

"The good news, Dougie, is that you continue to test negative for HIV."

"Okay, so what's the bad news then?" I clarified, seated shirtless on the crinkling paper of the exam table.

"You've tested positive for hepatitis-C antibodies, which means that we need to do some more tests. And because of that possibility, I'm erring on the side of caution and discontinuing the prophylactic anti-virals due to their potential impact on your liver." Over the next few days, I waited for the results of those tests.

Frustration because of anxious ambiguity.

Doctor Ross called me into his office. He didn't want to give me the results over the phone, which meant I already knew what he was going to say.

I'd been nauseous, but I figured it was the medication I had taken. Tessa thought I looked pale, even a little yellow. She just thought that I needed to spend more time in the sun. I'd been tired and a little fatigued, but aren't we all?

Doctor Ross told me I had "acute hepatitis-C infection," albeit "mild." He went on to explain that it was possible I might "clear" the disease—to test negative—after the acute symptoms were treated. He told me I needed shots of a medicine called "interferon," self-injected three times a week for forty-eight weeks. Then he asked me if I wanted to be off work. He told me I should take two weeks off to see how my body dealt with the interferon, which had potentially serious side effects: fatigue, depression, hair loss, severe muscle cramps, blurry vision, and many more. Of particular note: insomnia.

I took the two weeks off, and I said, "You don't tell anybody about this . . . anybody."

The good doctor told me some stuff that I already knew; the odds stated I was going to have a chronic infection for the rest of my life. With any luck though, I'd be asymptomatic. With God or The Creator or Whoever on my side, I'd never get cirrhosis or liver cancer.

Hey, I *might* not ever die a slow and horrible death.

"And, Dougie," Doctor Ross said, "you can't drink anymore."

Rad.

Ratchet had tested positive for Hepatitis-C, but nobody ever shared those results with my physician, just the results of the HIV screening. An "administrative oversight" they called it.

Frustration because I should have killed that piece of shit, and that I didn't haunted me for years.

I often wondered if Ratchet had similar thoughts about me, if he later thanked his lucky stars for the stay of mortality . . . or if he just didn't give a shit either way.

I spoke of the topic so often that Tessa finally told me, "You need to channel this aggression you seem to have developed into something that's better for you than endless rumination."

"I'll channel it right up in you," I answered.

"Dougie, I'm being serious. You sleep less now than ever. That's not good for you. You need to heal; you shouldn't even be working."

"I know. I understand. I'll think of something."

Half to appease her and half because she was right, I started murdering the heavy bag, running like a savage, trying to lift as much as I could over my head and/or skipping rope until I wanted to vomit on a near daily basis . . . after the meds—luckily—leveled out in my system and the side effects seemed more or less nonexistent. I wasn't sure if the exercise helped my mood, or helped my ailing liver, but it made Tessa happy. When all was said and done, that's really what mattered most.

CHAPTER 9

"What distinguishes us from one another is our dreams . . . and what we do to make them come about."

—*Joseph Epstein*

My final field training shift passed without exceptional or meritorious events. I contracted no new or exciting diseases.

"Congrats, Dougie-boy, you're done," Dean, who was back to working plainclothes, told me that day.

I headed home and had my nightly, after work whiskey, which I wasn't supposed to have. But, hey, habit and all. Soon, I slipped into bed after showering the day's unreasonably damp crackhead grime and precarious junkie searches off my body—rolling the dice over and over to dodge debilitating, diseased needles, and reminding myself that it still mattered. After reading a chapter of *Finnegan's Wake*, I laid down next to Tessa and tried to fall asleep, tossing and turning every five minutes or so.

It went on like that for hours, which wasn't anything new.

I'd had insomnia for as long as I could remember, on and off. But, since graduation from the academy, since starting patrol, since finding my rage and probably being doomed by it, since starting the interferon therapy, it seemed that the condition was steadily worsening. And on the days when I could sleep, the good days, I'd often felt like I could hibernate the rest of my life away. Yet, whether I'd slept too much, or too little, the result was always the same: I'd get out of bed after a lengthy internal struggle, shower, pound some coffee and head to work. Once there, people would generally feel the need to put on a sympathetic or concerned expression and ask one or more of the following questions:

1. "You look tired; is everything alright?"
2. "Did you get enough sleep?"
3. "Boy, late night last night? You look like hell; did your boyfriend keep you up? I told him to be gentle and to warm you up with a finger first."

I'd always preferred the third question because I felt no problem with saying, "Get fucked," which was my reflexive answer for all sarcastic and insult-based questions that concerned my appearance. The first question was almost as easy to answer; I'd just say, "No, I'm not tired. I guess I'm just ugly." But number two, well, that one was a problem.

If I just went the safe route and answered, "Did you get enough sleep?" with, "Yes," people wouldn't believe me and would ask a follow-up question.

The question was usually: "Really, are you sick?"

And, as this person obviously cared enough about me that they had a genuine interest in my well being, I no longer felt comfortable being an asshole by saying something like, "Yeah, I'm sick of you." Consequently, I'd usually play the safe route and tell a watered-down version of the truth such as: "I'm just slightly under the weather and didn't sleep *well* last night." Nine times out of ten, that would be sufficient to end the conversation about my puffy eyes or dark circles. Those odds made it the safest bet.

The problem arose with the *ten percent people*. Without fail, one of the previously mentioned ten would feel compelled to play doctor with me by asking, "Does this happen often?" Like they were about to crack the *Cohen Code* and solve all my problems, forever.

This would usually catch me off guard and I'd just go, "Yes." And then the bomb would drop. Then some well meaning person would feel compelled to enlighten me with their miracle cure for nights when they tossed and turned a few times, or when they woke up to take a leak more than once because they guzzled water right before bed. These people would say:

A. "Have you tried chamomile tea?"
B. "It's probably because of the caffeine/alcohol/red meat."
C. "Maybe you're stressed out."

And then, if I was in a particularly foul mood and I hadn't slept at all, or more than an hour or two, in my head I'd be screaming: *OH, FUCKING*

REALLY!?! I'M SUPPOSED TO DRINK A CUP OF TEA AND THAT WHOLE "IT DOESN'T MATTER HOW MUCH I SLEEP BECAUSE I WAS BORN WITH DARK CIRCLES UNDER MY EYES AND, FURTHERMORE, I USUALLY HAVE NIGHTMARES SO SLEEPING ISN'T REALLY ALL THAT RESTFUL IN THE FIRST PLACE"— THING WILL ALL BE BETTER? YOU MEAN THAT I SHOULD JUST THROW AWAY THE DRAWER FULL OF ELEPHANT-STRENGTH SEDATIVES BECAUSE YOU, APPARENTLY, KNOW BETTER THAN A DOCTOR? YOU'RE A GODDAMN GENIUS! REALLY, YOU SHOULD GET A NOBEL-FUCKING-PRIZE! GOD BLESS YOU, YOU SAINT. SOMEBODY CALL THE MOTHERFUCKING VATICAN! HAVE YOU THOUGHT ABOUT WRITING A BOOK?

That's what I'd be thinking, but I'd usually just say, "Yeah, I'll try that."

I knew that there were contributing factors to my insomnia: stress and/or anxiety. It probably was worsened by the injections, but I couldn't be sure. It could've been because of a schedule change that interrupted my normal circadian rhythm, like early morning court or mandatory overtime—or too much caffeine—there wasn't any mystery there. But that was only part of it. Absent those things, I still didn't sleep normally. This night wasn't any different; I was at least self-aware enough to know that I was preoccupied with work to such a degree that I couldn't quiet my mind.

For a period of about three hours, my consciousness drifted in and out of a state that wasn't quite dreaming and wasn't quite thinking. Eventually, I rose from bed to take a leak, got some water, took a sleeping pill, washed the pill down with another shot of bourbon and returned, trying to slip between the covers as quietly as possible. With every groan of the aging floor beneath my feet or squeak of the mattress, Tessa stirred and I winced, expecting that she must have been getting tired of the repeated interruptions.

If she did mind my insomnia, Tessa never let on. She just always seemed concerned about me. This instance was no different.

"Hey baby," she said from her side of the bed and placed a warm hand on my chest. "Can't sleep again?"

"Yeah, and I've got to be at work in six hours now so the prospect for a restful, healthy night doesn't seem so good."

She perked up a bit and looked up at me with those big eyes of hers. "Is there anything *special* I could do to make it better?" Her hand started sliding down from my chest, further south.

What a woman: willing to immediately go from fast asleep to jerking me off in the interest of my mental health. "No, baby," I said. "I'll be okay."

Tessa's eyes closed again and she resumed her dreams, what I can only assume were fantasies of sex, guitars, motorcycles, pinup girls, classic tattoos and mosh pits. I tried to think of sex, motorcycles, boxing, lyrics to my favorite Irish folk songs, food, naked girls, and tattoos—anything to get my mind away from work; I hated work dreams. I always figured that when one's mind is thinking of work and not getting paid, the mind is performing a disservice.

So I sat there and tossed and turned, thinking that I probably should have taken Tessa up on that hand-job. But then she would have smelled the whiskey on my breath and that would have required some explaining. She had been doing her internet research on my handicap.

After an unknown amount of time and despite my best efforts to the contrary, I finally drifted away into a dream about my work. This was the first occasion that I had this specific dream.

I later learned that just about every cop has the same one, more or less, with some changes in names and faces.

In the dream, I'm on patrol with Mark, my kind, worldly and laid-back third FTO. We are conducting a foot patrol down one of the Tenderloin's scummier blocks, where a dumbfounding assortment of drug-dealers and drug-users shuffle away from us as we make the corner, trying to look busy. We see a gigantic black guy, whose body is prison ripped and covered in bad tattoos of skulls, random female names—spelled out in cursive—and images of assault rifles. This mountainous man hands a rock of cocaine-base, crack, to a random crackhead in exchange for a ten-dollar bill. The crackhead puts the rock in is pocket and, as Mark and I start to advance, looks directly at us. The buyer's eyes go wide as he sees the two of us and promptly takes off running, down the sidewalk away from us.

Witnessing this spontaneous flight, the dealer turns to observe the source of his customer's fear: Mark and I.

The dealer doesn't make any attempt to leave. "What the fuck you gonna do, white boys?" he taunts. I see the fire grow behind his eyes, his chest juts forward and his muscles tense as he reaches his right hand out of sight, toward the small of his back.

"Mark!" I call out. My hand goes to my side and begins to un-holster my gun. Though I can't see it, I know that Mark is doing the same as I hear the cup he was formerly holding hit the ground and make a noise like a single blast on a snare drum.

The dealer takes a step toward us as he brings his right hand back into view; he's holding a silver, semi-automatic handgun. It looks like the same gun that Jameson Ratchet had. "Fuck you," he exclaims in a slow, distorted voice that sounds like a forty-five RPM record being played at thirty-three, and through soaking, shorting speakers.

"GUN!" I yell, watching the dealer bring his hand up, frame by frame. Everything goes black and white and for a moment no other sound exists but the sound of my breathing.

The dealer fires before my gun is even out of the holster. Mark is hit and falls to the ground. He immediately disappears, like Obi Wan Kenobi after his duel with Vader on the Death Star. All that's left of Mark is an empty uniform and belt, lying on the sidewalk where he once stood. Smirking, the dealer starts panning his gun toward me and all of the sudden we aren't on the street anymore; we're back in apartment 602.

"Stop," I say, "drop it!" I pull the trigger on my gun but it doesn't budge. I squeeze as hard as I can and feel only a slight give. The dealer levels his weapon at me and laughs, taking his time with my death. I pull and pull with all of my might but I'm still only halfway through the trigger's cycle. Everything is quiet. The scene begins fading from view.

"Stop, please."

He just smiles.

"Bang," the dealer says, as his face fades away into the darkness.

Everything goes black.

A noise that reminded me of a speeding car ramming an empty dumpster, my bedside alarm, jolted me awake. Good morning, Officer Dougie Cohen; welcome to your first day of probation.

CHAPTER 10

"You go out in that uniform, on the street—
it's like saying, 'I take on all comers.'"
—*Sgt. Peter Thoshinsky, SFPD*

Police a rough neighborhood long enough and you start to learn quite a bit about human nature, such as the dumbfounding ability of people to make excuses for their own misdeeds or the misdeeds of others.

"He don't have no gun!" squawking girlfriends, wives and *baby-mommas* say. "You planted that."

"Yeah, lady, right; I keep extras in the car for just such an occasion," you reply with a smirk but they never get the joke.

"You didn't get that dope off me, man," the suspect says.

"Dude, you just watched me pull it out of your pocket," you counter. You study the suspect's face and can see the gears turning behind his perspiring brow.

"These aren't my pants!" is his inevitable explanation.

The working cop learns about fear, mistrust and outright hatred; it's observable in the eyes of youths and adults. It doesn't matter if the officer—*you* for purposes of this demonstration—grew up in the same neighborhood or housing project. As long as you are wearing that blue uniform you are one of *them*, one of the enemy who takes sons, daughters, sisters and brothers away to jail; the people who are willing to say "NO" and refuse to entertain the outlandish, collective denial that urban violence and blight are the fault of everyone but the men and women committing the acts. As a cop, you are one of the people who remind others that they are responsible for their own actions and that our world has rules. This isn't necessarily accomplished by anything the officer says, but by what that officer represents.

Officers see countless examples of what happens when people give up hope. They witness the longtime effects of that hopelessness as it's passed down from generation to generation. Cops meet people who have no goals, no aspirations and no desire to ever leave the utter shit that surrounds them. So many young men who are just waiting for their turns to die but don't realize it; men who only care about being perceived as "hard" and making a quick buck by selling dope or victimizing those around them; people who have no qualms raping in place of seducing, maiming in place of conversing and killing another human being because they live on, or grew up on, a different block.

Yet, despite these issues, many people who reside in these areas still don't like to see the police. They want us out of the neighborhood and perceive the police as an occupying force that stands in the way of their desires. The citizens cry "harassment" when officers get out of their cars and detain the local dope-slingers and gangsters, telling them to get their asses off the corner.

The citizenry make complaints to independent watchdog agencies when their friends and loved ones violently resist arrest and the arresting officer has to use force. Yet, wait long enough and that same suspect will often wind up riddled with bullet holes on the same corner, gasping his final breath in the same cop's presence. Those same community and family members—who complained when the officer was out of the car and trying to decrease the available targets in the neighborhood—will wail in hysterics as they decry the lack of police presence in the area and proactive action to decrease the crime level.

"Why ain't you motherfuckers ever doing anything about this shit?" people scream as one cop performs CPR on the victim while his or her partner struggles to keep the hostile crowd at bay.

Hopefully, backup will get there soon and, hopefully, the paramedics will remove the obviously dead body so the crowd calms.

The next day, things will be somewhat tense and a shrine of empty, cheap bottles of booze and fifty cent candles will be set up where the victim was gunned down. Memorial T-shirts will be made bearing a picture of the deceased. The victim's often sordid history will be ignored by the media who will print that the dead man—who the coroner confirmed had rocks of crack in his mouth and several hundred dollars in his pocket when he was shot—was *"just turning his life around"* and *"not reportedly involved in gangs or criminal behavior."* The reporters get this information from the friends and family of the deceased and print it as if it's gospel, which wouldn't be a problem if so many people didn't believe it.

As if any grown man would tell his grandmother that he had raped, robbed and killed and that he was never going to change his ways.

Soon a retaliation shooting will injure or kill a rival thug or gang member or, if the God of Justice has anything to do with it, the suspect from the initial murder. The cycle continues indefinitely.

Ben Franklin once said, *"He that lieth down with dogs shall rise up with fleas."*

But the really sad thing about the situation, the one thing that jabs me in my side, is that before I ever get around to cleaning some clueless, ignorant, poor, goddamn murdered kid's blood off my boots, things are always back to normal in *The Hood*. People have forgotten all about *Big T*, *Joker*, or *Lil' Mack*; nobody learns any lasting lesson from their deaths.

There isn't any wakeup call to the community to change the culture, to end the cycle of death. And if there is, the people who are in position to change things, those doing the killing and dying, won't.

The victim's entire life will have amounted to a few minutes of cleanup, a series of crime scene photos and two paragraph police report because, despite all of the so-called outrage and accusations of the crowd at the homicide scene, there wasn't one witness. There wasn't one person willing to stand up in a court of law and be questioned for a little while. Fear of violent retribution and selfish shortsightedness keeps the people in line. Consequently, the report reads as follows:

> On the listed date and time, Officer Nichols #717 and I responded to a reported shooting at the intersection of Cameron and Sickles in the "Double Deuce" housing development. Upon arrival, I saw an unknown black male in his late teens lying prone on the ground in a pool of blood. The victim appeared to be wearing a ballistic vest. I rendered medical aid as Officer Nichols attempted to find a witness among the large and hostile crowd who threw bottles and rocks at the officers on scene and our patrol vehicles. The crowd eventually dispersed, somewhat, once the SFFD transported the victim to General Hospital. The victim was pronounced dead by Doctor Condescendo. I located a group of 7.62 caliber rifle casings in front of 154 Cameron, which were later collected by CSI Greenly who processed the scene. Officer Nichols initiated and maintained a crime scene log once the scene was stable. Despite the presence of over fifty bystanders, and despite repeated efforts to obtain further information, no person would come forward to provide any kind of suspect description.
>
> I notified the Operations Center of the incident. Inspector Espinoza of the Homicide Detail

responded and took over the investigation. I then responded to the hospital. Once there, I seized the victim's clothing and later turned it over to Inspector Greenly. Inspector Greenly retained all evidence. No suspects or witnesses were located in this incident.

A report such as this takes about twenty minutes to write if the cop is a slow typist; that's all. But if that same victim, a few weeks prior to being shot, got angry at his girlfriend, wife or baby-momma and smacked her across the face, then the reporting officer is looking at an hour of solid paperwork, minimum. And it's guaranteed to be even longer if an arrest is involved.

You've got the initial report to fill out, which must include the length of the relationship, whether or not the victim and suspect live together or have children in common. You must note if drug and/or alcohol intoxication was a factor in the event, and how many children were present. Include the statements of any kids if they are old enough to provide them. You must document if there was a prior history of documented or undocumented domestic violence, which there almost always is. Note if any restraining orders, temporary or otherwise, are or were in effect; note the demeanor of the victim and the suspect, and how the victim was medically treated; note who provided the medical care. Take photographs of the victim's injuries. Explain how the investigating officer came to the conclusion as to whom the "primary aggressor" was, and what the suspect's statement was—provided he was willing to give one and is in your custody. Then, obtain an emergency protective order (EPO), serve the suspect with it and drop off a copy to the victim with her multitude of referral cards for various advocacy groups, and instructions as to how to follow up with the investigation.

There are several other forms to complete: injury diagrams for the victim and suspect and a fact sheet, which summarizes some of the things that are already in the narrative of the police report. In a homicide report, to write: *The victim had several gunshot wounds to his torso* is sufficient enough documentation of injuries. Not so in a case like this.

Somebody, the investigating officer or the officer's partner, will have to fill out a booking card. Somebody has to remove the suspect's property from his person and he will then be booked on charges approved by your sergeant. The suspect is later transferred to the county jail, eventually sees a judge and is either remanded to custody, given bail or released on his own recognizance.

After the suspect is out of jail, which—in minor cases, such as the one described above—can be the same or next day, he usually ignores the EPO, calls the victim, says that he is "really sorry, baby" and goes right back home. Then freaky makeup sex is had on top of the coffee table, which is strewn with the various forms you, Officer, spent so much of your day filling out and delivering to the victim. That day or week or month or year later, the suspect gets pissed off at the victim again and punches her in the mouth. The victim calls the police and the cycle begins anew. The cops respond and the process is repeated.

After a while, one can't help but wonder why the hell the victim keeps letting the asshole back in. I mean, get a clue, right? But to think in such a manner is unhealthy. This may tempt an officer to simply blow the matter off. And that will undoubtedly be the instance in which the suspect winds up strangling the victim to death just after the police clear the scene.

For career longevity and from a moral standpoint, this is obviously a bad thing.

Folks who call the police on a regular basis often learn that the boys and girls in blue tend arrive quicker when someone is said to have a gun, for obvious reasons. Over time, this fact becomes apparent to entire communities and soon, amazingly, it seems like nearly every subject that a 911 caller is reporting, for whatever reason, has a gun. The police rush over, detain the guy or gal at gunpoint, and find no weapon. The 911 caller then laughs while swearing, "I thought there *really* was a gun, honest."

So sorry about the angry mob that surrounded you when you drew your gun pointed it at the suspect and ordered him down on the concrete in the cold and rain.

Provided there is no reason to arrest this person, the detainee is dusted off, apologized to and released. The former custody then marches right down to the Office of Citizen Review and makes a formal compliant against the officers who, so unjustly, detained him or her while he or she was, "Just minding my own business."

If I've learned anything about the world through policing, it's that everyone minds their own business: victims, witnesses and suspects alike—always.

So sorry about the lawsuit, really. Good thing you pay those union dues, right?

The real irony is that, in rough neighborhoods, lots of bad people have guns and have no problem using them to harm others. People usually just don't call 911 about these folks because they are either:

1. Too afraid.
2. Just don't care.
3. Up to equal amounts of no good.

Guns are everywhere. Finding them, legally, takes some effort.

CHAPTER 11

"The future is unwritten."
—*Joe Strummer*

The scheduled transfer to my probationary station was pushed back for about three months. I missed the boat because I was delayed in completing field training. All shifts that I'd missed had to be made up. First, there was three weeks for my hand to heal and to get used to the anti-HIV prophylactic therapy, and then there were two more weeks off to "adjust" to the interferon. After a few weeks of injections, my skin had resumed its normal color and my hepatitis symptoms were gone. The shots were doing their job.

I started my probationary period at the TL, working with Mark quite a bit, but no longer being graded, until the next big transfer came around. My classmate and friend, Matt Mathis, was already working in my new district, Southeast Station, when I arrived. Matt asked me about the medal. I filled him in, mostly.

I didn't tell anybody but Tessa about the disease.

The Southeast Police District of San Francisco was collectively known as the least desirable place to be a

151

cop in the city. It contained no less than three major public housing developments. And a good portion of the areas that weren't projects may as well have been; crime was just as prevalent. The African-American gangs in the area were so active and violent that a blanket of fear, hopelessness and complacency seemed to smother a substantial portion of the population there.

I didn't want to be transferred to Southeast, as it was so far removed from the vibe of working downtown— something I cherished when working in the Tenderloin.

Kiss the pretty girls, plentiful coffee and occasional smiling face goodbye, I thought.

Tessa didn't want me to go either. When I told her of the transfer she said, "I'm going to worry about you down there. That's a bad environment. I think it would easy to be a bad cop in such a place, surrounded by anger and negativity . . . and violence. At least in the TL, you can get out."

"I don't think that's really accurate," I replied in reference to the "bad cop" part. "A bad cop is gonna be a bad cop. No matter where he or she works. I'd like to think that you knew I was smarter than that, better than that."

"I do. Just don't get swallowed up by the place. You've given enough of yourself away already."

"I don't think you need to worry," I said. I didn't want to think to hard about what she'd just said. "I don't even look like Harvey Keitel."

I'd be lying if I said that I wasn't a little nervous about the transfer, being a white kid from Southern California who was totally unfamiliar with life in the ghetto. Yet, I knew I had no choice in the matter. Working in such a district, so I was told by the veterans of Southeast who went on to the "greener" pasture of the TL, would truly reveal what kind of officer I was going to be. I later learned that there were only two options:

1. The kind of officer who took his or her time in responding to all calls for service in hopes that the suspect wouldn't be there and always kept the car windows rolled up, so as not to hear screaming, gunshots or smell fire or weed. The same kind of cop that would look for the one non-thuggish looking driver, committing some sort of minor traffic violation, and ticket him or her accordingly rather than pull over a car that might actually contain a stolen gun, a sack of dope or a body.

2. A cowboy.

I got assigned to the early morning watch, "day watch," wherein the workday started at 0600 hours. Needless to say, I wasn't thrilled about the prospect of having to try and get to bed before dark everyday. At least Matt was working the same shift. That was a positive; as was the fact that the wee morning hours in any city, even Las Vegas, were generally somewhat slower, as far as crime was concerned. In theory, as a result of this slowdown, I'd be able to learn the district in a manner that was more nuanced and less of a trial by fire.

My first morning briefing—lineup—was casual and full of laughs and good natured ribbing. I was pleased that the few other cops on the watch—consisting of seven patrol officers, one sergeant and a lieutenant for two-hundred thousand people—all seemed to have senses of humor. The lieutenant assigned me to work as a third wheel, riding along with Matt and another cop, Sean O'Leary, in the southernmost sector of the district. After being dismissed from lineup, Matt, Sean and I headed to the equipment room to gather our car keys, a shotgun, some road spikes and a *half*-box of flares, as we were informed by the Station Keeper—the cop in charge of station operations, prisoners and equipment—that we were running low on the latter.

"Please tell me that there's a place to get coffee around here?" I asked Matt and Sean as we filed out of the equipment room to the parking lot, looking for our vehicle.

"No, I don't think so," said Sean.

"Obviously you aren't a coffee drinker?" I said. The injections were really hitting me hard with fatigue and I'd even developed slight anemia. It took every ounce of strength and will I had to drag myself out of bed and into work at such an hour . . . not to mention the gym too, four times a week. I'd promised Tessa.

"What makes you say that?" he asked, as Matt looked on, smiling.

"Because if you did drink coffee you would have finished that sentence by noting that it doesn't matter that there isn't a place to get coffee around here because San Francisco is only seven miles by seven miles and, at six in the goddamn morning, we can be just about anywhere in less than ten minutes. So let's, fucking, go downtown or something, man. Because I'm gonna drive you crazy if I don't get some caffeine in my system posthaste."

"Uh, okay, but I get to dri—" Sean said.

"I'm driving!" Matt called, snatching the keys from the peg board and running out of the room.

"Shotgun," said Sean.

"You can strap me to the fucking roof if you want, as long as we wind up at a coffee joint in the immediate future." I hadn't slept well the night before; this was probably apparent.

We loaded the car up with the necessary equipment and headed out. Matt, as per his standard operating procedure, hit the gas and spun the rear tires as we peeled out of the station's parking lot into the early morning darkness. A few harrowing miles later, I was trotting into a Starbucks with Matt—Sean stayed in the car; he really didn't drink coffee—and got my gigantic cup of motivation. Matt, per another one of his SOPs, loaded up on about ten dollars worth of pastries and a hot chocolate. Sugar was one of his primary nutrition sources. Despite such a vice, Matt had bright, shining choppers and imperceptible body fat. He could also run like a Kenyan. In the academy when I noted these traits of Matt, I surmised that scientists would be baffled by him, considering his fuel sources.

As we headed back into our district it became apparent that Matt was born to work at Southeast, judging by the fact that most of my coffee wound up on my lap after three blocks or so. Matt relished in the district's wide open streets, the ever present possibility of car chases and, despite his gawky, good-old-boy appearance, he was one of the most fearless cops I'd ever met.

The morning was typically slow and afforded Matt and Sean opportunity to give me the grand tour of the district. We started at the southernmost point, down by the municipal dump and recycling center, working our way north to Candlestick Park. I'd never been to the stadium and was surprised to see that, directly across the street, a state park bordered the bay: Candlestick Point Recreation Area.

We pulled into the park and I got out, making use of an outhouse therein. On the way back to the car, I stopped and read a sign that explained the origin of the park's name. Apparently, the area was so-named in times past, when aging wooden ships were burned just off the shore. The burning skeletons of the ships were said to resemble candlesticks as they sank down into the muddy silt below.

Turning a lazy three-sixty, I was both struck by the sublime, scenic beauty of the recreational area and the stark contrast created by the poorly maintained pavement, which cut an abrupt end to the greenery. The road beyond was terminated by a garish cyclone fence, which surrounded the incredible eyesore that was the stadium; a stadium that, frankly, hadn't mattered one bit since the San Francisco Giants had vacated it a few years prior.

"The Stick" wasn't even *Candlestick* anymore; rather it had been renamed with the namesake of the latest Fortune 500 Corporation that bought the place and really, truly, falsely believed that they wouldn't make the mistakes of the previous owner and delude themselves right into bankruptcy.

Yet, despite these meretricious landmarks, none could quite compete with the fortress-like Double Deuce Housing Projects: a horseshoe shaped compound of rectangular buildings, browning vegetation and wrought iron fences, which stood directly across the street to the north of the stadium. After concluding my brief moment of quietude and introspection, I returned to my position in the rear of the non-caged, four seat car and to my tour of the surreal surroundings.

I got in and Matt hit the gas, clouding the area to the rear of our vehicle with a moderate cloud of smoke before my ass hit the vinyl upholstery.

"Guess where we're going next?" Matt asked, smiling.

"To climb that barren hill behind the stadium," I deadpanned.

"I've done that, you know," Matt said. This didn't surprise me in the least and, honestly, I eventually wound up doing it as well . . . with Matt of course.

"Shocking," I said.

"It's time for project tour *number one.*"

"Double Deuce," Sean added.

"Yeah, dude. I think he figured that out," Matt stated.

"I assume that's the fucked-up looking cluster of buildings we're heading directly towards?" I asked.

"Yeah," Sean said, "I think the Navy used to own the buildings, back in the day."

"For fucking bombing practice," Matt spat out. The dick stole my line.

"You stole my line, dick."

The Double Deuce Projects had a single gate for access and egress. I later learned from one of the plainclothes guys at the station, Ken Byrne—who, like Dean, I greatly looked up to—that it wasn't always that way. Apparently, the tall, spiked fence had been built around the entire development to jam up the drive-through narcotics business but also, so I suspected, to direct the inevitable, cataclysmic explosion upwards.

The tale Ken told was exceptional.

Years prior to my arrival at Southeast, some member of the Board of Supervisors had decided that putting a fence around the development was a good way to reduce the high level of crime in the housing project. It had worked in other cities; why not here? Contractors were consulted, bids were given and eventually an army of migrant, illegal workers was drafted for the task.

"From the very beginning," Ken said, "there were problems."

"Problems? What kind?"

"First the locals started by stealing every tool and piece of personal property, everything that wasn't nailed down and had some sort of resale value or usefulness. In fact," Ken remembered, "the people from the projects stole just about everything: bags of concrete, cones, lumber, the water jugs for the workers, and hardhats; everything. It was kind of funny at first; for us at least." Ken went on, "Then the real trouble started. As the fence started to finally go up—obviously at a much slower pace than previously estimated—the local gangsters figured out that the fence was there to keep the dope deals to a minimum and began to harass, assault and, finally, *shoot* at the workers."

"No shit?"

"No shit. We'd get these calls regarding these mass raids by the gangsters and, as we drove toward the main entrance on Sickles, we'd see these poor Mexican guys running for dear life in our direction. Then, by the time we would get through the crowd of terrified workers into the project itself, the damage would be done and the assholes would have torn the fences down; the ones that were just built minutes before."

"So how did they get the fence up?" Matt, who was also in the room when Ken told the story, asked.

"The department staffed an overtime shift of four officers to baby-sit the workers, and the tools."

"Did you ever do the overtime?" I asked.

"Fuck no; you couldn't pay me enough to sit in 'The Deuce' for ten hours. There's a reason that it only costs five dollars a month to live there."

"Five dollars a month; is that true?" I asked in total disbelief.

"Not all the units are that cheap but it is the least expensive housing project in the city." Ken said. "Some people seem to like it, though. I mean, they're willing to kill other people over it."

"I reckon that implies an affinity."

Matt drove us toward the entrance of the projects. I was surprised to see a security booth between the entrance and exit gates. This booth was just big enough to fit an aging, hefty security guard and a small, archaic television. A blue steel revolver hung low on the security guard's hip and he had a look in his eyes, one which I never saw him absent of, that portrayed one part boredom and one part mortal terror. His expression was such a constant, that I often wondered if he was an animatronics figure—like in the *Country Bear Jamboree*—whose sole job was to push the "open" button for one of the two gates.

But this place was definitely not Disneyland.

"So, what does one need to do in order get that man to open the gate? Do you have to prove that you live here or something?" I asked Matt and Sean.

"Uh, I think you just have to drive up," Sean said.

"Okay . . . what's his job then?"

"Well, he, uh . . . he opens the gate and is a witness if anything happens," Sean replied.

"Is he a good witness?" I asked.

"I don't even know if he can talk," Matt interjected. "Somebody should teach him to, though; we'd solve a lot of homicides if he did."

"Effective," I said, as Matt meandered through the open gate.

"Make sure your window is rolled down when you're driving through here," Matt said.

"It's down enough, man; I can hear and smell just fine. We've been cops just as long, remember?" I qualified.

"No, I mean all the way down," Matt corrected. "The glass particles that fly out of the bullet holes won't blind you that way. Plus, you can return fire right back without sacrificing the first shot to break the glass." With that, Matt un-holstered his gun and put it in his lap.

"Oh."

Different world indeed, I thought.

Matt's normally hectic driving became a crawl as we slowly cruised the streets of The Deuce. The drab, concrete buildings were accented by a myriad of broken-down and derelict cars that littered the yards and streets. Dirty diapers and empty bottles of malt liquor were strewn about on various lots of dirt and dead grass in front of the many boarded up and vandalized units. The Tenderloin was bad but it was at least surrounded by "normal" people and civilization. We didn't "own" the streets in the Southeast, like at TL. Rolling through The Deuce, I felt tinges of fear— fear of the unknown; fear that never went away. I just learned to live with it.

Despite the early hour, a few thuggish looking young men were already posted between the buildings. These men kept far enough from the street to give themselves a good, running start—should the SFPD feel compelled to find out exactly why their jackets were hanging heavy to one side—but not too far away as to make a crack sale overly laborious or be too distant to return fire at a car executing a drive-by.

As we rounded the various corners, these men would slowly back away behind the building line and out of sight. I'd later learn that, once out of sight, some of these men bolted, running away as fast as possible; some of them simply ditched the sack of drugs or the gun they were holding, and walked right back. And some of them went inside their homes. There was one constant though: all of them knew that they had the home field advantage.

"Do you ever jump out on these guys?" I asked.

"Rarely," Matt said. "It's not like downtown. You've got to be smart about it down here. You've need to have a plan or be sneaky; or come in force. People get away in the projects. Watch," Matt pointed at the building line where one young man was previously standing. "He's gone already." I looked and, sure enough, there was no trace of the wanted and/or dope-dealing and/or armed (and/or just didn't have the desire to be stopped by the cops) man who walked away seconds before. "Plus, with all the unsolved homicides in this area because of the lack of witnesses, do you really think that yours would be any different?"

In the early morning fog, it was hard to imagine what a nightmare Double Deuce could be in the hot summer afternoons when enormous fights, multi-victim shootings, near riots and mass home invasions were common place. Though the decrepit surroundings and hard looks cast by the local hoods were unsettling, the area was quiet as most of the residents were obviously asleep. District wide, project drama usually didn't start until the afternoon, as large portions of the people who resided in the area were not exactly on a *working* schedule.

As we rolled, Matt and Sean told me a story wherein about seventy angry people charged into a single project dwelling, over on the north side of the development, and attacked the occupants therein. They said that it looked like the mosh pit at an enormous summer music festival had invaded an apartment.

"Only there was more screaming, and windows breaking and stuff," Matt added. Obviously there was little Matt and Sean could do. I laughed and wondered what, if anything, I would do differently. I didn't have a clue.

Our circuit/tour complete, Matt drove us through the open exit gate. I noted that the guard in the booth was sound asleep. I briefly imagined that the gate was the River Styx and that we had just emerged from Hades. This train of thought led my mind to wander into more comparisons with the three travelers in Homer's *Odyssey* and with the film *Oh Brother, Where Art Thou*, which was based on Homer's story.

I smiled. Lofty comparisons they were.

Then my mind wandered to other Cohen Brothers films, which I'd always liked and not just because of our common surnames. There was just something about being in the back of a car that made my mind wander.

Just about the time that I began to examine John Turturro's consummate perfection as "Da Jesus" in *The*

Big Lebowski, Matt pulled me back into reality with a sudden, jarring direction change.

"What the hell are *they* doing?" Matt asked as he maneuvered our car south on Hawes Street, toward the source of his obvious concern.

"Not sure," Sean said.

"Dougie, do you want to stop humming Credence Clearwater songs and join the rest of the group?" Matt mockingly asked.

"*The Dude* abides," I answered, quoting the main character in *The Big Lebowski*.

"Who's '*The Dude*?' Is he like Fonzie?" Sean asked.

"He's who Fonzie wishes he was," I said.

Pushing the thoughts of bowling, urine-soaked rugs and crazed Vietnam veterans out of my mind, I looked ahead through the windshield and saw a maroon Chevy Caprice stopped in the middle of the street, about two blocks down. A passenger in the vehicle was leaning out of a window on the right side of the car and extending his arms toward the east side of the street. I couldn't see what, if anything, he was holding. From that distance, it was difficult to tell if the vehicle's occupants were goofing off, talking to somebody or getting ready to do a drive-by. Matt accelerated forward and, suddenly, the Caprice sped off, making a left turn out of sight. It seemed that the latter suspicion may have been the most accurate. Sean picked up the radio.

"Charlie-fifteen-david," Sean said, breaking the morning radio silence.

"Go ahead," said the groggy dispatcher.

"Yeah, we're trying to catch up to a maroon Caprice that just took off from us. It's going from southbound Hawes to eastbound Jamestown, I think."

"Copy," replied the female voice, "do you need a code thirty-three?" The dispatcher asked, confirming if we wanted the radio channel to be secured of traffic not related to our incident.

"Do we?" Sean asked Matt and me.

"Nah," Matt said, "not unless we find it again."

"Negative," Sean said into the radio, "not unless we find it again."

"Matt, tell him: 'These aren't the droids you're looking for,'" I said, throwing in an Obi-Wan line. Neither of them got the joke as, likely, they didn't spend the formative years of their lives immersed in science fiction movies as I previously had done—and admittedly continued to do.

Blowing a stop sign in the process, Matt turned our vehicle eastbound onto Jamestown toward Candlestick Park. We spotted the Caprice ahead, still gunning the throttle.

"He's probably heading for the freeway," Matt guessed.

"Your guess is as good as mine, bro; just tell me when to get out and start running or shooting or whatever," I said, sounding calm and collected but consciously leaning forward in my seat, my right hand on the door's handle.

"Gotcha," Matt said as the car hit seventy miles per hour, heading down the hill toward the south side of the stadium. Matt and Sean both instinctively reached for their seatbelts. I considered doing the same but I feared that I would be caught up in the thing if I had to exit the car quickly: Murphy's Law of Patrol.

First day in a new district; don't look like an idiot.

To our astonishment, the Caprice stopped in a lane of traffic just around the corner on Jamestown, across from the southern entrance of the park. The brake lights were illuminated and the rear window tint was so great that I couldn't make out any of the occupants inside. Matt jammed on the breaks and hit the lights and siren as he slid in behind the Caprice, like it was home base. Having seen an abundance of pursuit videos during training, I knew that a suspect vehicle, which abruptly stopped in the middle of traffic when being pursued, was usually preparing to start shooting at the cops or otherwise baiting them for nefarious purposes. Keeping this in mind, I was out of the car and searching for cover before our wheels stopped turning. A tiny, dying tree was the only such object.

Matt quickly got out of the driver's seat, gun in hand. As he approached the Caprice, Matt concealed the weapon behind his leg—just in case. I watched as Matt made contact with the driver and exchanged some unknown words with him. Matt then held his free hand out, palm up, expectedly. The driver of the Caprice deposited the ignition keys on Matt's palm. Matt took the keys and placed them into his back pocket and then held his hand out in the same manner, once more. What followed next was not very shocking, as the driver produced a nearly empty, half-gallon of vodka. Matt promptly seized the bottle and poured it out on the ground below. Matt renewed conversation with the occupants of the vehicle, holstering his weapon in order to remove his pen and notebook from a breast pocket. I fixed my gaze on the back window, searching for motion inside and expecting that, at any moment, a barrage of gunfire would spew out toward me, Sean or our car. I figured I would probably be the intended target as I must have looked ridiculous standing behind such a pathetic piece of plant life.

Who could resist this shot? I thought as I tactically positioned my unshielded crotch behind the small trunk in front of me.

Ken Byrne—who had heard our radio traffic as we searched for and then found the Caprice—arrived to back us up. Ken was working by himself and therefore limited in his capacity; running through the projects after armed men, by oneself, was not usually considered a wise idea. Ken pulled his unmarked car behind our patrol car, exited and met Matt as he returned from the suspect vehicle in order to see what we had going on.

"I'll run the driver for you," Ken said; ever helpful. "Does he have any ID?"

"No, but I got his 'social,'" Matt replied. "The two passengers are both Samoan dudes, like the driver. I think they're all Double Deuce guys."

"Considering where we are and what their car looks like, I think that's a pretty safe assumption," Ken replied. He sat himself in the driver's seat of our patrol car and began typing in the driver's name, race, sex and date of birth—information that Matt had just obtained—on our vehicle's computer.

After about three minutes, Ken reached a verdict as to the next enforcement action to be taken, upon reviewing the information provided by the National Crime Information Network (NCIN) regarding the suspect driver.

"Everybody is coming out of that car, guys," Ken stated, and the four of us walked up to the Caprice.

"Does something not smell right?" I asked. I'd always wanted to ask that.

"Something stinks," Ken replied, hitting the ball out of the park. "Just kidding, the driver doesn't have a license and has a little warrant for the same, so we're going to go through the car and see if they don't got something a little more juicy."

I was relieved to finally get a good look at the three young men who occupied the Caprice—and see that they weren't, in fact, holding machine guns. Matt and Ken walked up to the driver's side and asked him to step out. The driver complied and was immediately handcuffed. Sean and I made contact with the front passenger, who seemed to be the oldest of the three, and the teenager in the back seat.

"What's going on, Officer?" the front passenger, a Mr. Valente Ia, asked.

"Nothing, bro. Hop out for me," I said.

"Alright, alright," Valente said. He then opened the door and immediately turned away from me, apparently familiar with the procedure. I quickly patted him down, checking for weapons.

"I'm clean. I ain't got nothing," he noted.

It appeared that he was right. I directed him to go sit on the side of the road under Sean's watchful eye. Valente did as instructed. I then turned my attention to the teenager in the back seat. I could see that he was wearing a rolled-up ski mask on top of his head—never a good sign.

"Jump out, man," I ordered.

"Fo' what?" the young man asked, feigning outrage.

I could hear Dean's voice in my head stating, *"There's always one in the group that is destined to fuck things up for everybody."*

I ignored his tone. "What's your name, bro?"

"Anthony," he spat.

"Anthony . . . what? Anthony Jones?"

"Anthony Smith," he answered, unenthusiastically.

"Mr. *Smith*," I said. "Please, do me a favor, as a man; get the fuck out of the car." I used to be so polite.

"Nigga, get out the car, nigga," the driver ordered. He then muttered, "You making this shit take too long, fafa." I assumed the last part was an insult.

"Ai polo lo kama!" Anthony said back as he slowly exited the Caprice. I patted him down as well. Finding nothing, I handcuffed the mouthy teen, walked him over to the side of the road and instructed him to sit next to his buddy.

"I'll stand with these guys if you wanna search the car," I said to Sean.

"Okay, what's the PC for the search?" Sean asked, seeking to collect and organize all of his legal ducks prior to diving into the vehicle's search.

"Um, at the minimum, the driver is under arrest for driving without a license and for having a warrant. Plus there's the whole *open bottle of vodka* thing and the fact that the car is a total sled, occupied by the expected unscrupulous element." In field training, I'd quickly found that the use of complex sentences was as good as speaking another language when in the presence of most suspects. Sometimes my coworkers didn't get the message either though. But Sean did.

"Cool." Sean walked over to the open door of the Caprice and, in a painstaking ritual that I could tell had been practiced many times over, put on a pair of latex gloves like he was about to conduct some sort of surgery.

"What's with the gloves?" I called over. Sean either didn't hear me or neglected to fall into the trap I was trying to spring.

"The car is clean, dog," Valente added. I wasn't sure if he was speaking literally or otherwise.

"Forgive us if we don't take your word for it." This marked the first instance that I used this line, which I used every day at work thereafter at least once.

Sean began searching the car with, what I assumed was, surgical precision. Starting with the passenger side, he opened the glove compartment and rooted through the various paperwork and accoutrements therein. While there, planning ahead nicely, Sean pressed the yellow trunk release button. Satisfied, Sean's hands moved to the center console and lifted up its lid. Finding nothing of consequence—a few CDs, some lip balm, et cetera—he ducked down and looked under the front passenger's seat.

"You've got some old McDonald's fries under here," he said to nobody in particular.

"Jack in the Box," I called back.

"Yeah, dats true," Valente chimed.

As Sean searched the car, I obtained the pertinent identifying information from the two detainees and began to run Valente and Anthony for warrants, via my portable radio. "Charlie-fifteen-david, can you run two?" I asked the dispatcher.

"Go ahead with your first subject," was the reply.

"First subject's last name is: 'ida-adam.' First name of: victor-adam-lincoln-edward-nora-tom-edward. He's a Samoan male with a dee-owe-bee of nineteen eighty, zero six, zero four. This is verbal information."

"Copy, go with your second subject."

"Last name of Smith: common spelling. First of Anthony: common spelling. He's also a Samoan male. Born nineteen eighty-eight, eleven, eighteen; that's verbal also. Can you run that one for an ID card as well?" A few moments passed.

"Charlie-fifteen-david, your first subject is showing clear at this time with an SF number of 707904. He has fourteen prior felonies and sixteen prior misdemeanors with a danger potential of ADW and carrying a concealed firearm."

"Copy, any record on the second?"

"Smith is showing no record of any kind, either in the local SF criminal database or for an ID card or driver's license." I figured as much. As he was a juvenile, this could have been due to his age. But it was most likely because he was lying to me, indicated by his rather unbelievable choice of a last name.

Sean's search continued to the rear passenger area of the Caprice, where he painstakingly examined every pocket of a jacket, which was crumbled on one of the back seats. Still empty handed, he moved on to the trunk. Hoping to find an AK-47 rifle, Sean was noticeably disappointed by the sole presence of a spare tire and the related tools. Undeterred, Sean closed the trunk and walked over to the driver's side door. Again, Sean hunkered down, removed his flashlight, and used it to illuminate the under seat area. A frown came across his face.

"It's clean," Sean said. I looked over at Valente and Anthony and could see relief dart across their faces. They had either hid whatever Sean couldn't find quite well or were just naturally shady.

"It looks like you weren't lying," I said and then called over to Matt and Ken, who were in the process of sitting the handcuffed driver in the rear of a recently arrived patrol unit for transport back to the station. I pointed at Valente. "This guy is good but the kid is showing no record."

"Where does he live?" Ken asked.

I turned to the young man. "Where do you live?"

"Double Deuce," Anthony said.

"Yeah, I figured. Where in?"

"Ten-two-five Cameron."

"Have you ever been arrested before; do you have an ID card in your name?"

"No, I'm only fourteen. I ain't ever been in no trouble. Why you asking me all these questions?"

"Because I've never met a Samoan guy whose last name was Smith?"

"Now you have—damn."

"So you say, yes. I'm not saying it isn't possible; I just haven't encountered it yet. See what I'm saying?"

"I feel you. Can I go now?" he said, cool as could be.

"Just let them go; there's not any PC to hold him anyways." Ken said. "If he's lying, we'll find him again later. We're taking the driver back to the station. Can one of you drive his car back so we don't have to wait out here in the middle of nowhere for a tow?" Sean looked over at me and grinned.

"Go ahead, dude. I'm not in the driving mood," I said to Sean. I looked down at Valente and Anthony. "Stand up, guys. It's time to go."

"We're good?" Valente asked.

"Yep," I said as I removed his handcuffs; Sean removed Anthony's. "You're free men. Fly, fly away."

With that the two of them began the long walk, I assumed, back to the Double Deuce.

Sean jumped into the driver's seat of the Caprice as I put my handcuffs back in their home on my belt. "Ten bucks says you crash this thing," I said as I walked back to our car and sat in the front seat, next to Matt.

"Ten bucks says he crashes that thing," Matt said to me.

"Make it twenty. By the way, I still have to pee. And quit stealing my lines. Also, by letting you know that I have to urinate, I'm not, in any way, telling you to drive any faster than you already do. I'm telling you to drive *smoother*."

"No, problem," said Matt. I somehow didn't believe him.

Sean, apparently sensing that Matt and I doubted his driving ability, which we didn't (we were just giving him shit), slowly—and I mean slowly—accelerated down the road, making the long loop around the stadium heading back past the Double Deuce and toward the station. About a hundred yards down, Matt flicked on our emergency lights and siren and pulled up behind Sean.

I picked up the PA microphone. Over the cacophony created by our car's wail, I did my best to harass my new coworker.

So far, I was enjoying the newfound freedoms probation offered.

"This is the police; hurry your slow-ass up. I have to take a leak!" There were a few, obvious advantages to being on the outskirts of Shitville at the crack of dawn. Paramount among these was the freedom to swear over the PA system and, in Matt's case, drive like an asshole.

Sean kept driving at the same speed. His only apparent response to our shenanigans and ridicule was the presentation of his rear facing middle finger out of the Caprice's sunroof. Inspired, I picked up the PA again.

"Yes, *one*: that is the number of hours it will take us to get back to the station at our current speed, which I must note you are currently dictating."

Matt—who was now giggling like a little girl—
suddenly pulled into the oncoming lane and accelerated
forward, paralleling Sean. Oddly, as we came alongside,
Sean abruptly hit the brakes and executed a screeching
halt. It seemed he was getting into the swing of things
nicely; Matt must have been rubbing off on him.

Matt stopped our car as well, next to the Caprice.
We both looked over. Sean had sublime look of horror
on his face.

Oh, what now? I thought and rolled the window down.

"What's up? Something bite your dick?" I asked.

"A gun just fell out onto the floorboard," Sean said,
flatly. Matt and I just stared at him for a few seconds,
reading his face for sincerity, not sure how to play this one.

"Seriously?" Matt muttered. I was glad he was the
first one to get fished-in by the obvious setup.

"Seriously," Sean said, reaching down between his
legs. Figuring we were about to be ambushed by a water
bottle or something, I began to roll the window up.

Not so.

Sean hoisted up a Mac-10 machine pistol by the
trigger guard and dangled it for us to observe. I turned
to Matt, whose eyes were now, also, growing wide.

"Sean doesn't carry that as a secondary gun by any
chance, does he?" I asked.

"No. I'm pretty sure those are really, really illegal."
Matt said.

I looked back toward the scene of the stop and could
see the distant figures of Anthony and Valente walking
west, toward the stadium, just about to disappear behind

it. I turned to Matt and said, "Take two." Matt nodded in agreement.

The one-hundred and eighty degree burnout that followed began on the blacktop of Jamestown's roadway, but finished on the gravel and dirt shoulder, near one of the gates to the ballpark. This abrupt exhibition of vehicular prowess created an immense billow of dust, which I thought to be an appropriate accessory to the (Dukes of) Hazzardian maneuver Matt was straining our poor, abused vehicle through. As I held on for dear life, I took the opportunity to ask a few questions and make a few observations.

"First of all, if those two lucky bastards weren't running before, they certainly are now." I glanced over at the other side of the stadium and couldn't see the targets anymore.

"No way; there's no way they can hear the tires squeal all the way across the parking lot," Matt argued.

"We'll see about that. Secondly, how did he fail to discover a gun that big on first time around, yo?" I wasn't sure why I felt compelled to add the word "yo" to the end of the sentence, but I did; I guessed the vibe of the area was already rubbing off on me.

"I don't know, man. But it's brutal," Matt said in a calm tone of voice that really didn't match the spastic contortions his arms were undergoing to maintain control of the steering wheel and therefore the vehicle itself.

"Those two idiots are probably still there, just out of sight . . . yo."

"Why are you saying 'yo' after everything?"

"Not sure, must be the drugs."

"You don't take drugs; you just drink too much."

"Eat a bucket of dicks, dude. How the fuck do you know that?"

Matt stomped on the gas and fishtailed back onto the roadway, streaking down the avenue toward the last known location of Anthony and Valente. To my surprise, as we rounded the huge expanse of the parking lot, I saw their bumbling figures slowly meandering up the hill behind the stadium, taking the long way home. I formulated a quick plan.

"Okay, we're gonna play it cool. Just slow up and I'll jump out and we'll offer them a ride back home. They might believe that," I said.

"Yep, play it cool . . . is there an alternate plan, yo?" Matt answered.

"You just said 'yo' too, dude."

"I did. I kinda like it," Matt admitted.

We closed in on the two suspects as they marched through the fog.

"You know, this whole 'playing it cool thing' is really kinda pointless if you don't slow down."

"Roger-dat," Matt stated and actually took his foot off the accelerator for a moment.

"Remind me to mark this day down on my calendar."

"What day is that?"

"The day you discovered that there is a pedal to the left of the one you seem so fond of."

"Dick . . . yo," Matt said, laughing. He slowly pulled our vehicle behind our two walking mistakes. Valente and Anthony both looked toward the source of the noise as gravel crunched under our car's tires, betraying our presence. Before forward motion had ceased, I cracked the door and readied my boot for landing on the dusty ground below.

"Excuse me," I called out as the car stopped and I exited, walking toward the two suspects. "You guys want a ride back to the Double Deuce?"

Matt jumped out of the car as well and added, "It's no trouble."

I expected to have to make a little bit more of a production in sweet talking these guys into the back of the car but, as it turned out, that was unnecessary.

"Yeah, das cool man, fo' real," Valente said. He backhanded Anthony—who still regarded Matt and me with an obvious degree of skepticism—on the chest, "Come on, nigga. I ain't about to walk that far."

I took a step toward Valente as Matt did the same toward Anthony. "Real quick though, we've gotta make sure you guys don't have any weapons before we put you in the back of the car; it's policy."

"No prob-lem, Office-sir." Though he'd been searched five minutes before, Valente complied and turned away from me, instinctively placing his hands in the small of his back.

"Turn around for me, man," Matt said to the younger of the two. Anthony complied as well.

I shot Matt a quick glance and we both, simultaneously, removed handcuffs from our respective belts and *hooked up* the two men in our company, bringing and end to the second round.

As I handcuffed Valente, he asked, "I needa get handcuffed too? I don't got nothing; you just search me."

"Things have changed, Sir."

"What's that then?"

"You know that thing that you guys were smiling about us not finding before," I announced. "Well, we found it."

He didn't say anything; he just sighed.

Once back at Southeast station "Anthony Smith" was discovered to be, after a little foray with the fingerprint ID system, Anthony Falele. Anthony Falele was found— through ensuing law enforcement database queries—to have a warrant for his arrest for aggravated assault. He was also sixteen and not fourteen as previously stated.

I conducted my first three interrogations that day. The driver, Anthony and Valente each waived their Miranda rights and agreed to talk to me about the day's events . . . and give me bullshit stories about how they had "no idea" that a gun was in the car, or how such an item could have wound up therein. Valente conspicuously added, "But if there really was one, it belongs to that little nigga, Anthony." We booked the whole trio on an array of charges and Sean wrote the police report, explaining my first gun arrest that didn't involve me biting the ear off of the person formally in possession of it.

The same night, when my shift was over, I told Tessa about the case over dinner at one of our regularly frequented eateries. At the conclusion of the tale, which I thought that I told wonderfully, she still had some questions.

"What's gonna happen to that kid, Anthony?" she asked.

"I don't know," I said. "I'm guessing that it'll be nothing of great importance. It doesn't seem that people actually have to bear the burden of their misdeeds here in SF. It also depends on the outcome of the other case that he had the warrant for."

"What do you think should happen?"

"I think he should go to jail for a while. He's young but he already has a history of serious violence and was rolling around in a car with two other assholes, obviously looking for trouble. They were probably looking for somebody to shoot."

"You don't know that," Tessa argued. "They could have just had the gun for protection." She was always such an optimist.

"Protection from who, the police? Three thugs, regardless of age, rolling around in a blacked-out Caprice, right after sunrise, with a bottle of booze and a loaded submachine gun does not a harmless social gathering make."

"People can change if they are given the opportunity."

"I agree, but if you don't see the consequences to your actions, what's the motivation?"

We continued the casual debate for a while before moving on to a different topic: what to do next. Tessa was wearing a tight, black tank top that she got at a concert we attended when we first started dating. She also wore some formfitting black jeans, a studded belt and black Converse sneakers. Her dyed-black hair was haphazardly spiked in random directions atop her head, in stark contrast with her pale skin. She was still my rock n' roll goddess; even though she may have been a bleeding heart.

"Let's just go home and fuck," Tessa recommended. She could always speak in that way, in such a vulgar and explicit manner, anywhere and at any time and I wouldn't care. Because, whenever she did, something stirred below my belt.

I made the universal signal for *"Check please!"* to our waiter, who nodded in understanding. "Deal," I replied.

When we got home, I barely had time to throw an old Ramones record on my turntable before Tessa was down on her knees in front of me and working Dougie Cohen Jr. to full attention. She looked up with those deep-blue eyes, as she deftly shaped me into the required state for activities to come, and said, "You're my hero, baby. You're my fucking macho pig. Do you want to run me through with your nightstick, Officer?"

Half-groaning, half-laughing, and one hundred percent turned on I replied, "Did you really just say that? My . . . nightstick?"

"Fine . . . baton then."

"Much better. Keep doing what you're doing, please."

After a few minutes, I removed my shirt and lifted Tessa up over my shoulder, carrying her into the bedroom. I pushed her onto the bed and quickly removed her shoes and pants. I stripped next. The increased time that I'd been spending in the gym apparently showed.

"You look so sexy, baby," Tessa said as I tore open a condom wrapper. She ran her hands across my newly defined abdominal muscles.

"It's only because you're touching me." It was a cheesy line but it worked in the moment.

I crawled behind her as she lay on her side. As we moved, I grasped her by the chin, turned her head and pressed my lips against hers for deep, open-mouth kisses. I cupped her gorgeous, blue veined breasts in my hands and groped her perfect ass as the intensity of the act built.

"I love you," she said as she started to orgasm, "forever."

As she convulsed and writhed through her climax, I came also. Soon, we both fell asleep while I was still inside her, my arms wrapped around her warm, dreaming body. My last conscious thought: *I should marry this girl.*

CHAPTER 12

"The art of the police is not to see what it is useless that it should see."
—*Napoleon Bonaparte*

Walk into any police department in America and you'll find a large concentration of either active or former military personnel among the ranks. Having never been in the military, I'm not really the most qualified person to make authoritative statements in regard to it—but you'll have to take my word for it when I say that I've consulted heavily with the servicemen and women in the department to help formulate the following opinions.

That, and I've watched a lot of stuff on the History Channel. Especially when I was laid up at home after being bitten, trying to keep the room from spinning due to the nausea brought on by the powerful, prophylactic anti-viral meds I was taking before I found out I had a different kind of deadly virus.

It's apparent that many aspects of military life translate well into police work: the familiarity with the chain of command, the confidence instilled by basic and advanced training schools, the empiricism of combat, the haircuts, the uniform thing, the familiarity with weapons, an understanding of fraternal social structures, and having been through boot camp—an experience that likely makes the police academy much easier.

I'll note that the similarities pretty much end there. In fact, I'd say it's probably distinctly more frustrating coming into policing from the military than, say, having been a garbage man. The reasons are pretty simple to surmise:

1. Respect is not only assumed in the military, it's demanded. When respect isn't at least shown—not necessarily believed—heavy shit can go down; sew chevrons on one's uniform sleeve and one can expect to be saluted by those lacking the same number of chevrons. Experience is displayed on the soldier's chest and the promotions are supposedly based on merit, conduct and experience as opposed to the things that get one promoted in a major metropolitan police department. These things are:

   a. You take a series of tests and score in the top ten of about two hundred other candidates.

   b. You take a series of tests, get an *okay* score, but are a black, female-to-male transsexual with psoriasis and a humpback. Or you are related to the right person or drank with the right person or are married to the right person's sister. Something such as that.

   c. You take a series of tests, get a mediocre score but are fellating or performing cunnilingus on the person in charge of the hiring.

    d. You take a series of tests and do poorly but file a lawsuit against the department and the guy/gal doing the hiring alleging bias, of some sort, against the single demographic that you represent.

    e. You take a series of tests and fail miserably but tell the guy who does the hiring that you plan to inform his wife of all the times you blew him absent the desired promotion, posthaste.

2. While a fair level of camaraderie exists in the police department, probably more so than in your average convenience store, I'm hesitant to compare it to that of barracks/platoon life. Hopefully and at the bare minimum, a cop will back up his fellow officers. And hopefully the act will be returned when and if it's needed—but that isn't always the case.

    A police station is a lot like a high school: Bill wants to fuck Sally, who won't be in the same room with Bill's partner because they used to fuck until one of them cheated, and now they insist that a supervisor must facilitate any and all interaction between them . . . but the supervisor is usually busy trying to mediate various conflicts spawned by political animals, who allege brutality/racism/sexism/homophobia on behalf of another coworker so they can leave the shift, station or bureau. Cops can be their own worst enemies.

    Police stations are riddled with cliques:

individual social scenes and members of special interest groups each vying for positions of power in the department. These include the "Black Peace Officer's League," the "Order of Native San Franciscan Police Officers," the "Latino-American Law Enforcement Officer's Association," the "Rainbow Pride Coalition," the "Asian American and Pacific Islander Police Officers Organization" and the "Assembly of Female Police Officers." Conspicuously absent from this list is the "Nonspecific American Mutt Copper Club," because nobody would really pay attention to what this group had to say in the first place. Those folks only get to be members of the plain-old, boring and un-sexy San Francisco Police Union—toward which I have no specific positive or negative feelings.

3. In war, the soldier is expected to engage the enemy and, provided the rules of engagement are adhered to, there isn't fear that some smarmy shylock in a boring suit, or a reporter trying to make a name for him/herself, will challenge the soldier with the idea that his/her client was a victim of brutality or (at the bare minimum) circumstance and therefore innocent. Nor will the family of the deceased, whose actions forced the soldier to use force and/or kill the enemy, organize mass demonstrations against the soldier or launch a campaign to get said person fired and reap financial reward from the government.

Yet, cops—like soldiers—learn to recognize what the bad guys look like even if the expected actions upon discovering the enemy are vastly different. I'd even hazard to guess that the working cop's intuition for such identification becomes far sharper than that of the average soldier. Most cops spend twenty-five to thirty years on the job as opposed to the four years most soldiers spend in the military.

The difference in my own perceptions of my surroundings on that first day on patrol with Dean, versus those a year later, was drastic. I became so proficient at formulating suspicion that I had trouble turning the ability off. I frequently couldn't exit the state of hyper-alertness that engulfed me when patrolling. Little, clandestine shots of booze helped, vacations helped more, and Tessa telling me to "Lighten up!" helped. But nothing got rid of it.

To the soldier, though not necessarily applicable to the public at home, there are two sides. One side is the side the soldier is on. The other side is the enemy. Life on the streets is different. As a working cop, you learn who the "shitbags" or "cronks" are, who the criminals are. You learn to see the people that pose the greatest threat to you and would like to see you dead and watch your world burn. These people aren't in the Middle East, or some Cold War era, Communist-holdover regime. They're right at home; they are in the movie theater with you; they are in the fast food line; they are at your local auto parts and electronics stores shopping with you.

And, as a cop, you are expected to be nice to these people, to presume their innocence and take their reports;

to rush to their aid when they are in distress—though it may just be karma catching up to them, finally.

You are expected to smile in the face of your prospective killer and make sure he doesn't get hurt while you are around.

To learn to identify these people, you need go no further than to your local criminal courts on a Monday or Friday, which are the busiest days. Park yourself on a bench where the preliminary hearings and arraignments are being conducted and you'll see a parade of humanity of several different types: thugs, gangsters, crackheads, junkies, drunks, street punks, hippies, illegal immigrants, jocks, disgraced business types and sex offenders—who usually either fall in to one of the previously listed categories or look like your creepy librarian or, well, like a greasy version of your creepy librarian.

After a week in this environment, you'll start to understand the consistency. You'll hear the same tones of voice and choice phrases over and over; you'll see the same inappropriate attire adorning poorly tattooed, prison built or beady-eyed frames. You'll see the families of the defendants present, all busy making excuses for their loved one's conduct, harassing the victim and/or the victim's family in the hallways, away from the prying eyes of the prosecutor, judge or bailiff; you'll see criminal proceedings as a sick sort of reunion and family bonding experience. You'll hear the smug confidence of a defendant celebrating victory in court due to some sort of procedural issue on the behalf of the arresting or investigating officers. You'll realize that the criminal element of the world, for the most part, has a certain, intangible quality that you can't really articulate but could easily point out were you to see it again.

As a cop, the jury sure isn't a group of your peers. Explaining the *"OH SHIT!"*-look that the defendant displayed upon seeing your patrol car, which led you to get out and detain him and consequently find the loaded gun, or sack of crack, is not easy.

For instance, how did you know to when to dole out your first kiss? How did you know when to round *first base*? How did you know when to try and steal third? I'm sure it wasn't something that you picked up immediately, but it happened—so I assume—and you did it again, and again, and again. Eventually, you probably got pretty damn good at knowing the right times for these acts, but I'm guessing that it wasn't, and still isn't, something easy to describe.

Learn to identify the antagonists and you'll realize how ridiculous it is when you hear people speak of cops "racially profiling" in San Francisco or the greater Bay Area. In reality, I've met very few cops who I suspected were racially profiling; criminal profiling is far more effective. Patrol the Southeast District and most of your contacts are going to be with black suspects; work in the Mission District and your gang members will be predominately Latino; police the Haight and you'll be chasing white, drug addicted, trust fund runaways; work in the South of Market area and you'll be throwing down with a multiracial cast of drunken idiots from surrounding cities, people who come into The City on Friday and Saturday nights to fuck the place up.

Want to know what a criminal looks like? Bam, now you know. Go out there and right some wrongs, Officer. Work hard and make good arrests but, listen to me, don't you profile.

One day, early in your career, you'll work with a seasoned veteran cop. This man will point out a guy driving by in a beat up car, as you sit down in a café for breakfast. This cop will say, in a hushed tone, "Over there. See that guy? That's the guy who shot me—son of a bitch."

And you'll reply, "No shit?"

"No shit."

"And he's out there driving around? He's out of prison? I don't get it, man. When did this happen?"

"Some years back. He was out of jail before my wounds were healed enough to come back to patrol. Crazy world, isn't it?" Then he'll go back to finishing his eggs and leave you to ponder the gravity of that statement. If you're me, you'll be thinking about Jameson Ratchet and how I'd react were I to see him drive by.

You may make a subconscious note not to sit with your back to the door anymore.

CHAPTER 13

"You flunked flank? Get the flunk out of here!"

—Shecky Greene in Mel Brooks'
History of the World: Part One

Toward the last third of my probationary period, my classmates—who, unlike me, were not injured and held back a grade—finished probation and were transferred to their "permanent" assignments. This third and final non-elective transfer was the last mandatory move to a new district station of a rookie SFPD officer's career. Mine was due in a few months. I'd just completed the initial interferon regimen when my classmate, Dave Costello, drew the proverbial short straw and was one of the five officers sent out to Southeast. Fortunately for Dave, he didn't seem to mind working in such an environment. Dave just saw an opportunity to do good police work and help a community in need.

Dave once said, "If I start to hate the drama, I can always put my name on a transfer list to go elsewhere."

I told him, "You should do that now; it's not like you're gonna be able to transfer out anytime soon and you may as well get a head start."

Dave was in his thirties and, despite his short stature of about 5'05", one of the strongest cops on the force, especially when the power-to-weight ratio was brought into consideration. Whereas I was always more of an overt clown, Dave was slightly less extroverted but no less entertaining, which was one of the main reasons why I liked him so much. To further illustrate why I found him to be good company, Dave could quote Mel Brooks movies endlessly and knew a lot about comics, things that had always been very close to my heart.

Dave was about as Irish by blood as I was—a bit more than fifty percent—but his father immigrated to the US in the sixties and still spoke with a brogue. David Costello Sr., and therefore Dave as well, still had close ties to family members on the Island. Further adding to his entertainment value, Dave could do spot-on impressions of his dad's manner of speaking that consistently cracked me up. Whenever I could, I'd goad him into having his "father" make our radio transmissions for us—especially when we were unit, *"Tree-charlie-fardy-far-dayvid."*

Dave also liked videogames and collected jazz recordings, favoring anything on the *Blue Note* label because they still produced quality vinyl albums. It was nice to know somebody who still owned a turntable, like me. Over the coming months, we became good friends both on and off duty.

Through my utter lack of seniority, I'd wound up on (what I soon realized was, judging by the facial expressions of my coworkers when I told them where and when I worked) the least desirable shift in the entire department: 1800-0400 hours, with a fixed schedule of Sunday, Monday and Tuesday off—as opposed to the standard rotating schedule most patrol officers were on. This meant that I worked every Friday and Saturday night, nights that were widely regarded as the worst time to wear a badge/star/shield/whatever.

Three other unlucky souls were assigned to this watch and, like me, staffed units without any sector or beat assignments. In other words, we had no specific patrol responsibility; our sector/beat was the entire district. These units or "power cars" were created to respond to high-priority calls for service, be proactive and help out where needed. I never could figure out why the shift was held in such disdain as, seriously, I loved it.

In the same transfer that brought Dave over, Matt was transferred to his permanent station, the neighboring Excelsior District, and that left me alone on the watch. I was partner-less and somewhat apprehensive as to whom Matt's replacement would be; luckily, it was Dave.

Because we had no beat assignment, we were also responsible for doing the prisoner transfer—if we didn't have a wagon working—and picking up the interdepartmental mail at the beginning of our shift. While I didn't really care for having to interact with the prisoners and bear the brunt of their incessant whining, I was happy to do the transfer as it provided me opportunity to stop at one of the million coffee shops in the general area of the Hall of Justice, where the county jail's intake facility was located.

Since the end of the interferon treatment, I'd needed less coffee as the fatigue that plagued me for the forty-eight weeks of hell was starting to resolve itself. The occasional nausea had abated itself too; I was even sleeping better. I saw Dr. Ross soon after the meds had run their course, and was subject to a blood test.

"Your liver enzymes are normal, Dougie. That's awesome; no more drugs needed unless you have a relapse," the doctor told me.

"Finally, man . . . I can't tell you how shitty that stuff made me feel. I probably still can't drink though, can I?" I asked, hopefully.

"No. Absolutely not. That could trigger a relapse and contribute to the development of cirrhosis or liver cancer—things that you're already very at risk for. This means that you could die if you drink. I know that sounds harsh; it's the truth. No booze."

"Alright, gotcha. Fucking killing me."

"And, as long as we're talking about it, I need to see you every six months for repeat blood work, to make sure you're still in the clear. And I also need you to be vigilant and aware of your body; look for abnormalities; be your own doctor." He went over the list of symptoms that I needed to look out for, signs that I could be getting sicker: liver pain, jaundice, dark urine, clay-like stool, diarrhea and abdominal bloating, to name a few.

So began the waiting game.

When I got home from the doc's office, Tessa greeted me at the door of our apartment with a warm embrace. "Thank GOD that's over!" she announced and, to my surprise, started to cry.

"Babe, what's the matter? This is supposed to be one of those happy moments," I said.

"I just . . . it was so hard, Dougie. It was so hard watching you be so tired and so angry all the time. And the stress; field training and fights and injections; it was really hard for me to witness." After a pause and a sniffle, she added, "I didn't know if we were going to make it."

Hard for you? I thought. I pushed the last part of her statement out of my mind, tried not to think about what would happed to our relationship if I had a relapse, and said, "I love you."

In day four of our first week working together, after lineup, Dave buzzed me into the holding tank at Southeast so I could handcuff the thuggish, twenty-something asshole therein and haul him down to county intake.

I told the prisoner that it was time to leave.

"Why I gotta go to eight-fifty?" the prisoner asked, referring to the address of the Hall of Justice, 850 Bryant Street.

"Don't know, dude. I'm just giving you a ride."

"Ain't it yo' motherfuckin' job to know?"

"Ain't you the asshole who got arrested? You tell me why you're here, dickhead." I was still a little cranky, since being medication free, but that wasn't anything surprising.

"Man, you bitch-ass cops ain't shit. Ya'll think yo' tuff but I've been up in this mix since I was eleven years old, motherfucker. Eight-fifty ain't shit and you ain't shit either."

"Whatever, dude, easy way or the hard way. Turn around."

The suspect turned away, continuing his tirade as I cuffed him up, "I've been banging, robbing and hustlin' fo' longer than you've been driving man. Take my ass to eight-fifty! See if I give a shit! I'll be out and gettin' some pussy before you even get off work, motherfucker."

He was probably right.

Deep breath, I reminded myself.

I shoved the mouthy cuss toward the exit door of the booking room and called over to my partner, "Dave, can you grab this gentleman's property envelope?"

Dave nodded in acknowledgement and began to say something but was, again, interrupted by Mr. Outrage, "Alright, playa—damn! You ain't gotta be so rough . . . shit." He then added, "Yo, but seriously, can you see what my charges are, Cohen?"

First they played innocent, then they got angry and then they asked for favors; never failed. I tried to hide my grimace. "Yeah, sure . . . Dave, what are his charges?"

Dave glanced at the suspect's red booking card—red indicating he was being booked for a felonious crime, "catching a *red card*" as it was known—and stated, "Let's see: we've got robbery, resisting, a warrant for dope sales for fifty-grand and a probation hold."

"Shit man, forgot about that warrant. Damn, they gonna extend my probation again. I just got that shit extended. Them plainclothes motherfuckers is ruthless." His tone then became slightly more somber as he shook his head from side to side, "And I had shit to do tonight."

One thing that began to weigh increasingly heavy on my mind, as my experience on the job accumulated, was the utter lack of efficiency in the local criminal justice system—as far as the prosecution aspect went. San Francisco seemed to be the best place in America to get caught committing a serious felony. The judicial system was so lenient that threatening to take a suspect to jail, the only *legal* leverage available to an officer, was like threatening to take a suspect to the DMV; sure, you would be there a while and it sucked to wait around doing nothing, but jump through a few hoops and you would be finished and back on the street in no time. Often, only the young suspects who hadn't experienced local judicial proceedings yet, and the dudes facing serious time, ran from the cops. Why waste the energy and risk the post-chase ass-kicking that tended to follow?

Any asshole that had been through the ringer a few times was well aware what a circus San Francisco criminal justice was and had little fear of punitive action. This was not to say that San Francisco's criminals were never sentenced to stays in prison, but the length of prior criminal history, and/or general heinousness of the act necessary to receive such punishment, was prodigious.

There were a number of different reasons for this standard of leniency: including the notoriously liberal, "anything goes" nature of San Franciscans, who most prosecutors believed—correctly in many cases—would never convict anyone of anything. This was especially relevant if the suspect was poor, an illegal immigrant, of the minority du jour or just "really, really sorry for stabbing that bitch." To complicate matters, San Francisco had well funded, enthusiastic and skilled defense staff and an abundance of heavily overworked and, in some cases, jaded prosecutors. The most dumbfounding factor—as San Franciscans had twice turned down legislation to correct the matter—was the physical lack of criminal courts to deal with the volume of cases heard on a given day.

Yes, there weren't enough rooms for the judicial process to take place. Bet you never saw that on *Law and Order.*

Dave and I drove the prisoner down to the county intake facility and booked him without remarkable incident, unless one considers having to physically inspect the guy's disgusting shoes and socks to be *remarkable*. It astounded me that grown men who spent so much time, praise, effort and cash on having the correct cars, expensive gaudy jewelry (read: ornamental dental inserts, a.k.a. "grillz") and designer clothes still had deplorable hygiene.

I'd first come across this phenomena earlier in life when I was working in the ER. Back then, it was a regular occurrence to treat a gang-banger, pimp or dope-dealer that'd been gunned down, only to discover that his socks were faded to brown from white, his underwear was yellow in the front and brown in the rear and his toenails were of comparable condition to those of homeless lepers from the Middle Age. Furthermore, I found it dumbfounding that these same, unhygienic men had often fathered several children in their short lives as—from what I understood—women had to have sex with these men for conception, pregnancy and delivery to occur.

I'd always been instructed to believe that women were not generally captivated by skid marks.

After a thorough hand washing, Dave and I headed back out to the patrol car and began the detoured trip back to Southeast. Dave wasn't a coffee drinker but was, thankfully, happy to accommodate my habit. Dave drove me to my regular spot, a Starbucks on Potrero Avenue in the Mission District. I picked up my usual boring cup of coffee with a moderate amount of half-and-half and an overpriced water bottle, which indicated on its label that I was helping save the world through its purchase. I was clearly one of the legions of consumers heartened to know that spending two dollars on a product, which cost roughly eight cents to produce, was not without profound purpose.

I liked this specific Starbucks more than others as it was one of the few places that I had never been subjected to the following statements, which plagued most uniformed officers wherever they traveled:

1. "I didn't do it."
2. "He did it." [Witty citizen then points to friend or bystander.]
3. [This is only said on Halloween but it's said HUNDREDS OF TIMES on Halloween. So I thought I'd include it.] "Nice costume."
4. "Officer, are you on duty because I have a question . . ." [I didn't really mind answering the questions; it was the "are you on duty" part that I found odd. The implication that I would make it practice to go about my day wearing a police uniform and driving a police car, were I not getting paid for it, was somewhat disturbing. I'm not sure why.]
5. "Excuse me, I saw one of your coworkers arresting a homeless man the other day, who took a swing at him, and the cop seemed very angry and threw the guy on the poor ground and put handcuffs on him and I don't think that's right. Don't they teach you aikido or something?"
6. "I smell bacon."
7. [This snide statement requires the presence of more than one officer to work.] "Boy, I hope there's no trouble anywhere else." [The usual, unofficial reply to this is: "Like you never take a break at work." Though, sometimes and especially on days when the injections had me feeling remarkably terrible, I'd mutter: "Go fuck yourself." Not recommended.]

This isn't to say that all interaction with the public in a nonofficial capacity was annoying or bothersome; it just often was and usually at the worst possible time. The one phrase that did not get old, that I never tired of hearing and had the effect of continually renewing my faith in the denizens of my home city, was: "Thank you."

Every once in a while a random person would approach me and I'd cynically assume, *Oh boy; here comes,* but then, *BAM*: "Thank you." The first couple of times, this totally caught me off guard. Consequently, I practiced a response, which I thought was adequate. I kept it in the front of my mind for just such an occurrence.

The citizen said, "Hey, Officer, thank you for the job you do."

I'd reply, "No, thank you. You pay my salary and I love you for doing so."

Another reason that I preferred this particular Starbucks was that I was expected to pay for the goods and services rendered. I was never one of those greedy discount hunters that many cops became after years of attending special *public service only* sales and getting free espresso drinks. Those men and women seemed to be experts at haphazardly telling salesmen what they did for a living and parlaying it into a modest discount on a new TV or whatever. When I went to a restaurant on-duty that knocked off a percentage from the bill, I always wound up spending more as I tipped whatever was discounted and then some. This isn't to say that I thought myself morally superior—okay, perhaps a little—but I didn't ever want to be accused of taking a bribe. That was a pretty good way to wind up fired or assigned to the "Rubber Gun Squad." And, though I wasn't going to be dining with the Rockefellers anytime soon, I certainly made enough to buy an omelet or a burrito . . . or a cup of coffee

After completing the transaction, I jumped back in the car with Dave and we headed back toward our district. While, cruising down Potrero Avenue, Dave asked me questions regarding my work experiences in Southeast and I fired back with questions about what it was like working in the Mission. Dave had many good things to say about his probationary station, but noted that it was impossibly busy and that the Latin gangs in the Mission, the red-wearing Norteños and blue wearing Sureños, were always in the process of finishing or renewing some sort of violent turf war.

"At least the assholes still wear colors out there," I noted. "That helps a lot with identification and probable cause." Before I'd even gotten into the department, black gangs had ceased wearing identifying colors as such activity was a very helpful accessory for police and prosecutors. "Not being able to understand what they're saying would suck, though."

"It did," Dave answered. "Luckily, most of the Norteños speak English even though they usually pretend they don't. The Sureños are a different story, though."

"I've heard that. I hear most of them are pretty *drippy*. Did you just talk a bunch of shit to them, when you thought they were faking, to see if they got mad? That's what I'd do."

"Yeah, I did that on a few occasions. Or I'd just talk to them in *Blazing Saddles* lines to see if their expressions changed. But you would be surprised how many of the Sureños really don't speak a lick of English. Most of them are *illegals* from El Salvador. That's where MS-13 is from."

"That's *the* big Sureños gang, right?"

"Yeah, they're huge. In ten years the Mission is gonna be a lot bluer. It was a good time to leave, while the getting was good."

"I hear that but, 'You've got to remember that these are just simple farmers. These are people of the land; the common clay of the New West. You know . . . morons.'" I'd been studying up on my Mel Brooks films to go tit-for-tat with Dave. The last time we had tried this, in the academy, he put me to shame. I was curious if Dave knew the line that followed. I didn't.

Right then, the sultry voice of the dispatcher interrupted. "Okay, in the Mission 'five car' we've got a report of a gunshot victim at 23rd and Bryant. Can I get a unit to start?"

"David-fifteen-david responding." The sector car answered, "Anything on the suspect; a direction of travel or description?"

The normal radio jamming caused by various units broadcasting that they were also responding to the call ensued.

"Units, standby . . . suspect is . . . described as a Latin male in his twenties . . . wearing a blue jacket, a blue hat and blue jeans. Last seen running north on Bryant. The gun is described as a handgun. No further."

I said to Dave, "I think I know what color the victim is wearing."

"Yeah, me too," he replied.

"Correct me if I'm wrong, but aren't we just about on top of this call?" I asked.

"Yeah, it's a few blocks away. Wanna head over there? We'll probably be the first ones on scene."

"Sure. Seems rather uncouth to not." I figured our sergeant couldn't get mad at us for helping out on such a call, though it wasn't in our district.

I was ready for an abrupt period of acceleration as Dave hit the gas. It was much smoother than what Matt would have done, which surely would have involved a nitrous boost and fire and spinning tires and pedestrians scrambling for cover. I had enough warning to extend my scalding hot coffee out at arm's length so as to minimize the damage of the fiery, staining liquid were it to make contact with my crotch and uniform.

"Dave, are you, uh, aware that I'm holding a hot beverage here?"

"Hang in there. We're almost there; three more blocks. You know most people would toss that out the window and get another one later."

"I ain't most people, son."

The 911 dispatcher broadcast an update as the 911 call-taker relayed the information to her: "Units, updated suspect description on the shooting at 23rd and Bryant: Latin male, late teens or early twenties. Suspect is wearing a blue hat, a blue jacket and dark pants; now last seen running eastbound on 23rd toward Potrero. The 911 caller saw the suspect put the gun in his jacket pocket."

Dave slowed his response to the scene in obvious realization that, provided the 911 call was relayed promptly and the suspect information was good, we could be about to drive right past the shooter. As Dave hit the brakes, I clenched my teeth to stifle the horrific scream that almost eked out when and eruption of boiling coffee splashed on my hand. As I rapidly formulated the appropriate slew of insults to launch at my partner, dispatch spoke again.

"Okay, units on the shooting at 23rd and Bryant, can we get a unit to go by 20th and Potrero? Another 911 caller is saying he saw a man with a gun run into the Laundromat there. The guy with the gun was supposed to be dressed all in blue."

I looked to my right and saw that we were flying by a Laundromat. I then looked up at the street sign and saw that we were approaching 21st Street.

"Dave! Dave!" I said excitedly.

"Whatcha got?"

"Dude, the Laundromat. The one dispatch just mentioned. I think we just passed it. Spin around."

"On it."

Unlike Matt, Dave was generally capable of slowing our vehicle in a manner that didn't cause groups of pigeons to rocket upwards from their perches on the telephone lines overhead. He hit our overhead lights and pulled to the road's right shoulder. Throwing the car into reverse, Dave backed up about a hundred feet until

Daniel B. Silver

he was two buildings down from the Laundromat. Dave brought the car to a quick halt.

"Okay, a Latin dude in blue, with a gun, right?" I clarified so the suspect's description would be fresh in our minds—as is the expected job of the officer who isn't driving the patrol vehicle.

"Yep, sounds about right," Dave said as we threw the doors open and exited, drawing our side-arms in the process.

Dave and I quickly jogged up to the closest exterior window of the Laundromat. I peered in and saw a rotund Mexican woman folding clothes on the table nearest the door. Her two young children were seated next to her, behaving themselves but looking bored.

I whispered to Dave, "One lady, a Latin female, and her two kids. I don't see the suspect but I can't see the whole inside, obviously."

A voice barked through my earpiece. "David-fifteen-david is on the scene," I heard the initial responding officer broadcast. Almost immediately he keyed his mike again, "David-fifteen-david, emergency traffic! I've got a man down, not breathing, with a gunshot to the head. I need an ambulance; we're starting CPR." He sounded stressed. Shootings happened with reasonable frequency in the Mission but the Latin gangs were notoriously bad shots. Because of this, they often tended to "wing" or graze just about everybody they shot at, sparing rare occasions such as this. Part of me thought that the units in the Mission—who shared the same radio channel as Southeast, meaning that I had to listen to them gab to

206

each other all night—just yelled over the radio and drove everywhere with their lights and sirens on out of envy that they didn't work where the real shit went down. But that opinion wasn't entirely accurate, obviously.

"An ambulance is already en route, david-fifteen-david. I'll update," the dispatcher said, calmly. She then relayed his message, "Units, clear the air; david-fifteen-david has located the victim. This is a good two-seventeen."

"Okay, so," I said to Dave in reference to the last update, "looks like this could be interesting. Let's head them off at the pass, shall we?"

"Head them off at the pass? I hate clichés!" Dave appropriately quipped and walked past me with his gun pointed down at the ground. I followed behind, giggling despite the danger. We cautiously approached the front door.

Dave and I took positions on either side of the entrance. I peered around the frame and waved to the two children; the kids stared back at me with looks of absolute boredom on their faces. Dave also looked in and gestured to the two youngsters with his free hand, trying to get them to come toward us, to safety. They didn't budge. In a similar effort, I made a variety of hissing noises with my mouth that were meant to transcend cultural boundaries and get the attention of the mother, who was still in earnest concentration on the laundry before her.

That didn't work either.

"Fuck it," I said to Dave and walked in. I mumbled, "You'd think that if he was in here they probably would have run out screaming or something?"

"What?" Dave asked.

"I said: 'The sheriff is near.'"

"You sure you didn't mean to say: 'Excuse me while I whip this out,'" Dave countered.

"'Somebody go back and get a shit-load of dimes!' Okay, enough. Let's go."

Despite the current breakdown into comedic quotations, we were still somewhat focused on the task at hand and still had our guns out of their holsters, but we hid them behind our legs so as not to freak out the kids or their mother. A series of large, yellow support beams—the center row of washers and sections of counter—obscured the back half of the room from full view. Yet, considering the attitude of the sole patron and her two kids inside, I tended to think the rumored, armed suspect probably wasn't present.

"Dude, would you hide in a Laundromat after shooting somebody?" I muttered to Dave under my breath. "I really don't think he's in here."

We walked straight past the family—whose facial expressions seemed to indicate that the presence of uniformed policemen in their Laundromat was a fairly regular occurrence—and continued toward the back of the room, moving briskly. We were both, by this point, reasonably sure that this was probably a bogus call; or the guy was gone. Dave forked to the left side of the center row of washers, dryers and counters; I took the right.

As we advanced, Dave began to whisper, "This speech comes to mind right now, Dougie: 'Men, you are about to embark on a great crusade to stamp out runaway decency in the West. Now, you will only be risking your lives, whilst I will be risking an almost certain Academy Award nomination for Best Supporting Actor . . . .'"

"Dude, do you know that entire speech?"

"I know more than you."

"I need to step up the studying."

As we walked to the end of the row of appliances, toward the last prospective hiding place, I glanced over at Dave and shot him a look as if to ask: *Find anybody?*

I could see him slow down, just a tad, and bring his gun up slightly. Worried that Dave had just seen something I hadn't, I looked back toward the rear of the room. Right then, a dryer door clanged shut, somewhere ahead of us.

Shit, I thought. *That probably isn't a midget doing his laundry.*

Dave and I both immediately froze, right before rounding the final corner. Simultaneously realizing that somebody, likely the suspect, was hiding just out of sight and that we were about to place ourselves in a crossfire situation, I pointed at Dave and made a hook motion with my left hand, signaling him to continue his course. I then pointed at myself and then at the counter, making a *walking* motion with my first two fingers.

Dave nodded in understanding.

I checked my grip on the gun, nodded three times and, after the third nod, I vaulted to a standing position on top of the washers and dryers, channeling my newfound energy. I bounded forward toward the unsecured area as Dave moved to do the same. In three steps, I towered above a Latin guy, about nineteen, wearing a blue hat, a blue jacket and blue jeans. The suspect was breathing heavily, obviously covered in sweat and crouched down on the floor. Out of the corner of my eye, I saw Dave round the corner and see the guy as well.

In response to the racket I made clamoring across the sheet metal washers and dryers, the young gangster looked right up at me, square in the eyes. For just a moment, the three of us froze in silence. Realizing that he had just finished shooting another human being and probably wouldn't object to doing it again, I began to formulate a command to yell as I brought my gun up. I figured, rightly, that this was a good choice of action.

Seeing this, the suspect lashed out toward the door of the drier like a desperate man being carried away by a flash flood grasping for a thrown safety line. Establishing a satisfactory grip on the plastic handle, he started to pull the door open and reached for the pistol he had just stashed inside—or so I figured.

"DON'T MOVE! NO SE MUEVA!" Dave yelled, bringing his gun up and pointing it at the formerly hidden Sureno.

Reflexively, I leapt down feet first and landed both of my boots on the suspect's chest, sending his body crashing toward the floor. This probably wasn't the smartest thing to do as I was now in Dave's line of fire but, once airborne, I couldn't take it back.

I heard a metal clang inside the dryer as the suspect's gun fell away from his grasp. Underfoot, the Sureno came down in a heap. I rolled outwards, off the suspect and onto the floor, scrambling to my feet.

I hoped to hell that Dave wouldn't shoot me by mistake if the bombardment didn't stick. Fortunately, it did and I could tell the move caught Dave by equal surprise.

"Oh, DAMN!" Dave said, enjoying the show, which made me feel pretty cool. Dave ran up and slammed the door to the dryer closed, concealing the gun inside. The gong-like report of the dryer door shutting immediately preceded Dave grabbing the dazed and coughing man by the leg. Dave ripped the young gangster away from the concealed gun with his considerable strength. Dave dropped down next to the suspect and flipped him over onto his face, like he was pulling the rug out from under the guy.

I hastily got back to my feet—years of skateboarding had finally paid off—and ran over to help Dave handcuff the shooter. Once the suspect's arms were secured behind his back, Dave and I both slowly rose back to our feet and caught our breath, our gazes still fixed on the prone suspect in admiration of our work. Then I remembered that I should probably tell somebody what we were doing. I reached for my radio mic and keyed it.

"Charlie-seventeen-david to headquarters," I said.

"Charlie-seventeen-david standby, a unit just came on scene at the Laundromat where the homicide suspect may be hiding and is going in to search."

Both Dave and I looked toward the front door and saw two cops come cautiously walking in, guns drawn. Seeing us, they both stopped short and displayed confused looks on their faces.

"Uh, well, you can cancel that unit. We've got one in custody in the Laundromat at two-zero and Potrero. I think we might have the gun in here also . . . sorry we didn't put it out sooner; we were driving by when you put the call out. By the way we have sufficient help now." I waved at the two cops and smiled as they holstered their weapons, looking a little miffed.

"Copy that. Charlie-seventeen-david advises they have a possible suspect in custody, regarding the shooting at 23rd and Bryant. Does a unit have a witness for a cold show?"

Dave and I smiled at each other, proud of ourselves.

"Coja a sus madres!" The custody gasped from the floor.

A lieutenant at the crime scene broadcast an update: "David-two-hundred," he announced, "the paramedics are advising me that this has now been deemed a homicide. Can you raise somebody from the Gang Task Force and advise him that a Southeast unit has a suspect detained regarding the incident, and where."

"Ten-four," the dispatcher answered.

"Epic drag there, Dave," I complimented.

"Nice jump," Dave returned. "But your landing could use some work."

"Everyone's a critic."

"Oh, and the next time," Dave added, "you happen to find yourself pile-driving a murderer into the ground you say, for me, for all of us: 'Piss on you; I'm working for Mel Brooks!'"

CHAPTER 14

"The police are the public and the public are the police; the police being only members of the public who are paid to give full time attention to duties which are incumbent on every citizen in the interests of community welfare and existence."

—*Robert Peel*

Put on the uniform and jump into a radio car. It doesn't matter if you drive or not; unless the rare, hypothetical situation described in the first chapter pops up. You remember, right? It was the one with the drunk guy and the copious spitting.

Early in your career—when everything is relatively new—and on busy nights, you'll feel fine; the radio will be the master of your destiny and you won't have time for timidity or feel overwhelmed. You'll have fun and needn't worry about what lies before you; the dispatcher will direct you where to go like the trade winds picking up your spinnaker.

After a short time on the street, you'll figure out that only so many things necessitate your presence or intervention. Small constants in a job full of variables, a static line above the abyss of limitless, endless drama. You could wind up going from emergency to emergency: homicides, shootings, stabbings, reports of shots being fired, gang fights, fights on the street, fights in bars, and fights in houses—between husbands and wives, or boyfriends and girlfriends, or any combination thereof. You'll respond to robberies in progress, burglaries in progress, laptop thefts in progress, bicycle thefts in progress, auto thefts in progress, auto burglaries in progress, and reports of drunk or reckless drivers. And let's not forget the people reported to have guns, people reported to have swords, people reported to have knives, the structure fires, vehicle fires and "explosions" (usually just some jackass with an M-80). You name it; the public has it in store and in stock.

It's equally likely that it could be one of those lame days, in which you schlep your beaten, sticky patrol car from *blah* call to *blah* call: domestic disputes, pay disputes, suspicious people, suspicious vehicles, homeless complaints, kids skateboarding (the lamest of all police calls, if you ask me), youths doing graffiti, junkies shooting-up, crackheads smoking-up, and tweakers tweaking in every direction. It could be a call about an out of control teen running away for the millionth time, a missing family member that's been absent for about twenty minutes, a drunk on a bus, a guy peeing on the sidewalk, or a guy who took five Advil and called 911 because he wanted attention.

Be it "hot" call or "cold" call, you'll take reports: homicide reports, robbery reports, burglary reports, domestic violence reports, theft reports, lost property reports, missing person reports, rape reports, molestation reports, death reports, embezzlement reports (*Wait, why did you give your son the car if he's on parole for car theft?*), identity theft reports, battery reports, sexual battery reports; the list goes on and on and it's all equally dull for the most part, after you do one a few times.

But it sounds so interesting on TV, doesn't it? So, how does it get so boring and stressful at the same time?

It gets boring because only so much can happen on patrol. Sure, the extremes of what can go wrong are horrible and terrifying: you get beaten, stabbed or shot to death; you get in a terrible car wreck or purposely run over; you wind up in a coma or paralyzed. A commercial airliner could crash into a major city center. Maybe two idiots in body armor with assault rifles storm a local B of A? That's all happened.

But, most of it is just drama; endless, mind-numbing, hair-pulling, ridiculous drama. If you're me, that's what you dread the most.

Guns and knives: bring 'em on.

Child custody disputes: put a rope around my neck, please.

In theory, it's a different story when one becomes a detective, where you work a "good" case from the beginning to the end—whatever that may be. You wrap your brain around the case. You delve into it and live it for a portion of your life. Writers always use detectives as protagonists for that reason; every serious case is a journey. The work is often emotional and it's heavily romanticized by the public and media. The same people who "hate fucking punk-ass cops" often feel differently about detectives; they are perceived to be of a different breed. Investigators aren't just another blue uniform taking away a family member in handcuffs or writing a traffic ticket.

In most large police agencies, the detectives are assigned to units that specialize in certain types of crime. In these situations, the crime itself becomes personal, the specialty of the person investigating it. A specific kind of tragedy or injustice becomes the investigator's responsibility to correct. And, when the case all comes together and the bad guy goes to jail, there's no feeling comparable in other lines of work; that's satisfaction from a career.

It's not so in patrol; at the most, you're a part of the initial investigation and will never hear or see the outcome: it's just another victim of a robbery, another man dead in the projects, or another house ransacked by some drug-hungry asshole. You're only a part of any arrest or any investigation for a few hours at the most, discounting the potential court appearances later down the road, where you have the opportunity to learn what became of the case.

Of course, you can be the master of your own destiny. That's when the shit really tends to hit the fan: when you have the opportunity to be proactive and to stir up the hornet's nest. When that radio is silent at three in the morning and all you have to do is drive around and get in to trouble, or when you're assigned to a specialized assignment and exist solely for the purpose of arresting people, is when the real anxiety hits.

When you have downtime to think about the all the problems that you are responsible for solving, that's when you start to feel overwhelmed; that's when you start to realize that you, Officer, are the center of attention wherever you go. That's when you feel the many expectant stares.

Pop quiz:
Consider for a moment an average intersection in a big city. On the northwest corner of this intersection stand six people. They are described as follows;

- Person #1 is an attractive, nineteen year old Asian girl. She is completely naked.
- Person #2 is a white homeless man in the process of pissing on a bus shelter.
- Person #3 is a man of indeterminable race in a clown suit drinking shitty vodka from a brown, paper bag.
- Person #4 is a shady looking Latin guy who is wearing a long coat in the mid-day heat, a rolled up ski mask on his head and has one arm buried in a bulging pocket.
- Person #5 is a uniformed white, female police officer.
- Person #6 is her also uniformed black, male partner.

Question: Which of these people is the average citizen intently observing? Take your time.

Answer: If you chose the two cops (numbers five and six), congrats. You're a winner. Sure, the first four options may all be interesting people to check out; a person may be near-incapable of tearing his or her eyes away from the sight of a gorgeous, naked female or a vodka-loving clown; it doesn't matter. He or she will, in this case, watch the cops. No matter how interested a person is in a given incident or situation, the same person is generally even more captivated by what a cop is going to think or do about it. Will the cop laugh? Will the cop keep walking and not pay any notice? Will the cop trip and fall? Will the cop remove his or her baton and start beating the naked girl, the clown, the minority suspect—at least one who differs demographically from the officers in question—or poor homeless man? People want to know, especially in the age of cellular phone cameras. Somebody wants to see somebody else go to jail. Somebody wants to witness the next Rodney King beating. Somebody wants to shoot the next internet video of some bonehead cop accidentally hurting him or herself. Somebody wants an example of how their tax dollars are being wasted on lazy cops who "never do anything" and just keep walking. The public is watching.

If you're a perceptive officer, you'll also realize that the big black and white car, the creaking, leather gun-belt and the shiny symbol on your shirt don't just make you the star of the show; you are also a target. All the cool toys you worked so hard to get in the hiring process and academy make you "The Man" and every rebellious teenager, gangster, thug, political science major and politician up for reelection doesn't really give a shit what happens to you. In fact, a good portion of them would like to see you suffer; they would like to see you hurt and even like to see you die.

You could be black as night, first generation Latin or a Jew just off the boat—fleeing the new *Fourth* Reich—it doesn't matter. You're blue. You don't have a name, a religion or even a skin color. It's socially acceptable to hate cops. Go see a modern action film and watch as cop after cop is blown away by the misunderstood, persecuted, patent leather-clad protagonist. "Fuck the po-lice," people say, sing and write on walls, in magazines, and in the lyric booklets of bestselling albums. This causes boring spokespeople and pundits go on TV and decry the offensive lyrical content, which doesn't do anything but increase sales of the media in question.

Whether or not the individual officer takes offense to such sentiments doesn't matter. It's just another brick on the stack of anger that forces drops of perspiration out of the skin under his or her Kevlar vest, like rivets in the dispassion that cops tend to wrap themselves in. And, if a constructive outlet for this anger isn't found then it will probably drive one to drink, drive one to violent outbursts, and/or fill one with self-loathing and self-doubt.

It may just change you into somebody you don't like anymore.

Daniel B. Silver

Holes may develop in the boat keeping you afloat the murky tide, which flows through the city streets.

Outside forces could muck up the moral compass.

You'll come back to work, day after day, "pushing" a patrol car around, arresting the same suspect again, and writing the same report for a hundredth time. After a while, when you're getting out of the car and trying to breathe away the unknown situation that awaits you and forcing it to a certain place, somewhere behind the metal trauma insert in the level IIIA vest—the same place that you'll draw on when the shit hits the fan and you're struggling to survive—you start to respond to the seemingly endless hard looks with smirking, challenging grins.

And when your boots hit the ground, when you are in a hurry to get to a call or to grab a suspect before he jumps on the train, one thought will race through your mind in response to the palpable disdain of the citizens around you: *Put up or shut up, man. Just get the fuck out of my way.*

CHAPTER 15

"Dreams are today's answers to tomorrow's questions."

—*Edgar Cayce*

In the dream, I'm ten years old and I'm supposed to read a book to my fifth grade class. It's a harmless piece of children's literature, one that has some sort of grand moral lesson to impart upon the reader, such as: *"Look both ways before crossing the street,"* or *"Don't short-change the blind."*

I'm standing in a drab, yellow classroom with filthy acoustic tiles and shitty, age inappropriate crayon drawings adorning the walls. A line of aging computers with green on green monitors sit on a long desk against the back wall of the room. Six rows of bored looking students are seated before me and I can hear toes tapping, noses blowing, chewing gum snapping and binders sliding back and forth across worn, wooden desks. An overly tanned and bespectacled female teacher sits to my right, audibly clearing her throat in a practiced and overtly dramatic manner, prompting me to begin.

But I don't. I'm just standing there, frozen in my own thoughts, holding a thin book in my hand and staring at the dense, foul smelling carpet under my feet.

"Dougie," the teacher says, "read. It's your turn."

"Uh huh," I reply, bringing the book up to my face. But it isn't a children's book; it's my highlighted copy of *Fight Club*. In the real, waking world, I'd written a bunch of quotes from the same book on the walls of my apartment's bedroom—back before I applied for the department, before I met Tessa. This somewhat explains why the novel keeps popping up in my dreams. This probably helps clarify why I applied to the department.

Every man needs a right of passage. Until that happens, there is no man.

The teacher clears her throat again, "Begin."

I was pleased when I discovered that Tessa was a modern literature fan and didn't mind my spouts of writing on the walls when the muse moved me; especially pleased because this occasion was also the same time she was ever in my bed.

"Hey, Dougie, 'I want to have your abortion,'" Tessa said, quoting Marla Singer, the main female character from the same book.

"Oh, 'Marla, you tourist,'" I answered before pulling her shoes off and throwing them over my shoulder, followed by the rest of her clothes.

It was a good night.

Back in the dream, back in what was not turning out to be a good night, I open the text to the first page and start to dictate it to my young classmates: "Tyler gets me a job as a waiter, after that Tyler's pushing a gun in my mouth and saying the first step to eternal life is you have to die." I glance up for a moment; the students are all gone now. I continue to read, "For a long time though, Tyler and I were best friends . . ."

The students fade from view and now I'm outside myself, looking at the ten year old me standing there, reading out loud. Non-dictating Dougie Cohen is wearing a police uniform; my SFPD uniform and my goofy service cap. I'm standing in front of the younger me, the little art fag me who loves drama class. And I'm listening to my prepubescent voice say the following words, which are totally out of order with the book, but it doesn't matter: "If I could wake up in a different place, at a different time, could I wake up as a different person?"

But I don't wake up. I keep dreaming some sort of meandering, random narrative that switches between the first and third person.

Later in the dream, I'm out on patrol with Mark, my third phase FTO. We are walking a beat down one of the Tenderloin's scummier blocks, where a dumbfounding assortment of drug dealers and users shuffle away from us as we make the corner. The reoccurring cast of the dream is trying to look like they always do: busy. Mark and I see a gigantic black guy whose body is prison-ripped and covered in bad tattoos of skulls, random names—spelled out in cursive—and images of assault rifles. This mountainous man hands a rock of cocaine base to a random crackhead, in exchange for a ten-dollar bill. The crackhead puts the rock in is pocket and, as Mark and I start to advance, looks directly at us. The crackhead's eyes go wide as he sees the two of us and he promptly takes off running, down the sidewalk.

Witnessing this spontaneous flight, the dealer turns to observe the source of his customer's fear: Mark and me.

The dealer doesn't make any attempt to leave. "What the fuck you gonna do, white boy?" he taunts. I see the fire grow behind his eyes. His chest juts forward and his muscles tense as he suddenly reaches his right hand out of sight, toward the small of his back.

This is usually where the dream goes to shit, but this time it's different. I don't call out Mark's name; I don't hesitate; I don't feel fear. My gun is out of the holster before I can even think about it and I'm snapping the trigger back, again and again and again. Red mist pops out of the dealer's back as I fire round after round into his muscular frame. The dealer falls to the ground as my weapon's slide locks back in the empty position. I look at Mark, who's just standing there with a vacant look on his face, his coffee still in hand. I take a step forward, toward the fallen man and the blood pooling under him.

I drop the empty magazine to the ground and it goes: *"tock."* I casually remove another, fresh clip from my belt and insert it into the magazine well of my pistol. I hit the slide release with my right thumb and listen as it claps forward, chambering another round. Again, I'm ready to fire.

A few more steps forward and I'm standing directly over the fallen dealer who makes pathetic attempts at breaths, clinging to the last vestiges of life. But I don't feel anything. I don't care. I don't call him an ambulance or scream on the radio that I just shot somebody. I just point my pistol right at his head and, for a second, I think about closing my eyes before pulling the trigger again.

But I don't. I look him right in the face.

It's me again; I'm ten years old. I'm looking up at myself from the perspective of the dealer, holding a smoking gun. My face and uniform are spattered with blood. I'm surrounded by the cold winds of violence and rage. I'm eye to eye with wrath.

Ten year old me says, in that little art fag voice, "Bang."

I wake up thinking that I really need to stop working so much. And that I should write some happier shit on my walls.

CHAPTER 16

*"Every time I see Bono in those big fly glasses
and tight leather pants, I just can't hack it. I
can't see that as solving the world's problems.
He's crushing his testicles in tight trousers for
world peace."*
—*John Lydon, A.K.A. "Johnny Rotten"*

There are a few distinct and differing options available
to an officer—*you* for purposes of this exercise—when
confronting a subject who is armed with a firearm of
some sort and either pointing it at, or shooting at, you:

1. Completely ignore all of your training. Effectively
   bury your survival instinct and utterly fail to
   preserve your own life by freezing up. Stand
   there, jaw agape, hands and forearms clenched,
   eyes wide, totally motionless. Then, let out a
   garbled half-command, half-yelp of some sort,
   which likely translates into "stop" or "don't" or
   "please stop" or "please don't." Then receive a
   volley of bullets from the muzzle of the suspect's
   gun into your quaking body. Hopefully, your
   level IIIA ballistic vest will keep any of these

rounds from killing you, provided you don't get hit in the melon, liver, femoral artery, descending aorta or inferior vena cava. If that happens, well, lights out and game over. This course of action is not generally recommended, unless you're one of the people who insist that chamomile tea will magically cure my chronic insomnia, when high dosages of potent narcotics barely have any effect.

2. Pray. Some would argue that the spiritual benefit of prayer is comparable to the benefit that rigorous exercise has on the living body. I'm still not totally convinced either way; you can't be sore if you don't exercise. Granted, I exercise compulsively but I really wish I didn't, so I wouldn't be sore all the time. A vicious cycle. Regardless of one's opinion as to the power of prayer, I'm hesitant to suggest this is a good activity to undertake immediately *prior* to being shot. After being shot, it seems pretty reasonable. If rabbis, priests, clerics, witches or other spiritual leaders take issue with this, feel free to email, phone or write me and let me know you're opinion so that I might dismiss it as drivel.

3. If available, rapidly move to a position of cover: an object that is capable of stopping a ballistic projectile, like a bullet, or at least vastly decreasing its capacity to kill or maim. If no cover is available, move to a position of concealment: a place or area that shields or obscures one's body from view thereby decreasing the accuracy of

the rounds currently being fired at you. During said movement, draw your sidearm, point it at the threat, give a warning if possible—be able to articulate why you were unable to give a warning if you choose not to or are otherwise unable to—and initiate deadly force application procedures (shoot the guy).

After the suspect is down and provided you haven't been hit and incapacitated, make a tactical approach, kick the suspect's weapon away, handcuff him and call for immediate assistance and an ambulance. Be prepared for every cop and their mothers—not really their mothers—to respond to the scene and for a brief period of chaos and confusion.

Soon, a supervisor will remove you from the scene. After being removed, you can expect to have your weapon taken away from you by a crime scene technician and replaced with a loaner. Your union representative will sit by your side and read you of your rights as an officer—prior to ensuing interviews by a detective from the department's Homicide Detail, a lawyer from the City Attorney's Office, and later, an investigator from the Office of Citizen's Review. During the OCR interview, the investigator will assume you murdered the suspect in cold blood, so it really doesn't matter what one says to this person, but try to do your best anyhow.

A one paragraph news story will air the next

day stating that an officer-involved shooting occurred, where it was, and that it is currently under investigation by the noted agencies. You will read this story and be amazed how little information is actually in it.

You will then be given ten days of paid administrative leave. During the first few days of this time away from work, you will likely be contacted by a myriad of coworkers and supervisors, all of whom will wish you well and express their concern for you, which feels weird because you are the one who survived. If your partner got hit or, God forbid, died in the encounter, each call will make you feel worse. For the sake of this exercise, this didn't happen, though.

About three days into your leave, the phone calls will subside and you will try not to read the new story in the newspaper, which names you as the officer involved in the shooting and describes your length of service and current assignment. The story will feature interviews with the family members and/or loved ones of the man that you killed. It will state that these people really have "no idea" why their blessed little angel was taken from this world by the cruel, calloused hands of a rogue, murderous officer. You read on, only to learn that—just like nearly every single one of the people killed by the police, nationwide—the deceased was *"just turning his life around"* and *"didn't even own a gun."* Inevitably, people will protest your continued employment at San Francisco Police Commission hearings, and a website or organization will be established in the memory of the criminal you killed because, so we are led to believe, *"He was really a great guy!"*

You'll be sued and, as it was a "good" shooting, the department will settle for an undisclosed amount of money rather than bother going through the even *more* expensive and time-consuming process of lengthy proceedings in a civil court. For years to come, people will pick apart and second guess your actions. Eventually, you will return to work, feeling very out of place for a while. Perhaps you'll experience some behavioral or psychiatric problems. Maybe you won't be able to get *it* up anymore. But, if you're smart, you will not retreat into a bottle or take up some other form of self-destructive behavior.

Hopefully and despite warnings to the contrary (*Don't discuss the case while it's still under investigation!*), you'll talk with people about what happened and engage in regular exercise. Hopefully, the little "funk" that you are in will subside with time and you'll soon be your old self again. Hopefully, you won't dread the job; it won't fill you with anxiety. Hopefully, you'll *keep on keepin' on* with only a mild amount of lingering mental disquietude.

This is the way it's supposed to go, the way

your training is supposed to steer your actions. The rest of the baggage that goes along with killing a suspect in an officer-involved shooting is just par for the course. You need to realize this and push all of it out of your mind when back at work because, though unlikely, it could easily happen again. Keep your mental eye on the prize because survival is more important than being demonized and vilified by the media and in court. Despite this, I can't really say I recommend going through such an experience but, in this situation, you don't really have many options.

And, hey, you might even get a medal one day.

4. Plow into the asshole with your car. If you ever get the chance, totally do this one; it fucking rules, man.

CHAPTER 17

"Imagine the powerful rage when someone crosses the passion between a man and a woman or a man and his city."

—*Frank Miller*

It was August in San Francisco, which meant that on any given roadway one could observe some sort of midsized sport utility vehicle, caked with dirt from a Northern Nevada desert, passing by. Such vehicles were usually piloted by some white chick or dude, inevitably gabbing away on a cellular phone. The same automobiles often had some sort of symbol, quote or would-be sound bite scribbled in the dust, such as: *"Blackrock City, USA"* or *"Burn to live; live to Burn."*

This evidence added up to one conclusion: somebody just had just gotten back from Burning Man, an annual gathering in the desert outside of Reno—a gigantic campout party with music, fire dancing, drugs galore, floats and theme camps. A festival populated by yuppies, hippies, burnouts and eccentric artist types. I imagined that there were a handful of lecherous creeps in there as well, due to the high concentration of naked people, but I couldn't confirm this.

At the end of the festival, a giant wooden construct, humanoid in shape, was set ablaze while a group of psilocybin and ketamine influenced minds creamed themselves with delight.

I had never been to Burning Man as, frankly, hippies made my blood pressure shoot up to unhealthy levels. Burning Man was chock full of hippies. But, from what I understood, Burning Man wasn't all hippies; it was also full of monster trucks shooting fire out of their grills and naked girls blown out of their minds on ecstasy.

So I imagined that it wasn't all bad. Tessa was definitely interested.

"I really want to go to Burning Man this year," Tessa would often say. "We should both go."

"Oh yeah," I'd usually reply, "that'll be a blast. You can do a bunch of drugs and get naked and I can get wicked sunburn, lose my job and get really dehydrated. I'm totally there."

"You don't have to be 'on duty' all the time," Tessa once said. "Your days off are your days off. Turn the other cheek once in a while. Experiment, nobody will know. It won't kill you."

"That's easy for you to say; you didn't take an oath. And you aren't gonna wind up on the front page of the paper if you get caught on film hanging out with a bunch of sweaty dopers."

"Dopers? Who says that?" She shook her head from side to side. "Seriously, you're such a cop." I could tell

Tessa didn't mean that as a compliment, which kind of annoyed me. I let it slide.

Having stood up in front of a room full of proud parents and bored politicians, having raised my right hand and swearing to uphold the laws of the State of California, I'm pretty sure that I wrote myself the anti-ticket to Burning Man for the duration of my current state of employment. Plus, I was in a committed relationship and said ecstasy-addled women were likely quite un-showered, two important aspects that further lent toward bowing out of attendance.

And I hated camping.

Much like hippies, spotting one of the aforementioned dust covered yuppie-wagons rolling around my beloved (kinda) city's streets was annoying. It's not that I was bothered by the disheveled state of a once-proud automobile; I was tired of the attitude that came with it. The people who attended Burning Man whom I did like, well, you never would have known that they attended the festival—if you didn't ask—as they didn't spend the entire rest of the year talking about it and planning for it. But many regular attendees couldn't go ten minutes without relaying some sort of anecdote or story that reminded everybody around them that they yes, in fact, went to Burning Man that year—and it was "amazing."

"Also, you should totally go because it was amazing."

"Man, these I.T. issues that we've been having between our branch and the main office, these totally never happen at BURNING MAN—where I just was by the way. Hey, do you

like this coffee? Some guy at BURNING MAN turned me on to it. It's amazing, isn't it?"

I hate the word "amazing."

I had a lieutenant once who used to be a detective. She told me a story about a victim of a serious assault and a robbery who refused to come to court and testify against his attacker because he *had* to go to Burning Man. Couldn't miss it for anything. *"Gee, pa, hope you don't kick it in late August or you're on your own for that funeral."*

One thing I often heard spoken by "Burners" was that the sense of community was special. They said that people forgot their problems and just reveled in brotherly love when at the festival. They said that radical creativity was the norm and that it was *special* (read: AMAZING!) because of that.

Start a revolution; start a utopia; start a movement. Create your paradise with likeminded people. Make it sovereign, a country full of citizens committed to living with a mutual understanding with the same morals, and the same ideals. Sure, it might work for a while, but the next generation will have a few rebels and a few rabble-rousers. And with each successive generation the paradigm will gradually shift.

Congratulations Burners: you get the Thousand Year Reich.

You get the Empire of Nippon.

You get North Korea.

"If the entire world worked like Burning Man," the dirty car guy said, "there wouldn't be any more war or starvation or poverty because people share things when they're out there; people take care of each other. People all understand the common good. It would be perfect and beautiful."

And I always replied with the same line: "Make Burning Man its own country, add a hundred years, and you get Liberia—only with different drugs."

I told this theory to Tessa and she just said, "Well, scratch that place off the list of places I'm taking you."

My partner for the day, Marty Sammy (a nickname evolved from Martin Samson), and I were patrolling the streets governed by Excelsior Station. I had recently followed Matt to Excelsior after my probationary year at Southeast. We "partnered up" immediately, but Matt had taken the day off because it was his birthday. I could only assume that he had big plans for the day, likely consisting of eating a ton of cake and doing burnouts in his Mustang.

I was driving the radio car and we were headed south on San Jose Avenue, just south of the border with Mission Station's territory, which was delineated by Army Street. We had one side of the roadway and Mission had the other. Army Street had long since been renamed Cesar Chavez Boulevard, but nobody called it that; way too many syllables.

This part of San Jose Ave was divided by a concrete barrier, meaning that one could only make a u-turn at an intersection. It was about 1930 hours, the end of rush hour, when Marty and I saw a red Nissan SUV driving the opposite direction, covered in dust. Though the setting sun shone in my eyes, I could still spot a prospect on approach.

"Okay, here we go. Here's one," I said to Marty, pointing at the oncoming car.

"Here's one: what?"

"A Burner Mobile; I fucking hate Burner Mobiles."

"You mean like Spicoli's van in *Fast Times*?"

"No, not that kind of Burner. Good reference, though. Point for Marty Sammy." The car passed and I saw a reasonably fit, reasonably attractive, affluent-looking white chick. She was holding an expensive PDA/phone up to here ear and chatting away. Then I saw the trademark finger-written graffiti on the side of the SUV and said, "I mean the kind of Burner that goes to fucking Burning Man every year and won't wash their car until July. Those people make me insane . . . and, we have a winner. Let's go find something to ticket her for."

"You've got issues man. She might be hot though. If that's the case, you can pull her over but you can't ticket her."

"Yeah, well, the captain wants traffic cites; I'm gonna give him traffic cites. So sue me if I profile yuppies to do it. I bet her name is like 'Amber' or 'Zoe' or something."

"You probably dated her."

"No . . . maybe her fat friend, Kirsten, though."

"I thought her name was Ally?"

Unfortunately, the next intersection was about a hundred feet down. I still had to wait for oncoming traffic to pass before I could get to the northbound lanes and go after Amberzoe's dirty SUV. Precious seconds passed and, finally, I turned our car in the right direction. I jumped on the gas and weaved through traffic, headed toward my prey. A smile cracked across my face as I snaked through the cars in a manner that brought the games Frogger, Asteroids and Centipede to mind. Soon, I was only two car lengths behind the dusty SUV and could make out the text *"Best Burn EVER"* scrawled in the back window.

All traffic stops on vehicles like this usually went the same way:

Officer Cohen: "Ma'am, do you know why I pulled you over?"

Driver: "No."

Officer Cohen: "Because you were speeding."

Driver: "No I wasn't. I wasn't driving any faster than anybody else."

Officer Cohen: "Because your registration is expired then."

Driver: "Um, I don't think it is. I just renewed it. I even put the tabs on."

Officer Cohen—"Seriously though, would it kill you to wash your car?"

We were closing in fast when I heard the dispatcher tell us that she had other plans for us, "Henry-eleven-david, can you handle a wellbeing check on a possible suicide at 3350 Mission Street? It's an A-run."

"NO! What!?!" I called out, slamming my hands down on the steering wheel. Out of the corner of my eye, I could see Marty picking up the radio mic to acknowledge the dispatch. "Dude, come on," I pleaded, "I need this." Were I able to force tears out, I would have done it then.

"The eleven-david copies. We're responding," Marty answered. "I'm sorry, Dougie."

"Fucking balls, Marty Sammy. What's wrong with you?" I replied and, at the next intersection, jammed the car through another quick u-turn. "I hope dispatch knows what I sacrifice for them."

About a minute later we rolled up at the scene. I saw a Chinese man in his forties, who was wearing a pair of painter's overalls, standing outside a house bearing the numbers *3350*. The house was set back from the row of buildings, obviously built years before the rest of the block. It was small, dirty, paint flaked, decrepit and surrounded by a small dirt lot with sparse, dying grass near the old concrete walkway to the (equally old) front door.

I got out of the car and the man approached me. He seemed fairly calm. He started to speak.

"I call you because my friend he, uh, say he gonna kill himself earlier today and I tell him not to do it but now door to house lock and he no come out."

It seemed pretty straightforward so far.

"Why does he want to kill himself?" I asked.

"Because, he say it about money and wife."

"Okay, fair enough. Has he tried to kill himself before?"

"Yes, earlier today I find him inside with a how-you-say, string? Yes, a string around his neck hanging from stairs and I grab him and shake and say, 'WHAT

YOU DOING' and he say he wanna die." The man pantomimed grasping his poor, distraught friend by the shoulders and violently shaking him as he spoke, which was hysterical.

I could hear Marty start to snicker and shot him a look as if to say: *"Don't make me laugh, dude."*

Consummate professionalism abounds, I thought.

"So, then what happened?"

"Well, I tell him that he stupid because life (sounding a bit more like "rife") good and he come to my apartment and we have a dinner and some beer. I tell him to look on bright side of life. Then he leave."

"So you gave the guy a pep talk after you found him hanging by his neck, brought him to your house and gave him some booze and then let him leave," I deadpanned.

"Yes, basically that it."

I turned to Marty—who was now whistling Monty Python's "Always Look on the Bright Side of Life"—and said, "Reasonable."

"Oh, yeah," Marty said, "a few beers, a little pep talk; All good."

"Okay, Sir," I said to the caring friend, "we're gonna head inside and look for your buddy. We need you to wait outside for us though, okay. I don't know what we're going to find in there but, whatever the case may be, we'll let you know."

"Okay, I wait."

"Ready?" I asked Marty, knowing the answer.

Despite Marty's go-getter attitude and youthful enthusiasm—even I was two years older than him—he was quite superstitious and got creeped-the-fuck out by situations like this, which was an easy quality to take advantage of.

"Dude," Marty said as we walked the concrete path to the front door, "he better not be dead in there."

"Oh, don't worry, Marty Sammy" I said in the deepest, creepiest voice possible. "He'll probably still have enough life in him to be twitching and convulsing a little."

"Don't say shit like that."

"What, the guy with the chainsaw inside probably *doesn't* have a mask made from human skin." I pushed the door open, slowly, hoping it would make a loud creaking noise, which it did.

"Oh, man," Marty grumbled.

It was totally dark inside. I pulled out my flashlight and took a step in, smiling when the hard wood floor groaned under foot. "Did you hear that?" I asked Marty.

"WHAT? Did I hear what!?!"

"Shhh," I hissed. Then, as if blessed by the God of Comedy, I farted—a barely audible squeaker of a thing.

"Oh, that's it. You're going in by yourself. You're an asshole." Marty pulled his undershirt up over his nose with his free hand and drew his flashlight.

Despite his protest, Marty still followed me in announcing "POLICE" as we did so. We split up.

Our flashlight beams swept from side to side in the darkness, looking for a body. I flipped a few light switches without effect.

"Okay, this sucks," I heard Marty yell from the other room as he clomped through the house.

"What sucks?" I called back, wincing and closing one eye as I opened a closet and peered in, half expecting a swarm of bats to come shooting out.

"Here we are, in a creepy-ass house and the lights don't fucking work and we're looking for a bod—JESUS CHRIST!!!"

"What, dude, what?" I trotted toward the commotion, reflexively removing my gun as I went. "Are you alright, bro?"

"Yeah, I'm good . . . I'm good. He's not."

I rounded the corner and saw the body of a Chinese man in his mid-forties with an extension cord tied around his neck. The cord was anchored to the banister of the stairway that led up to the second story. The dead man was facing the wall and his neck was elongated to such a degree that I imagined his head had a very good chance of popping off if pressure was applied to his feet. His skin was ashen gray and, the most impressive—and oddest— part of all: he knelt on the ground, which meant that he had *leaned* into his death; it meant that he had a long time to think about the motivating factors that led him to suicide and just went ahead with it anyway.

So much for pep talks, I thought.

Though I didn't really want to, I felt the dead man's neck just to be sure. He had no pulse and was cold to the touch.

"Guess you found him. Good job on not shooting the corpse when you were screaming like a little girl," I congratulated, giving Marty the thumbs up. He flipped me off in return.

"Dude, this is so creepy. And you're touching it . . . him. That makes you creepy."

I sighed and said, "Don't make fun. It's a sad moment. Dying here, all alone, after you already cried out for help; the flame of your life snuffed out by a few feet of extension cord, a stairway and dogged determination not to stand up—sad."

"I'm sorry. I guess you're right; it is kind—"

I farted again.

"DUDE, stop that! You really are an asshole!" Marty exclaimed and charged out of the room.

"You were totally going along with that 'sad' stuff . . . pussy."

Over the next hour I briefed the dead man's friend, his arriving family members and our patrol sergeant of the incident—common practice in all death cases. Marty called for an ambulance to pronounce the guy and the paramedics called for the coroner's investigators to take the body away.

Though I made light of the man's death, his tragedy, it was sad. And, honestly, it was pretty creepy.

After the coroner's deputies took the corpse away and the required interviews were taken care of, we left to grab some takeout and then headed back to the station, so I could write the report. Just before this, while still at the scene, I approached the dead guy's buddy and patted him on the shoulder.

"You did what you could man, kinda. You almost did a really good job today. You shouldn't feel very bad for a really . . . *really* . . . really long time."

"Okay, thank you," he replied, oblivious.

I was munching a burrito with one hand and trying to hunt and peck my way through the suicide report's narrative when the "FOUR-OH-SIX!" came out. That's when the frantic dispatcher's voice relayed on all SFPD radio channels that an officer was putting out THE code. It was the *"Oh Shit!"* code; the *worst possible scenario is currently happening at my location* code; the *drop whatever it is that you're doing and RUN to your car because IT is ON* code.

No matter where you were or what you were engaged in, you responded to a four-oh-six because a cop needed your help in a bad, bad way. The four-oh-six didn't mean the cop was in a little fight, a minor tussle, or a wee donnybrook. The four-oh-six didn't mean that the cop had rolled up on a robbery in progress or just witnessed a school bus ram into a concrete wall at sixty miles per hour; that's what a "code thirty-three" was for: an emergency. A four-oh-six meant that the officer had been shot or currently was being shot at; it meant she'd been stabbed and was bleeding to death; it meant that she was looking at a man who had a bomb strapped to his chest and was holding a whole building hostage with a finger on the detonator switch.

The shit wasn't hitting the fan. It already hit the fan and the inner workings of the fan were pretty well fucked.

I'd previously filled out the report's heading page, the property listing, and the victim and witness information pages. I should have been working on the narrative portion but I was totally uninspired and toying with the idea of writing a joke narrative—something I did occasionally and left out for other cops to see and debate about who wrote it and weather or not it was, in fact, real. But I wasn't really even set on doing that. In about twenty minutes, I'd written the following:

> On the listed date and time a Chinese guy hung himself because the pep talk that his friend gave him didn't work. Richard hung himself. Richard hung himself. It happened just the other day. Needles something something something something. Hooray. Now, I'm fucking bored. I'm really bored. BOREDBOREDBORED. I'm hungry too. And bored. bored. bored. bored. HUNGRY. BORed. Fridayfridayfridayfridayitsfriday.
>
> BOREDBOREDlajfsaljdfsaljfaslkj kjfsadlkjfsaljdfpwoieoijnfnvnvhfjfjjeijf ijefijeijfpoaijfpoiejawfweopijfwapoiefijndnburrito. Burrito burrito carne asada deliciouso. I've got to take a whiz and thdf

"Marty Sammy!" I called out. "Get me a diet Coke, wouldja?"

"You gonna give me some money or—" he started to answer from the other room.

"UNITS: FOUR-OH-SIX AT LATONA AND THORNTON; FOUR-OH-SIX LATONA AND THORNTON!"

That's how it sounded.

Upon hearing the dispatcher's excited message, Marty and I were out of the report writing area with sufficient velocity as to leave behind a jumbled mass of flying papers and overturned chairs. We bailed out of the station at full clip through the large, metal front door with adequate force (so we later learned) as to jam up the latching mechanism, which later spawned a midnight call to the department's on-call repairman.

As I had the keys to the patrol car, I hopped into the driver's seat and put the vehicle into motion.

"Seatbelts," I said to Marty as he switched over our vehicle mounted radio to Southeast Station's frequency. I was all of the sudden glad that I had trained at Southeast. If one wasn't familiar with the area, Latona and Thornton were not easy streets to find.

"Check," Marty said, bracing himself in his seat.

"And make the calculations for the jump to hyperspace, bro."

"Uh, okay?" Marty, obviously, wasn't as big of a *Star Wars* fan as I.

I threw the patrol car into drive and hit the gas, leaving behind a thin strip of rubber on the ground of the station's parking lot as I sped out onto city streets. I switched on the emergency lights and the siren. As we left the station's long driveway, I glanced up at the rearview mirror and saw another patrol car—staffed by Mike Trujillo and his third phase trainee, Jason Abram—following us to the incident scene.

I hit the freeway at about sixty and was pushing the car up to one hundred—indicated by our used and abused

patrol car starting to shake violently at about ninety—
when the primary unit at the incident scene finally came
over the air, gasping out a transmission.

"OFFICER NEEDS HELP! I'VE GOT SHOTS
FIRED . . . AND A SUSPECT IS DOWN . . ." There
were a few deep, audible breaths and then he continued to
speak, "I've also got two other victims . . . I shot the guy
who shot them . . . I think." He paused for a moment and
then said, "He was shooting at me . . . I think he's dead."

It sounded like Dave.

Breathe, man, breathe, I thought.

The usual radio chaos that accompanied any serious
incident followed, garbling further transmissions;
specifically if there was more than one suspect, where
said villain might be and if he or she was armed.

"Headquarters, what district are Latona and Thorton
in!?!" an unknown officer, from one of nine possible
stations currently sending officers to Southeast, asked.
Obviously, he must not have had a map in his possession.
Otherwise, I thought, *to transmit unnecessary radio traffic during
such an incident, when your dumb ass is probably miles away, and
you won't have a chance of arriving at said incident while it's still
active, would be a really fucked thing to do.*

"Where does he think it is?" Marty said to me, "There
are only two districts on this channel."

"That dude probably never worked down on our
side of town." The strain that I was forcing our car's
big engine through was obviously generating some high
temperatures, as hot air blasted out of the interior vents.
"Hey, can you turn the heater off?" I asked Marty as the

car finally pushed past the century mark, causing the violent yaw to suddenly cease. I had found it best not to question as to why this phenomenon happened, choosing simply to ignore it and pray for the best.

Marty switched the air off and caught a glimpse of Mike and Jason in the rearview. "The new guy is keeping up pretty well," he said.

I didn't respond as I was busy taking an evasive maneuver to avoid a minivan, stubbornly decelerating to the speed limit, as if the speeding patrol cars approaching were for him.

"Charlie-two-david to all responding unit—" the transmission broke as the dispatcher keyed her radio mic to respond and then let it go, realizing her error.

"Say again, unit. You were covered. Is any officer injured? Are you alright?"

"No, headquarters . . . I think . . . I think I'm fine," he took a few breaths and his tone of voice normalized somewhat. "Yeah, shots fired and suspect down. He tried to kill me. The car is all blown to hell and my ears are ringing really bad. Sorry if I'm yelling."

"Copy, the ambulance is en route. Are there any additional suspects?" the dispatcher clarified. She was doing a good job, considering the circumstances.

"Ten-four, there were, uh, two or three black males—all in dark clothing. I think they took off running southbound on Latona and then headed east on Thornton, but I don't know if they were related to this or not."

"Shit," I said to Marty, "looks like the fun's not over yet, Marty Sammy. By the way, I loaded slugs in the shotgun."

"Sweet," he answered. Marty clicked open the car's shotgun retention latch and pulled the weapon free.

We exited the freeway and hit Southeast's streets, headed for the crime scene. I decelerated markedly, wary of the myriad of other cops who were going to be zipping through oncoming intersections—in the wrong direction—likely confused as to where they were going. In what seemed like a matter of seconds, we parked about a block away from Latona and Thornton and bailed out of the car. Marty racked a round into the shotgun's chamber, which announced: *chak-chack*. I drew my forty-cal and we sprinted to the scene, hoping that there would be a piece of something left for us to get.

We first saw a patrol car in the middle of the intersection. It had been blown to shit; the windows were shattered and the bodywork was full of bullet holes. The passenger side door was wide open. I later learned that the officer had bailed out of the car on that side, ripping the onboard computer's keyboard off its mount in the process. A black male, who was clad all in black, was prone and handcuffed down on the sidewalk in a pool of blood. A sawed-off pump shotgun lay on the ground next to the dead man. I wasn't sure if I was imagining it, but I thought I saw smoke still coming from the barrel. Dave was standing nearby, pacing back and forth in the middle of the street. The slide of his pistol was locked back; he'd shot empty. I ran over to him.

"Dude, are you alright?" He didn't answer. "Dave . . . DAVE!" I announced and grabbed him by the shoulder. His dilated pupils darted from side to side and I could see that he was still breathing fast. "Dave, take a breath, man. Concentrate, you need to direct us."

Dave nodded. Looking into his eyes, I could see him start to come back from wherever place he had just retreated into. His brow unfurled, slightly.

"Yeah, yeah, I'm okay. I'm okay. He just started shooting as soon as I rolled up, man. I didn't have a choice."

"I know; you did good." Out of the corner of my eye, I saw Ken Byrne jogging up. He had recently been promoted to sergeant and was back in uniform. "Dave, talk to Ken. He knows what to do. Are there any more suspects?"

"I don't know. I saw two or three more people down the block when the guy started shooting. They could have been shooting too; I don't know. I was right around the corner when I heard the shots. I drove up and saw the two bodies and then the guy with the shotgun starting peppering my fucking car with fucking buckshot."

"Okay, we're gonna go look. You might want to reload, dude. You're empty."

Dave looked down at his gun and said, "Oh, yeah."

Marty and I jogged down the block, east on Thornton. We saw a crashed 1990's Impala, which was hood-first into a house, its stereo playing loud hip-hop as if oblivious to the carnage around it. Feet away lay the two bodies that Dave had spoken of. They were prone on the sidewalk, motionless under the surreal, amber glow of a nearby magnesium light. They appeared to be two young Samoan guys, men whose blood, guts and brains were splattered all over the concrete.

"Guess those are the two Dave was talking about?" Marty asked, rhetorically.

"That's probably a safe assumption," I pointed at one of the bodies. A portion of the dead man's face was gone. The part that was there looked like Anthony Falele, the teenage thug from Double Deuce that Sean, Matt and I booked over a year prior. "I think I know that du—"

Suddenly, another frantic voice came over the air, "JENNINGS AND VAN DYKE, TWO RUNNING— GUN, GUN!"

We knew that we'd never make it the necessary five blocks on foot to where the chase had just started. Marty and I turned around and sprinted back to the patrol car. We jumped in and I slammed the car into drive before the doors were closed, peeling out again and barely avoiding several other police cars doing the same thing.

"SOUTHBOUND JENNINGS . . . BLACK MALES IN DARK CLOTHING!" the pursuing officer updated.

I mashed the accelerator down and, about ten *long* seconds later, we saw a patrol car backing down Jennings, paralleling a uniformed officer who was chasing two shadowy suspects. I leaned the gas again as they rounded the corner, out of sight for a brief moment.

Just after Marty and I lost visual contact, we heard a series of pops. At the intersection ahead, I saw a parked vehicle's windshield shatter. The pursuing officer's voice crackled out of our radios announcing, "SHOTS FIRED!"

The San Francisco Police Academy's *Emergency Vehicle Operations Course,* or "EVOC," teaches new cadets that if one plans on staying in one's own lane and not barreling into oncoming traffic, one can only take a level, ninety degree turn at a maximum speed of twenty-five miles per hour. When I was first told this, it didn't seem true; twenty-five is pretty damn slow. Hell, I'd hit forty-something on a bicycle when I was a teenager. Granted, I was going down a long hill and pedaling my ass off.

But the demonstration proved the theory, soundly.

EVOC instruction was at Pier 89, near the Hunters Point Naval Yard, an old, condemned and heavily protested against area—due to findings of nuclear contamination and the surrounding community's outrage in regard to this. (Though, despite this outrage, nobody seemed to care that a police station was actually in the naval yard itself, rather than simply *nearby* as were said protestors.)

The ninety degree turn course was comprised of a T-intersection, which was delineated by small, orange cones. We students each had our own decommissioned patrol vehicles. We idled there, blasting the AC and wearing goofy, white helmets awaiting our respective runs through the course. The instructors stood nearby and called out speeds and turn directions. They started at ten, then fifteen, then twenty, then twenty-five, then thirty and then thirty-five for dramatic effect—as any speed over twenty-five, at the minimum, caused one's vehicle to drift into oncoming traffic or, worst case scenario, cause a massacre of coneage.

"Each of those cones is a person," the instructor would say. "And you just killed them. Remember that."

I did.

I could tell by the white-knuckled hand in my peripheral vision that Marty thought I was going too fast. That and he announced, "Dougie, you're going too fast!" as I barreled toward the source of the gunfire, just around the corner and out of sight.

"No way . . . I've got it, man."

I pulled left into the oncoming lane—thankful that it was late and there wasn't any traffic—in an effort to elongate the turn as much as possible, hoping to avoid slamming in to whatever was on the other side.

Halfway through the maneuver, I was pretty sure that Marty was right about my driving. Our patrol car slid to the outside of the roadway into the oncoming lane. As we came around, I felt the world slow around me. I saw the pursuing officer ducked down behind his car's hood, which was stopped backwards and on the right side of the street. The vehicle's rear windshield was marred by bullet holes.

I saw the shooter in the middle of the street, with his gun raised toward the pursuing officers. I didn't really give a shit anymore about making the turn as my attention was immediately glued to the pistol in his hand.

I took my foot off the brake and held the wheel fast as the patrol car careened off the parked vehicles to my left, shearing several side view mirrors in the process.

"Cars! Gun! FUCK!" Marty called out as he scrambled to rip his seatbelt off.

The suspect's weapon swept toward Marty and I as he saw the new vehicular threat streaking toward him. His eyes grew wide and I imagined that a trigger-pull was likely in progress when the fender of our car made contact with the gunman's lower half and sent him rolling across our hood, much like a matador seconds before deciding on retirement. I broke, hard, and the suspect's contorted body launched onto the street. Marty was out of the car before our forward momentum even stopped and trained his sidearm at the man. I was slightly behind, though. I had to climb out the passenger's side door, as Dave had earlier done. By the time I was out, and saw the suspect's gun on the ground nearby, Marty already had the moaning and bloodied guy in handcuffs.

"Do you need an ambulance, Sir?" Marty asked, in a somewhat mocking tone.

"Not as bad as yo' partner needs drivin' lessons, motherfucker," he groaned in response. He was quick witted. I had to give him that.

I heard rapidly-approaching cop-footsteps—indicated by the creaking of leather and jangling of keys—to my right. The officer that was formerly driving the reverse-pursuing patrol car, and his partner, came running forward. I was relieved to see that the driver, Norbert Chu (everyone just called him "Nordman"), who I knew from my time at Southeast, was okay—as was his partner (who I didn't know). The anger that seethed from them was palpable, intense and quite understandable, considering they had just been shot at and had likely seen their respective lives flash before their eyes. Marty obviously saw this too, and jumped back from the handcuffed suspect as Nordman and his partner buried their boots into the former-gunmen's stomach.

"Motherfucker!" Nordman seethed.

"Bitch!" his partner added.

I looked down the block and saw a bunch of cops taking the other suspect into custody at gunpoint, his hands up in the universal sign of surrender. Apparently, all that man's fight was gone.

Never one to miss an opportunity to get the last word, I walked up to the now whimpering arrestee, as Nordman and his partner snatched the limp man from the ground by the handcuff chain. The smell of *ass* in the air was enough to tell me that the man had shit his pants.

I leaned in close to the guy and said, "Hey fucker, as long as we're in the mood to trade advice, it looks like you could use some toilet training." I was pretty stoked about that line.

After a late night of speaking with detectives, writing a lengthy statement and helping book evidence, I left work and made a quick stop at a local jewelry store. I picked up an item that I'd ordered a week earlier and headed home, several thousand dollars poorer. Once there, I joined Tessa in bed at about 1000 hours (10AM). She stirred lightly as I crept under the covers. When I reached over to turn the lights off, she brought her back against my side.

"I was wondering if you ever were gonna come home," she said in that adorable half-asleep and half-awake voice that I was so fond of. "Is everything all right?"

"Yeah baby. I love you. Go back to sleep."

She arched her back in a stretch and pressed herself against me. "Okay," she said. Soon we were both asleep, still touching, breathing with synchronicity.

We both woke up at about three in the afternoon and Tessa made our "morning" pot of coffee. Over coffee and the paper, which was miraculously still in the lobby of our apartment complex, she inquired why I'd been home nearly eight hours late.

"Dave blew a guy away last night who had just killed two people and was shooting at him," I told her.

"No shit? Dave . . . as in *the* Dave? The same Dave who was just over here a few weeks ago playing videogames with you? The guy you were arguing with because you thought the 'Master Chief' would totally kick the 'Arbitrator's' ass, or something?"

"Yeah, Dave, my classmate. He fucking lit a guy up last night with his handgun. We drove over to help out and wound up catching one of the other suspects that just did a double-murder with the guy Dave shot. It was pretty awesome; I rammed the guy with the patrol car while he took some shots at two of the dudes at Southeast. And, I'll note, the Master Chief would totally rock the *Arbiter*, any day."

"God . . . is he okay?" she asked, ignoring my videogame joke.

"Dave's fine. I mean, he didn't get hit and blew the fucker away, so that's making him feel pretty good about the whole thing."

"What do you mean? He isn't upset because he had to take a human life? I mean, it sounds horrible. I can't even imagine what must be going through is head right now."

"Well, he seemed pretty stoked that it wasn't a piece of copper and lead. And he killed a double murderer; that's like winning the big game in police work. He didn't just catch the guy, he took him down and kept the asshole from killing again—killing Dave himself, not to put too fine a point on it. I don't see what the problem is?"

"I can't believe you're being so cavalier about this," she was starting to get riled up at my attitude but, then again, she wasn't just forced to ram a gun-wielding murderer with a vehicle to save her life. "What if that had been you instead of Dave? Would you be 'happy' about it?"

"I don't know. But if it was as righteous as this, I'm pretty sure I'd be buying cigars for my coworkers. That's score one for the team right there. I certainly wouldn't go on TV and give the public crocodile tears about it. Fuck those guys; they started shooting first."

"You're being really cold and it sounds sick. I thought you were past this point in your life. I had *hoped* that your unreasonable rage had subsided."

"Past-fucking-what? I'm not sick and there's no 'unreasonable' rage here. I'm just not about to lie to the world and tell them that I would feel bad if I had to kill somebody that was trying to kill me."

"If who you were when I met you could hear you now, speaking about killing a human being like it's punching a time clock . . . I don't think he'd have much good to say about your opinions," she spat.

"I'm sorry, did you just come back from a night of death and mayhem and potential FUCKING lethality? You're the fucking punk rocker!" I called back. "You're the one who is always talking about social injustice! It doesn't really get much more cut and dry and 'socially just' than this, does it? I just don't get you sometimes."

"Wow, Dougie, wow. I can—"

I interrupted her response. "How is my opinion a surprise after getting a potentially fatal disease from a piece of shit that I talked about killing for almost a whole goddamn year? I still wish I could kill that motherfucker! You think I'm not pissed about having to wear a rubber for the rest of my life? I'm out there doing what I can to keep you safe, to keep us all safe, and you're here telling me I'm some sort of sociopath for doing so. What the fuck is that about?"

Her voice changed. I could tell I'd hurt her. "Dougie," she said, "I'm the *'fucking* punk rocker' who you fell in love with," she made that little quotation mark sign with her hands, "and I'm also the woman who loves you and doesn't want you to turn into an asshole. But maybe it's too late for that?"

Ouch, I thought.

Predictably, she jumped to the worst possible conclusion. "Do you even want me anymore?"

I took a deep breath and remembered the little box in my pocket. I looked Tessa in the eyes and tried to pull back my words with a softened gaze. I reached out to embrace her, wanting to stop the argument before the day was ruined. I was tired, cranky and still angry that some shitheads had tried to kill three of my friends. I was still angry that, again, I had opportunity for some sort of revenge and drove right past it.

I made a mental note not to talk about work with her anymore, if at all possible. She pulled away before I could complete the hug.

"Just leave me alone!" she said, retreating into the kitchen and putting her hands up to her now crying face.

"Babe, stop . . . I'm sorry."

This was going nowhere good, fast. I retrieved the item from my pocket, moving toward her, slowly.

If she says yes now, we'll last forever, I thought.

"I said leave me alone!" she yelled as I approached.

"Catch," I said softly and tossed the jewelry case toward her. "I'm sorry, baby."

Instinctively, she pulled her hands away from her face and caught it. She sniffled and asked, "What's this?"

"That's proof."

"Of what?"

"Of how I feel about you; proof that I want to spend the rest of my life with you. That's my own psychiatric insurance policy because keeping you around keeps me grounded, keeps me sane. I love you, Tessa, and if you're making a mistake by being with me then I'm sorry but I want you to keep making it."

She opened the box and saw the ring inside. Her tears slowed. Like every cheese-ball scene in every romantic comedy that I despised so much, she ran toward and put her head against my chest saying, "Okay, yes, yes, yes, you fucker . . . at a time like this . . . I'm sorry. I love you, too. You're not a total asshole."

I lifted her off the ground in my arms saying, "I didn't even ask you anything."

CHAPTER 18

He seems to be completely unreceptive
The tests I gave him showed no sense at all
His eyes react to light; the dials detect it
He hears but cannot answer to your call
  —The Who, "Go to the Mirror Boy"

Nationwide, when new officers graduate their respective police academies, there usually exists a ceremony of some sort. At the SFPD this ceremony is called, aptly enough, "graduation." It works like this:

1. The soon-to-be cops/soon-to-be ex-cadets (hereafter referred to in a variety of differing ways, but mostly as "graduates") show up early at some civic auditorium in their dress uniforms.

2. A dress rehearsal of the ceremony itself is conducted. Laughter and anticipation abounds.

3. The group of graduates is ushered backstage into a small room and given sealed envelopes, which contain loose ammunition, extra handgun magazines, keys, a canister of mace and a list of important department phone numbers. The

graduates are instructed to leave the envelope in the room until the completion of the ceremony.

4. Unloaded handguns are issued—one at a time, accompanied by many "ooes" and "ahhs"—along with a state certificate, which signifies completion of basic police academy curriculum. This certificate is commonly known as the "bailout certificate," as one would only need to ever show it to anybody in the event that they were not going to complete the department's Field Training Program (due to poor performance or personal reasons) and were seeking employment with another, less-stringent/less-hectic/less-insane agency.

5. By this time, the auditorium is generally filled with parents, family, friends, department leaders, and representatives from the city and/or state government. A shitty recording of the national anthem gets played over aging, crackling speakers.

6. The graduates march through the auditorium, in formation, and take their designated places at the front of the room, standing at the Position of Attention. Some sort of nifty chant or drill—specific to each class, though it usually involves the class number and the words "honor," "pride," and "dedication"—is then performed for the audience.

7. A (probably Catholic, as he kind of reeks of Jameson and not Bushmills) priest leads the room in prayer for the safety of these new, fine officers.

A surprising amount of people know the biblical verses by heart and speak along. Agnostics such as me wing it and hope nobody notices.

8. The graduates raise their right hands and take the Oath of Office.

9. Badge pinning time, followed by copious handshaking and picture taking. Self-explanatory.

10. The rookie marches out of the auditorium, jogs to the small room, retrieves the appropriate envelope and places the contents in their proper places on the department-issued duty-belt.

11. The new officer loads his or her gun, takes it home, removes all of his/her gear and enjoys the next thirty-six hours of drama-free, low-danger living because, after that, it's thirty years to retirement. Hopefully, one will advance in rank (i.e. sergeant, detective, etc.) over this period, so one doesn't have to have forty to fifty-plus hours per week, ten-plus hours per day, of the same shit . . . over and over again.

12. At the start of the game, parents, family members and loved ones are proud. The rookie's elation and happiness makes those close to him or her feel good. It gives those loved ones hope and it calms their anxiety. They don't know, and the rookie cop probably doesn't either, that he/she is now a twenty-four hour officer of the law, which means that regardless of the day—or level of intoxication—cops are expected to conduct their personal and professional lives in a certain

way. It's expected that an exemplary measure of integrity and ethics will govern the officer's day-to-day business. It's even written down that an officer will not *"do anything to bring discredit up on him/her, the badge or the agency."* And if they don't, if they fail to live up to that standard, it can be big news—deserving or not: *"Officer arrested for drunk driving: news at eleven"* vs. *"An officer is under investigation for posting erotic pictures of himself on an adult, personal ad website. When asked, the officer—a ten year veteran—refused to comment but undisclosed sources within the department indicated that the officer recently underwent a divorce and is 'extremely lonely.' Disciplinary charges are pending further investigation."*

13. Even though the rookie may be a third generation lawman, he/she doesn't have firsthand knowledge or understanding of what being "on the job" entails. Rookies don't know about the long, involuntary hours and work-related commitments. They don't know about the prevailing negative state of department morale. They don't know that their pre-police career relationships and marriages have a good chance of falling apart (so say the statistics). They don't realize that over the first year of duty, despite what they may feel toward their significant others, they are probably not going to be as sensitive or understanding of the minor personal troubles of these people as they once were. (The general exception to this rule being if the significant other in question

is themselves a cop, paramedic, nurse or other commonly shit upon, jaded and oft slandered and/or libeled professional that I have failed to mention here. I'm still not sure if firefighters fall into this exception as, usually, everybody loves them.)

14. And when that person, that lover, wife, husband, girlfriend or boyfriend is complaining about their rough day at the office, or about the dishes that are always in the sink, the officer may one day snap and say, "Did anybody spit on you today? Did your FTO scream at you to 'get the fucking report done,' the one where the guy tried to take your head off with a right hook, while your boss stood behind him and laughed? Did you get accused of being a racist because you arrested a guy for a hit and run that somebody else sent you to? Did an independent watchdog agency—comprised of persons who have limited knowledge of what you actually do for a living—serve you with papers ordering you to explain yourself to them for something that you did at your job? Did you get stuck with some diseased junkie's needle? Did you get fucking shot at? Did you shoot somebody else? No? Then please just leave me alone. Spare me the nonexistent problems." The rookie might say something to that effect; he or she might make a huge scene or start a blowout fight and come across as a horrible, narcissistic dick . . . but they'll probably just bottle it all up instead. That's

what they'll do once they go around the block a few times. That's what they'll do if they're smart.

15. Learning to bottle it up: that's the final stage of graduation. Self-explanatory.

CHAPTER 19

"If you want a happy ending, that depends, of course, on where you stop your story."
—*Orson Welles*

The line appeared ready.

At least, that's what my training and experience led me to believe: that the line of men and women standing with holstered guns, facing the sides of turned-away paper targets, roasting in the midday heat (or as near a facsimile as San Francisco could provide), were ready to—upon the swivel of said targets to face said men and women—remove their guns and:

A. Fire two rounds into the black circle, smack dab in the middle of the target's center mass, and one through the outline of the head.

B. Fire two rounds into the gray part of the target (nowhere near the middle) and one completely over the head, thereby severing the rubber band that suspends the target and then look back toward the instructor—currently standing a few feet to the rear and shaking his head in disbelief at the utter improbability of the shot and/or poor marksmanship—and give a sheepish, embarrassed grin as the target flops around in the wind.

C. Fail to get one's gun out of the holster in time, due to operator or equipment error, and then panic-fire five rounds—two more than prescribed—in the general direction of the target as a whole, not just the gray part.

Obviously, choice A was the preferred course of action but, hey, nobody's perfect.

At least the line appeared ready.

I knew that much because everybody was facing the same direction, everybody was standing in single file and nobody had their hand raised, which indicated the need for assistance from one of the staff members—those lucky devils in the red hats to the rear, coasting through their last years before retirement by shooting guns and kicking back.

As the line was ready, at any moment the target would turn and I would perform the Seven-Step Draw: a technique taught in combat handgun courses to remove the firearm, bring it out to point, engage the threat, and tactically re-holster the weapon.

The seven steps explained (for purposes of this demonstration, the shooter is right handed):

1. The left hand slaps the front of the stomach—to ensure clearance from the line of fire—as the

right hand moves back to grip the weapon and unsnap it from the holster.

2. The weapon is drawn and immediately pointed at the threat/target, held in a hip-shooting position, which enables one to immediately fire with reasonable accuracy at nearby persons, objects or animals.

3. The weapon is brought out to *point* (held out, at arm's length) and a two-handed grip is established.

4. Two shots are fired. This pair of shots is also commonly referred to as a "hammer pair" or a "double tap."

5. The weapon is lowered slightly, and a side-to-side scanning motion in order to assess additional threats and break tunnel-vision is initiated.

6. Upon determination that the threat has been eliminated, the weapon is brought back to the hip-shooting position.

7. The weapon is de-cocked, holstered and secured.
The line was ready.

Furthermore, I was ready; I was not only prepared to do my seven steps, I was going to fire an additional round as that's what the Range Master—he who was in charge of the firing drills and the control the targets—had just ordered via the range's PA system.

"Okay, this course of fire will be from the seven yard line," the Range Master said. "This will be two handed, natural-point shooting but try and pick up your front sight if possible." I was with him so far. "Once the target turns, you will have five seconds to fire two shots to the body and one to the head. You will then scan, de-cock and holster a loaded weapon. I will repeat that . . ."

"Yeah, yeah, yeah; it's my day off. Let's get this show on the road," I muttered.

"Again: two shots to the body and one to the head; five seconds. Scan, de-cock and holster."

"Yes, I've got it."

"The line appears ready."

"Yes, we are all ready. We all know this."

"Who are you talking to, Cohen?" Kevin O'Malley, one of the range's staff members, asked.

"Nobody, bro," I said without turning—for that would have been bad and meant that the line was not, in any way, ready. "I'm just babbling to myself."

I wasn't always so impatient during my bi-yearly shooting qualification, I just had shit to do and, as I had previously, audibly complained, it was my day off. In other words, I was doing mandatory work stuff but not getting paid, which was lame. And that wasn't to imply that I didn't enjoy shooting, quite the contrary; it's just that I *personal* stuff to do after the qualification. In fact, I had *wedding* stuff to do. It had been three months since I proposed and things between Tessa and I had never been better. I was anxious but very excited. I was getting married.

Soon.

Prior to leaving for the range, my fiancé reminded me that I had to take her to the Marina District to get a certain brand of eye shadow. I was not entirely sure why, exactly, I was drafted for this task but I thought it best not to argue. I figured that there was plenty of time for that after the wedding, which was less than a week away.

"The line appears ready," the Range Master's voice announced.

Finally, I thought and lowered my center of gravity, just slightly, waiting for the target's turn. And I waited, eyes fixed forward.

I exhaled my breath and held it.

I opened and closed my right hand, loosening my fingers.

And I waited.

After fifteen or so seconds I started to think that something must have been wrong with the equipment—something that would, no doubt, be resolved shortly—and drew in a shallow breath. Keeping my gaze on the target and my hands just in front of my chest, I stayed prepared to draw and fire. The Range Master's microphone clicked on and then, abruptly, off. I figured he had resolved the problem and canceled his announcement.

After twenty more seconds, I began to suspect that something was completely broken and stood fully up, shaking out my hands and legs.

Figures.

Growing more and more annoyed, I cheated a glace toward the control booth, located just over my left shoulder. Upon turning, I noticed that Kevin, an Irish cop if there ever was an Irish cop (one who didn't actually work in Ireland), was running up the small set of stairs toward the Range Master's seat. Through the bullet resistant glass, I caught the tail end of the Range Master's face falling forward onto the control panel in front of him. He was in obvious distress. That's why the targets hadn't turned. It all made sense.

Ironically, as I realized I should probably do something productive in such a time of crisis, the *thunk* of the Range Master's forehead hitting the control board must have hit the magic button. The targets turned and twenty cops opened fire.

Shit.

Despite being otherwise ordered, I abandoned my lane and hurried toward the booth, past the determined and grimaced faces of my fellow shooters. I bounded up the small staircase and joined Kevin in the booth. I could see that he was a little flustered as his coworker/friend/boss was totally unconscious.

"KEVIN," I announced over the final shots of the volley, which quickly came to a close. I removed my hearing protection. "Need some help?"

Kevin turned his face to me, his hearing protection still affixed to his head. "Get an ambulance," he ordered.

TAHK-TAHK! went some lag-behind's gun.

"I don't have a cell phone." Kevin didn't hear me. I reached over and pulled back one of his earmuffs. "Dude, I don't have a phone. You call; I've got him."

"Okay, fuck, okay," Kevin said and took a step back, removing his cellular phone from his pocket.

I could see that the Range Master was pale and dripping with sweat. Having seen such a signs a number of times in the past, I felt comfortable stating, "He doesn't look so hot."

I grabbed the limp body before me by the shoulders and pulled him back to an upright position; his head flopped back, looking up toward the ceiling. I could see that one side of his face was dropping off to the left. Placing the pointer and middle fingers of my left hand on the fallen man's neck, I noted a bounding pulse, a sign of a sky-rocketed blood pressure. I could hear Kevin behind me, speaking in a harried manner to the 911 call taker. "Kevin, tell them that he's probably having a stroke."

"Oh, God," Kevin said out loud. "Another officer is saying that he had a stroke. That's bad, right? Oh God!"

I grasped the Range Master's head between my hands and thrust his jaw forward with my fingers, making sure his airway stayed open. The gurgling noise that had mired his labored respirations decreased significantly. I took the opportunity to look down at the man's name tag. It read: *C. Burns*. I realized that I never knew the Range Master's name prior to that moment. In fact, as far as I knew, he lived in this booth—as it was the only place that I'd ever seen him.

"She wants you to tilt Charlie's head back and open his airway," Kevin ordered, relaying the instructions given by the 911 dispatcher.

"It's already done, Sir."

"Give rescue breaths if he isn't breathing."

"He's breathing fine." I was glad that this was the case, partly because I really didn't feel like putting my lips on Charlie's; he was not a pretty man.

"She wants you to make sure that he has a pulse by feeling his carotid artery."

"Yeah, he has a pulse."

People who are breathing have pulses, I thought, somewhat sarcastically. I had prior knowledge of this phenomenon. I didn't bother to point out this obvious fact as Kevin was, no doubt, distraught. And justly so, don't get me wrong.

I looked through the bullet-resistant glass of the control booth as I stood there; I'd run out of first aid options. Some of the cops on the firing line were milling about, still awaiting instructions for the next course of fire and, likely, wondering why the targets still faced them. Others were looking into the control tower with obvious confusion. Two officers, however, were sprinting toward us looking even more panicked then Kevin. Panic, in such a situation, is contagious.

Uh oh.

"They're on their way," Kevin said behind me.

"Yes they are; two of them," I muttered.

"I hope they get here soon."

"I'm not talking about the ambulance crew. I'm talking abou—"

It was too late. Two slightly overweight, female cops—who I'd never seen before—were now arriving at the booth.

"What's going on?" the blonde officer asked, feverishly.

"What happened?" the redhead added.

"Everything is under con—" I started to say.

"Charlie is all fucked up!" Kevin called out, loosing his cool.

"Oh my God!" Red keyed her radio microphone, "Dispatch, dispatch, we need an ambulance out to the police range. THE RANGE MASTER IS DYING!"

The dispatcher was unable to answer due to the congested, screeching sound of multiple cops keying their microphones at once. I couldn't hear them, but I already knew what they were saying: that they were on the way to assist, en mass. Their hearts were in the right place but their presence was superfluous if not a detriment.

Great.

"I already called for an ambulance. You two: help me move him," Kevin ordered, while nudging me to the side.

"Move him—where, to a hospital? The ambulance is on its—" I started to argue.

"Goddamn it!" Kevin said, his cool clearly blown to hell at this point, "We need to lay him down."

"I'll get some blankets," the blonde officer chimed in.

"Let's just wait until the ambulance gets here guys. He's breathing okay and I can manage his airway fine in here. Plus, laying him down is only gonna increase the blood flow to his head, which is the last thing he needs."

Kevin paused and his expression went from one of panic to a blank slate. He stared at me coldly for a few, long seconds. I met his gaze and gave him a look as if to say, *"What? I'm trying to help here."*

Kevin's stare met mine and then a look of profound sadness came over his face. His eyes moved down my arms to my hands as they cradled the—in all probability— dying man's head.

Kevin leaned in close to the Range Master's face and he, ever so lightly, kissed his forehead. He then whispered into the obtunded man's ear, "Don't die, baby. Please don't leave me yet. I love you."

I'm not positive, but I'm pretty sure that my jaw scraped against the floor right then. A part of me badly wanted to say, "Oh, gnarly," as it would have been a perfect instance in which to quote Jeff Spicoli, but I resisted.

A crowd had gathered outside the booth, a now silent crowd at that. The only break in the silence was the faint sob and sniffle of the redhead to my right.

Kevin was gay; the Range Master, Charlie, was his lover. This was a really moving moment. This was one of those Oscar Clip moments.

All I could think was: *Awkward.*

Thank Christ the ambulance showed up a few minutes later.

After Charlie had been carted away, I did my best to make a silent escape from the worried throng of cops that remained at the range. They kept asking me what had happened and/or, "Are those dudes really queers?"

A little over an hour later, Tessa and I were driving through the Marina, the hoity-toity area at the north end of SF, en route to a particular makeup place, which, so I had gathered, had a particular kind of makeup for my particular wife-to-be.

During the drive over, I briefed Tessa of the day's excitement. As we circled the neighborhood in search of a parking space large enough to park my modest Toyota pickup, that I purchased just after my probation ended, I still couldn't abandon the subject.

"I mean Charlie and Kevin: they're gay. Man, I had no idea; it's so weird," I said to Tessa—just before I spun the truck in a fast one-eighty, diving into an empty space on the opposite side of the street.

"I don't see what's so weird about it," Tessa answered. "It's just tragic. What if Charlie dies? Kevin will be all alone . . . they've probably been together for years and years."

"It's weird because you don't know them. Kevin is a grizzled looking paddy, who probably starts and finishes every meal with four fingers of Jameson. And Charlie, he's like some old Korean guy or something and not a very fit or attractive one at that. You know, I'd never even seen his face, really, until today when I was holding it in my hands. It's funny; he's always in this little control booth at the range. I kind of figured it was like *The Matrix* or something—like he was plugged into the range and the range was plugged into him. Like they were symbio—"

"Yeah . . . and?" she interrupted, stopping the tangent. Over the years, she had become quite adept at that.

"What do you mean 'and?' And nothing. And they are an Irish dude and a Korean guy who just happen to be old, gay cops. That doesn't strike you as *unique*? I mean, what the fuck kind of music do they listen to? Is there an Abba record where they cover 'The Auld Triangle'?"

"I think they're brave. Love happens; you can't always fight it."

"Yeah, as brave as one has to be when they're sitting on an arsenal of firearms. And old Irish dude cop on old Korean dude cop love doesn't just 'happen.' At least, it doesn't in my world, man, not between those two. Gross."

"It's not 'gross' and you know what I mean. They're brave to have followed their hearts and let love take its course."

I backed the truck into the empty space and turned off the motor, shutting the engine off.

"That's like the queerest thing you've ever said."

"God, when did you turn in to such a homophobe? You used to be so open-minded."

I could tell she was a little offended. "What are you talking about? I'm not really a homophobe and I'm still open-minded. You know I don't care if two dudes want to hump; I'm just taking the piss because they're an unlikely pair. If I was a gay guy, I'd be going out with one of those dudes who go to the gym all the time and take their shirts off at night clubs."

"This is just an example. You say off-color things all the time and you're consistently and overtly insensitive. I don't know if you're serious or not. I'm just amazed at how much you've changed over the last two years—your politics, your temper, your attitude." My expression started to turn sour; this was totally coming out of left field. She went on: "And I still love you, Dougie, I do. I just worry about who you're turning into sometimes. I worry that I won't know you anymore soon; that I won't be able to keep up with the change. And, I'm only bringing this up now because we're getting married in a matter of days."

"Trust me, I haven't forgotten."

"I'm serious; I need to know that when we do this—when we take our vows—that you are going to be in it for the long haul." She paused. "I need you to tell me that the man I marry is going to be the same man one, five, or ten years later—the same man forever. I need that stability."

Sensing that we had officially transitioned into Tessa's patented *Serious Conversation Time*, I took my hand off the door handle and put my right arm on the back of her neck. "I'm still the same guy, babe. I still love you. That's not gonna change. You're my support network, you know? I need you."

"I know you do. You just seem so angry and depressed still. And, God knows, Dougie, I understand. I've been with you through all the shit that this fucking city has thrown on your shoulders."

"Well, work is stressful. I think it's taken its toll on my personality. If I'm kind of a bastard on the exterior, it's just because I have to act a certain way at work and sometimes it's hard to turn off—you know: looking at the world through skeptical eyes. Police culture is . . . weird . . . different."

"I've gathered that."

"I could be wrong, but I feel like you're gonna drop a bomb on me here, out of nowhere. If that's the case, just let me have it." That probably wasn't the smartest thing to say but I did. My dad used to tell me that you shouldn't plant the seeds of things you don't want to see grow.

279

"Dougie, I need you to trust me and to talk to me. I need you to let me into your whole world, not just the world at home where it's only you and me. I have a stressful job too; I'm familiar with the feelings." She stopped talking and searched my eyes with her own. I worried that the subtext of what she was saying was: *"I'm having second thoughts."* After years together, I had become at least somewhat used to reading her mood.

"Baby," a knot started to form in the back of my throat, considering the possibility that she had such doubts. Perhaps, I was being too fatalistic. "It's hard to . . . to talk about exactly what makes me feel the way I do, but you and me are still the same. Believe that, please."

"I do, just open up now and then. It's not just for me; it's for us. We can't just be about sex until death do us part." She smiled a little half-grin.

"I'll try." With that, I pulled my hand back and opened the door. We lucked out and got a parking space on the same block as the cosmetic store, which Tessa sought. Union Street, The City's showcase of yuppiedom, was bustling; the unusually bright sun seemed to act as a giant magnet for consumers of designer clothing and Italian sunglasses.

That Tessa, out of nowhere, had suddenly brought up such a serious subject because of a stupid anecdote felt really weird. After exiting the car and meeting on the sidewalk, I grabbed her hand.

"You know, feel free to bring up stuff like this when we aren't surrounded by the beautiful people. I'd really hate to cry in front of them—the moisture might fuck up their wiring," I said.

"You don't cry anymore."

"Not often; not for a while but I can."

"I sometimes wonder if you're still capable," Tessa replied.

"Okay, well, you're in a mood—aren't you?" I felt myself getting slightly annoyed and thought I'd make a go at changing the subject. "You know SF cops aren't supposed to go anywhere NEAR Union Street anymore." I didn't work.

"See, this is what I'm talking about," she snapped, "you and your seeming inability to take anything seriously. What is it about your job that you think makes . . . ?"

Tessa kept lecturing but I didn't hear what she said as, toward the beginning of the sentence, I had clued in on two totally out of place crackheads—two sweaty, skinny, dirty-looking black guys in greasy, tattered clothing. Their eyes were darting up and down the block. The two men were huddled in close, like they were in a final quarter huddle and getting ready to make a play to score. One looked to be about fifty, though he was likely in his late thirties, and the other appeared slightly younger, by about five years or so.

I saw one of the men glance at an affluent looking woman who was clad in a combination of Dolce and Gabana sunglasses and Prada shoes. She stood just a few feet away from them. She was trying to flag down a taxi and, as she did, she lowered her expensive purse down to her side. I felt an obligatory tinge of guilt, assuming that

281

the two black men approaching her were up to no good. But the cop in me shoved that feeling aside.

The two conspirators, looking at the affluent woman with marked interest, promptly broke their huddle and hurried toward her. I could see that she was focused on passing traffic. When they neared her, one turned his back and glanced up and down the block. Satisfied, he mouthed a few words to his compatriot. Though I was about sixty feet away, I could tell what he said by watching his lips.

He said, "Let's go get that shit."

Son of a bitch, I thought. *What is it with this day?*

As they broke into a quick jog while staring in the general vicinity of the chick's purse, I clued back in on what Tessa was saying. She closed her tirade with, "I don't want to go shopping with an insensitive jerk. Please quit being one."

I got angry and said, rhetorically, "How's this for you?"

On or about the utterance of the word "jerk," the younger crackhead ripped the purse from the aspiring fare's shoulder as the older one shoved her down to the ground.

Robbery; felony; Penal Code section 211: the unlawful taking of personal property from another by means of force or fear.

The crime complete, the assailants ran directly toward me. Though I had left my gun at the house after getting home from the range, instinct, habit and/or outrage superseded sound tactics. I pushed Tessa into an open lingerie store and muttered, "Call 911."

I charged forward toward the thieves, who were both looking back over their shoulders at the screaming victim, laughing. But then they brought their eyes forward and saw me. I pulled my badge/star/shield/whatever, which was held on by a chain around my neck, out from under my shirt. Only about twenty feet from the two men, I announced, "STOP, POLICE!"

The two men slowed for a moment. Their expressions of elation turned immediately to surprise. The older, wiser lookout abruptly changed direction, running into the street. At close to full sprint, I clued in on the younger guy, the one who had the purse clutched to his chest. To my surprise, this man didn't adopt a new path or try to juke or dodge me, sending me running by. He stayed his course and ran straight ahead, determined.

In the brief moments before impact, I thought of the sled push event from the SFPD obstacle course.

"Whatever you choose to do make sure you PROTECT YOUR FACE upon impact," the sergeant had said.

With five feet between me and the thief, I brought my right elbow and left forearm up in front of my face. My dad taught me the position when I was about thirteen; in boxing it was referred to as a "crab guard." By luck, fate, or random chance, my elbow connected with the crackhead's throat. By irony, paradox or derision, the force of the ensuing collision caused my right arm to jam my scarred right hand into the bridge of my nose, breaking it. A spontaneous eruption of blood shot down my face.

At the moment of impact as white light exploded in front of my eyes, when my nose broke and the blood did cascade onto my white Fred Perry polo shirt, I was reminded a video game that I used to play as a kid. It was called "Joust."

Mash buttons like crazy and hope you win. No real skill to it. Just throw it down and pray for the best.

Kamikaze.

"Go fucking crazy!" Ozzy had announced at the Black Sabbath reunion show Tessa and I saw over the summer.

As good a plan as any.

And when our two bodies hit and I came crashing down on top of the much taller man onto the pavement below, when I heard the crack of his head hitting the pavement, when I landed on him and rolled off his limp body, when I grabbed the purse off his chest and got to my feet, all I could think to do was "talk shit" and get the last words in.

I should have kept the thoughts to myself, but I didn't. I was injured and furious, damaged and fierce.

I said, "Didn't see that coming did you, motherfucker? How does it feel now, huh?" I spat a gob of blood and saliva into the street.

Looking up, I saw the other man still sprinting past Tessa around the corner. I considered chasing him but the white-hot fire behind my eyes—a byproduct of my bleeding and broken face—stayed my feet.

I handed the victim back her purse. She grew silent and regarded me with an expression that was one part disgust and one part thanks. I limped in circles around the suspect, walking off the pain while spitting more blood on the ground and moving my jaw back and forth to make sure it wasn't broken as well.

The victim removed a silk scarf from around her neck and approached me, holding it up like she was going to give me first aid. "God, you're bleeding," she said.

"I'm fine. I'm fine. Just don't touch me."

She continued forward, "But you're bleeding a lot. Here," she reached for my nose with the scarf.

"No, really, I—"

"I insist; it's the least I can do." She continued to advance.

"Ma'am, GET BACK! I have a communicable disease. You don't have gloves on."

She pulled her hand back and tossed me the scarf, backpedaling away. "Oh . . . I'm sorry. Here, take this."

"Thanks."

Tessa walked up to me. She gazed down at the unconscious man, the loser of the contest. He was still in the same position as when his head had hit the ground, vacant eyes open with rasping, labored breaths. The treating physician later stated he had a "fractured hyoid bone" and a "subdural hematoma." In layman's terms: a broken bone in his throat—a pretty important one at that—and a ruptured blood vessel in his head from contact with the sidewalk. He'd survive, but always have some sort of neurological deficit, which would enable him to collect taxpayer money for the rest of his life. Way more than the value of the purse he had tried to steal. But that wasn't illegal and not my concern.

"I will protect life and property; preserve the peace; prevent crime . . ." I said when I took the oath on graduation day, with Tessa, my parents and an auditorium full of proud and/or worried faces watching. *"Enforce criminal laws and ordinances; regulate non-criminal conduct as provided by law . . ."*

A look of concern for the supine thief washed over Tessa's face and then, like someone had turned on the fire sprinklers in her head, she held out her cellular phone toward me. Her face went blank.

"While on duty, devote my entire time to the completion of this mission . . ."

"Your coworkers are on their way," Tessa said, coldly. "And I can't marry you."

"This I swear before God and country."

CHAPTER 20

*"Death is not the greatest of evils; it is worse
to want to die and not be able to."*
—Sophocles

There are two distinct and opposing options available to
a uniformed patrol officer who hears a series of gunshots
coming from a nearby location:

1. Roll the patrol car's windows up and promptly
   drive in the opposite direction.
2. Roll the patrol car's windows all the way down, in
   an effort to pinpoint where the shots are coming
   from and, once the general direction is decided
   upon, drive toward them.

For the purpose of this demonstration, I am the
officer in question.

In the rainy, cold November night, the series of
gunshots I heard could only be coming from one place.
The City's largest public housing development was only
four blocks to the west. The precise and non-panicked
series of about five shots were obviously being fired
in the Visitacion View public housing development.
And, as these shots were spaced by about one second,

and continuing, I could only imagine that they were being fired at a stationary target, like a downed human body. Considering the two rival gangs located in the "Veevees"—creatively known as the "Lower Corner Gang," because as they hung out in a geographically lower portion of the projects, and the "Hilltop Gang," for a reason that should now be apparent—were blowing each other away on a near nightly basis, I thought it reasonable that my assumption was correct. Consequently, I picked up my radio microphone and keyed it.

"Three-henry-three-david," I quickly uttered.

"Go ahead," the dispatcher answered.

"I'm hearing gunshots in the Veevees—so far about ten. I'm en route to the area to investigate and will be arriving in a matter of seconds."

"Copy," the dispatcher said. "Units, three-henry-three-david is hearing shots in the Visitacion View projects. He's a solo officer unit; can I get a unit to back him."

As I neared the projects, the shots stopped. I turned my high beams on in an effort to blind any possible lookouts and conceal the light-bar on the top of my vehicle from ready view.

Since Tessa cleared her belongings out of our apartment—in what can only be described as record fucking time—I had been working alone after canceling most of the days off I had previously scheduled for the wedding. I even picked up a few overtime shifts. I figured that being at work was probably the best way to avoid dealing with the repeated phone calls of family and friends wanting to know, respectively, "what happened" and/or "how you fucked that one up?" And, as I was frankly miserable, I didn't feel it fair to take out my emotional wreckage on a well-meaning, concerned coworker. So, I was flying solo, as it were.

And then, when I got home in the early morning hours after my shift was over, I'd drown myself in bourbon and watch movies that catered to my overwhelming state of self-hatred and depression. So far, I'd watched: *2001: A Space Odyssey*, *Akira*, *Leaving Las Vegas*, *Fight Club*, *Taxi Driver*, *Apocalypse Now*, *Quadrophenia* and *The Harder They Come*.

Since Tessa left, I didn't even bother hitting the heavy bag in the morning, going for a run, or skipping rope. Nor did I attempt one unnecessary pushup or sit-up. I couldn't find the energy.

Despite the booze and the pills, I had slept about one or two hours per night on average.

In the morning, I got up, drank a huge coffee, swallowed a few aspirin, and ate cold pizza that I'd left sitting out on the counter from the night before. Maybe I'd find another picture of Tessa and burn it or simply toss it in the trash. Perhaps I'd spray-paint over the quotes on my walls that Tessa liked so much. I'd not open a window when doing so, blatantly violating the instructions on the back of the can. I'd fail, again, to shave for the whateverith day in a row.

Prior to leaving the apartment, I'd dab some makeup that Tessa forgot to take with her on my deeply bruised eyes and face so the lieutenant wouldn't pull me off the street due to injury. As you may have already guessed, I looked liked hell. But plausible deniability was all a boss needed to turn a blind eye to a subordinate's *issues*. The SFPD had nothing if not familiarity with *issues*.

Then I went to work, looking at the world through a haze of confusion and drowsiness that seemed like I was wearing someone else's reading glasses.

Issues.

As I pulled into the projects, on the lower corner, I noted an utter absence of people out where the usual gangsters and associates were known to congregate. In fact, I didn't see anybody out at all. This was a bad sign, one that lent merit to my belief that a gun was, in fact, being fired nearby. Over the years I'd learned that the only real way to get everybody indoors in the projects was to discharge a weapon. Nobody wanted to be the straggler who was stopped and questioned by the police or themselves a victim of said gunfire. I gave one last transmission as I stopped my vehicle.

"Hey, guys," I broadcast to the backup units responding. "It's dead down here. Headquarters, I'm gonna be out on foot between the buildings on the lower corner; Copy?"

"Ten four; three-henry-three-david is going to be out on foot at the lower corner."

As I pulled my keys out of the ignition and turned my vehicle's parking lights on, to mark my general location, I heard a voice call out over the radio, "Cohen, be careful. Why don't you just wait for us . . . ?"

The voice trailed off when I trotted into the "cuts"—slang for the areas between buildings in the projects—and turned to a western direction, toward where I thought the shots had come from. I drew my handgun with my right hand and held my flashlight in the left. As I expediently advanced forward, I heard a door open to my right and brought my gun around to face the possible threat. I saw a small black kid, not more than five. He didn't say anything, just poked his head out and pointed to the west, guiding me where to go. He wasn't yet old enough to hate me. History, experience and perception, distorted though it may have been, hadn't taught him that white men in blue uniforms were anything to fear.

Even if those white men looked as haggard, beaten to shit and poorly made up as I did.

I heard a female voice say, "What the fuck you doin,' little nigga? Close dat door! They shootin' out there."

I frowned, feeling sorry for the kid having to grow up surrounded by shit and likely doomed to a life of the same. There wasn't anything I could do about that, though, other than try and catch the man responsible for the evening's terror.

I keyed my radio and whispered, "Three-henry-three-david, there's definitely merit to shots being fired. I'm being directed toward the general direction of the playground on the lower corner."

As the dispatcher repeated my transmission, I pressed forward toward the building that was just in front of the playground, a frequent hangout for Lower Corner members. As I neared, I heard young men's voices from the area, laughing. I slowed and leaned against the building, pausing momentarily to take a breath and steady my shaking hands. I needed a drink.

I readied myself to round the corner by raising my gun up and supporting it with my opposite forearm. I held my flashlight parallel to the weapon's barrel, so they would always be pointing in the same direction. Moving out, away from the building line, I slowly crept around the corner in a wide arch with my weapon pointed ahead. The edge of the jungle gym came into view and a gunshot rang out. It was close, close enough that I could see the muzzle's flash on the buildings around me. I flinched and stopped my advance, contemplating retreat behind the building line. For a moment, I thought about waiting for backup: the smartest option.

I starting to bring my flashlight hand up to my chest to key the microphone and call for help.

The light illuminated my face for a moment and I caught a glimpse of my reflection in someone's kitchen window. I didn't speak. I thought of Tessa. I knew that she wasn't perfect, but I couldn't help but think she was the best thing that ever happened to me. I believed myself lost without her, lost in this job, lost in this world.

I was lost in my own head.

I remembered that my work, my "shit-magnet" persona, my increasingly rough exterior, and my utter failure at effective communication had driven my love away.

I remembered that I was standing there in the night, in the middle of Crap Central and no matter how hard I worked it never seemed to change. It never got any better. The streets never got any safer.

All the anguish I'd witnessed. All the rage I'd absorbed. All the spiteful words and looks directed toward me—despite the passionate duty, the trips to the emergency room and those lives laid down in service of the same people who despised us . . . I just didn't feel like the job was worth it anymore.

In the fleeting moment that I saw my face, I could see poison flowing through my veins.

I sneered and started to run forward into the unknown.

The San Francisco Police Department trains its officers to make silent, stealthy approaches to crimes in progress when the suspect may still be on scene. Instructions as to the proper way to respond to urgent calls for service are as follows:

1. Avoid using the lights and siren. If unavoidable due to heavy traffic, shut down the lights and siren at least five blocks from the call.

2. Try to park the vehicle out of sight of the call location, such as around the corner and/or behind the building line.

3. Keep the vehicle keys in a pocket or in the department issued key-keeper—a leather holster worn on the belt—not jingling on a belt hook.

4. Upon exiting the vehicle, close the door quietly. Lock the doors so that the car will still be secure if the door doesn't latch entirely.
5. In darkness, use the flashlight sparingly. Allow one's eyes to adjust to the ambient light if possible. If one needs to briefly illuminate an area, keep one eye closed. This retains night vision.

As I began to charge into the playground toward the source of the gunfire, I didn't really care who was there: a group of armed men, a pack of wolves, and/or a bunch of angry Apache warriors with an Apache attack helicopter—it was all the same. It was a good day to die, and I didn't really care what happened to me.

It wasn't superfluous; it was duty. It wasn't self-destruction; it was bravery. It wasn't suicide; it was martyrdom.

After rounding the corner, I was somewhat disappointed to only see a group of four hoods, all of whom were wearing black puffy coats and in their late teens. One was taller than the rest and he was standing closest to a little thug with dyed red dreadlocks. And that little thug, the blessed salvation, that ticket to bagpipes and mile-long, thousand car funeral processions, was holding a Glock handgun. The slide wasn't locked back, indicating that he still had ammunition to spare. The four of them all stared at the ground, studying the supine, lifeless body below them. They stared at the man they had murdered or watched die with uncaring eyes.

I lowered my gun to my side, pressing forward toward fate, toward Jameson Ratchet take-two with

worse odds, toward the sequel: *Jameson Ratchet: Reloaded.*
The oft imitated sound of a single blast of the marked
patrol vehicle's "wail" siren tone—the one that goes
beeooowwwrrrr—picked a rather inopportune moment
to activate less than seventy yards to my right, out
from the street. Some clueless coworker of mine, some
overanxious, well-meaning fuckup wasn't paying attention
to department policy and let the whole neighborhood
know that the police, the "five-oh," the "po-po," or the
"one-times," were on scene. The multiracial bunch of
men and women—who came to work for fifty hours a
week and donned armor and girded weapons, in order to
serve and protect—had arrived.

Hooray.

In other words: *Clear the fuck out!*

Upon the first escalating tone of the siren, the murder
party of four began to scatter in opposite directions, two
to the north and two to the south. From a distance of
about one hundred feet away, the bastard with the red
dreadlocks and the gun turned and saw me. His eyes went
wide. While he broke into the first jogging steps of his
flight from the scene, the gun he held came up at arm's
length and pointed directly at me.

For some stupid reason, all the personally ruinous
thoughts I'd just mustered took a back seat my collective
training and experience. Almost involuntarily, I saw the
gun, I saw the killer in front of me and I started firing at
my would-be deliverance from the misery I'd manifested
for myself as of late.

So much for bagpipes; so much for heroism; four hollowpoint handgun rounds streaking toward the general vicinity of the waste of space before me blew that idea away.

They did not, however, blow him away.

As I took off running after the shooter and his taller comrade, I recalled the academy's week long Basic Handgun Combat Training Course.

"You guys are going to put a whole bunch of holes in a whole bunch of targets," Kevin O'Malley said. "But those targets will be stationary and it won't be after a long car chase or a hair-raising foot chase. Your hands will not be shaking and your adrenaline will not be coursing through your veins. You'll just be standing in a big line with a bunch of your classmates shooting the prescribed number of rounds into the instructed area of the target and reloading when you go empty, at your leisure, without any bullets coming right back at you. It'll be fun.

"Keep in mind," he said, "keep in mind that officer-involved shootings on the street are a whole new ballgame." He was right about that.

The line wasn't ready.

I yelled, "SHOTS FIRED! OFFICER INVOLVED!" into my radio as I chased the two young men through the projects. I reeled in my panic. "Foot pursuit," I relayed, "headed south, along the building line!"

The furious bedlam that answered let me know that the other officers in the area heard my transmission and, likely, the gunshots. Distant, approaching sirens shook the night awake.

The two suspects rounded a corner, briefly out of my sight. Seconds later, I slowed to hit the same corner, brought my gun up to point and illuminated the area with my flashlight.

"Watch the corners, Mr. Cohen," Ken Byrne used to always say, regarding pursuits in the projects. "You never know who's waiting on the other side."

The sound tactics I now made use of as I chased the suspects tipped further in their favor the odds of escape. I was by myself, burdened by twenty-five extra pounds of uniform and gear that they weren't and I'd been drinking/not-sleeping the last several days of my life away. The listed factors—when weighed against my above-average speed and conditioning—put the three of us on even ground. As I ran, the hundred foot head start that they had on me closed only marginally.

A nearby, amber-hued streetlight transformed the two gangsters into silhouettes of violent ghosts that I desperately hunted. The surreal glow reflected off the rain, making the whole scene seem like a staged shot from a Scorsese flick. Beyond the two men, at the next street, a patrol car streaked by with its lights and siren on.

"Unit on Camdale," I called into my radio, "STOP! We're coming right toward you!"

If there was an answer, I didn't hear it. But as the radio car continued away, out of my sight, I figured that they didn't. Ahead of me, I saw the shorter of the two silhouetted men make a furtive move with his right arm and heard a metal object bounce across the pavement.

"POLICE," I screamed, "STOP!"

I continued to run as fast as I could, leaning forward on my toes and striking the ground with only the balls of my feet. I slowly gained ground. If I could keep them in sight for another hundred yards, I knew that I'd be right on top of them. As the two suspects approached the end of the building line, rounding a small, bushy tree out of my sight, I passed the Glock, which had been discarded on the concrete below. Barring some concealed weapon—or other random happenstance—it seemed my destruction would be postponed for the evening.

I passed the same tree, slowing as I did so and rounding the corner in the same tactical manner as before. My gun led my body onto the sidewalk of Camdale Street. The two men were no longer in sight. I started to spin, scanning the landscape for closing doors, fresh tracks in the mud, cars that one could hide under—anything. I trotted into the street, looking back over my shoulder from where I had just come to see if they had doubled back; nothing. I ran across the street and looked behind the buildings searching desperately for any sign of them.

Nothing.

I muttered audibly, "Where the fuck are you?" Then again, louder, "WHERE ARE YOU?"

I looked and looked but they were gone, disappeared into an unknown unit in an unknown building—one of a hundred possible. Sure, were this Iraq, I could have kicked in every door; we probably could have napalmed the whole block, but this was SAN FRANCISCO.

It's impossible to write a hundred search warrants at once.

I updated dispatch of my status and the suspects' last location, waiting in vain for another officer to pick up the chase. But nobody found the killers. Yet another crime that would hinge on the unlikely prospect of getting DNA evidence off the weapon or the even less likely circumstance that a witness would come forward. And I was RIGHT THERE when it happened.

Right there.

I jogged back to recover the gun.

All the time in the gym, I thought, *all the training in the academy, all the awards, the medal, the attaboys: none of it matters.*

I still wasn't superhuman. I'd shot and missed; I ran and lost. I couldn't even destroy myself correctly.

What would Bruce Wayne say? Who would he let escape?

As officers began to arrive and search the area, including cops from several neighboring districts, all I could think of was my failure. Some poor schmuck lay dead in the middle of some bombed-out, Beirut-looking projects, in a fucking playground, and I couldn't do shit about it.

If only that unit on Camdale would have stopped, I thought.

I retraced my steps and stood by with the gun. Over my radio, I heard a voice say that the two other suspects, the ones who I didn't chase, were in custody and had been hiding in some bushes just north of the playground. I broadcast where I was and that I was guarding the probable murder weapon.

"Henry-three-david, what was the final disposition of the two suspects you were chasing?" the dispatcher asked.

I paused and stated, flatly, something that working cops hated to say: "Lost in the area."

I heard Dave's voice behind me ask in a concerned tone, "Dougie, Jesus Christ, we thought you got shot there for a while. What were you thinking chasing those guys by yourself? You've got some balls, man." He paused for a few awkward moments of silence and asked, "You're okay though, right?"

I didn't know how to answer a man who didn't fail in the same circumstance. I just said, "Sure, man. I'm fine."

CHAPTER 21

And I shall hear, tho' soft you tread above me
And all my dreams will warm and sweeter be
If you'll not fail to tell me that you love me
I simply sleep in peace until you come to me
　　　　　　—"Danny Boy," Traditional

Seated shirtless, wearing only my boxers and a pair of black socks, I couldn't help but think that I should put on something a little more presentable for the occasion. I took another long pull from the bottle of Jim Beam in my hand and put it down on the floor of my bedroom, next to the bed where I was seated. I contemplated pulling my dress uniform out of the closet and giving it one last showing but quickly dismissed the idea thinking it rather trite; it had already been done in *A Few Good Men*.

That and I didn't want to polish the shoes that went with it.

Instead, I donned a pair of blue jeans that were draped over a nearby chair and then decided I should probably put my current favorite song on, favorite because it catered to my misery and loneliness, because it reminded me of Tessa as just about everything else did. The song: "Dirty Old Town" by The Pogues.

I always had a thing for Irish music, perhaps because of the family bloodline; perhaps it was another clue as to why I joined the PD in the first place. God help me, I'd never even been to Ireland but had every Chieftains album and read Irish history books for fun. I put the song on repeat and became acutely aware of, and simultaneously disgusted by, the shamrocks tattooed in the pits of my arms.

Fucking poser, I thought. *Typical American boy: trying to belong to something unique, something special, and ignoring what he already has.*

Was that the real reason I joined the force?

The first song on the CD started to play and Shane McGowan, the band's lead singer, began to sing: *"I met my love by the gas works wall, dreamed a dream by the old canal; kissed a girl by the factory wall—dirty old town; dirty old town."*

I stumbled back to my bedroom thinking about all the events that led up to Tessa's love for me fading away: biting that homicidal tweaker's ear off; my changing politics; how jaded I became; how she finally witnessed the reality of my career choice—my life and identity—and was disgusted by it. She was disgusted by me.

My alcohol soaked brain compared the love Tessa and I had to a tsunami. First, you're overwhelmed by the onslaught and then equally fucked by the riptide.

Mr. McGowan went on: *"Clouds a-drifting across the moon, cats a-prowling on their beat; spring's a girl in the street at night—dirty old town; dirty old town."*

As I sat back down onto the foot of my bed, I briefly fantasized about running away and joining the French Foreign Legion—or becoming The Punisher and exacting revenge and violent justice on the evil men of our society. But then I remembered that I was probably the last person who should decide what the composition of justice was—my mind tainted by years dealing with "cronks" and "shitbags" and "assholes" and every other nickname for "criminal" common in Cop Speak.

I recalled that the one thing I tried to commit to that really mattered, something more important than a job: that goddamn girl. She didn't even want me. I remembered all the self-doubt and self-pity and self-imposed torture I'd been partaking in since she left. And I felt even more pity and doubt and disgust with myself.

How pathetic, I thought. *Some man you turned out to be, sweet-cheeks.*

And I decided to just get this thing over with so I could sleep for once, as I hadn't in days, as I hadn't in a manner worth remembering since that warm body was no longer laying next to me. I picked up my duty weapon from the bed next to me and felt its weight in my hands.

The song went: *"I'm going to make me a good sharp axe, shining steel tempered in the fire; will chop you down like an old dead tree—dirty old town; dirty old town."*

I thought, *At least I won't miss this shot.*

There are a few distinct and differing options available to a man who has lost his mind, has been drinking for a week, has slept for about six total hours in the same time frame, believes that he is a rapidly sinking ship—a failure at the things that matter—and holding a .40 caliber automatic pistol, which is fully loaded and has a chambered round, ready to fire:

1. Take the weapon, put it into the mouth, exhale sharply, bite down and pull the trigger. Die. Be discovered an unknown amount of time later, the exact time of discovery dictated by the following factors:

    a. The person(s) in the neighboring apartment(s) actually hear the gunshot and, believing it actually is a gunshot, call 911. The responding officers then, hopefully, knock on some doors and interview some neighbors. One of these neighbors may or may not report that the guy who lives next door—the one with all the tattoos whose fiancée recently moved out—has been blaring music all day and his recycling has been filled with empty bottles of whiskey. These same officers will do the proverbial math, call the self-congratulating jackoffs from the fire department and make entry, thereby discovering the brain matter and clotted blood adorning the bedspread, under the head of the dead body. Hopefully, these officers will not have known or worked with the dead man because that would be awkward and really un-cool. But, you know, fuck it. It's not like the dead guy will be around to feel bad.

b.   The smell becomes overwhelming.

2.   Put the gun down, pick up the phone and get some help. Quit wallowing in depression and masochism and realize that life doesn't always work out in your favor; sometimes it downright blows but if you never fail you'll never succeed. If you are never miserable, you will never be happy. If you never hit rock bottom, you'll never find the motivation to change. "What doesn't kill you . . ." and all that bullshit. Just pour the bottle out, go down to the gym and hit the heavy bag or jump some rope, whatever. And maybe, when you're done being a useless, manic drunk, and get your brain chemicals squared away, you'll meet another girl. Maybe you'll actually grow up and stop pretending to be an adult. And if you hate your job so much, just quit.

For purposes of this exercise, we'll assume the man in question chose to proceed with option number one.

I stopped staring at the pistol and began to bring it up to my open mouth, desperately hoping that the gun would fall to the floor after the bullet passed through my brain, so that I wouldn't be discovered by a bunch of fratboy firemen sucking on a .40 caliber cock. I could just see the "jakeys" stomping into my room and finding all the books, graphic novels, comic book posters and my writing on the walls drenched in my blood and tissue. I could just imagine them banging the hell out of my door frames with their entry tools and axes, laughing at what a nerd I was. I could just picture them all seeing some brainless, dead cop on the ground and not getting it, not understanding the events that led up to that point. I could just imagine them all back at the station after the coroner took me away lounging in their big taxpayer-bought recliners and stuffing their faces and slapping each other on the back because some sports team won some contest and who gave a shit.

I knew they wouldn't care and I knew why, but in my current emotional state, I didn't feel the need to empathize.

Because fuck those fags, I thought.

As the front sight of the gun tapped my upper teeth, I drew in a deep breath and tried to psych myself up. My eyes caught a picture of Tessa up on the dresser, looking sultry and gorgeous. That was all the psyching-up I needed. I canted the gun to the side and inserted it in my mouth.

Just prior to pulling the trigger, I remembered that I forgot to write a note but pushed the thought out of my mind. There's no point to writing a suicide note other than to let detectives know that it's not worth investigating. There's no mystery in the act: people kill themselves because they are miserable, feel trapped and want an out. Sometimes, people kill themselves because they can't sleep and sometimes they kill themselves because they can't live with who they've become when they're awake. The note is just icing for parents and loved ones, a physical object to confuse them even more.

"Know that this isn't your fault," the notes read. *"And I'll always love you all."* I didn't feel the need to explain myself. Even I wasn't that big of a drama queen.

With the gun still in my mouth, I tried to say "fuck it" but it probably sounded more like "frrrggh iff." My drunken mind forced a chuckle at the sound I produced, which also sounded funny, and I decided to take one last drink. Gripping the weapon's handle with my right hand, I reached down and picked up the bottle of whiskey with my left; the gunpowder residue and oil tasted terrible and I figured bourbon would be a welcome replacement. I unscrewed the cap and brought the bottle up to my lips, trying to simultaneously keep the pistol in my mouth and take a swig out of the bottle—as if I was worried that I'd lose the nerve if I removed it.

Quit procrastinating, dude, I thought. The phone began to ring. Unsuccessful, I took the bottle out of my mouth and closed my eyes, pouring the contents out on my face and down the front of my body. Some of the liquor splashed into my eyes and it stung, badly. I threw the bottle down and it shattered on the floor. I closed my lips and mouth around the gun, holding it in place so I could use a nearby T-shirt to dry my burning eyes.

Great job, asshole.

The phone continued to ring.

I took a deep breath and squeezed my eyes shut, discarding the wet shirt to the side.

I moved my finger to the trigger as the machine picked up.

"Hello, you've reached Dougie Cohen's fucking goddamn shit phone. Tessa doesn't live here anymore. Don't leave a message because I don't want to talk to you. Eat a dick," my prerecorded voice said.

Motherfucker, I thought, *I always forget to mute the machine.*

The caller started to speak, breaking my concentration. It was Matt's voice and he sounded distraught.

"Dougie. Dougie, are you there? Dougie, pick up . . . asshole. Put the fucking bottle down and pick up, it's important . . . fuck, guess you're not in."

Matt sounded weird.

"Listen: Dave's dead, bro. They fucking ran him down with a car. A fucking carload of bank robbers crushed him against a wall fleeing the scene, man. He was all fucked up. He never even got a shot off. I never even got a shot off and I got there right as they killed him, man. I saw him die, Dougie. The fuckers all surrendered when their car broke down. They're all still alive . . . fucking pussies."

The ending of the song approached, repeating: *"Dirty old town."*

The gun fell to the floor, chipping a tooth on the way down and I lay on the bed, eyes wide open with my gaze fixed on the ceiling; my head absent any new holes. Matt went on after a pause; I could tell that he was crying.

"What are the fucking odds? He barely escapes death a few months ago and now . . . I'm SO FUCKING PISSED RIGHT NOW." I heard a banging noise in the background like he punched the wall. He continued after a deep, sobbing sigh. "Give me a call, Dougie. I need to talk to somebody. Call whenever you—"

The cordless phone was on the bedside table, next to me. I picked it up and put it to my ear, switching it on.

"Dirty old town."

"Matt," I said, trying to keep my speech from slurring like one of the thousands of drunks I'd stopped in their weaving cars, rolling my eyes as they tried to talk their ways out of a DUI. "Matt, it's alright, man. Tell me what happened."

Matt just sobbed.

"Dirty old town."

CHAPTER 22

Walked out this morning
Don't believe what I saw
A hundred billion bottles
Washed up on the shore
Seems I'm not alone in being alone
A hundred billion castaways
Looking for a home
—The Police, "Message in a Bottle"

It was a cloudy day, but thankfully rain wasn't forecast. The layer of gaseous moisture between me and the sun's rays meant that I didn't have to squint at the SFPD's Honor Guard: the six sharply dressed men of fierce military bearing who were currently carrying my friend's coffin down a long promenade toward the luminous oak doors and grand entryway of St. Mary's Cathedral. Thousands of men and women stood in platoon formations on all sides of me, forming a long track of blue uniforms. I, like most everyone else standing at attention and in ranks, wore my dress uniform—complete with the modest collection of campaign ribbons and awards I'd accumulated over the

310

years, little "chicklets" that indicated I had done, or had been present during the doing of, something cool.

Moments earlier, Dave's coffin was gingerly removed from the back of a highly polished hearse. Its slow parade ensued, down the long aisle formed by the bulk of the SFPD, various officers from other agencies around the state, local politicians (looking obviously uncomfortable but obligated to be present), media representatives and Dave's friends and family. Out on Geary Boulevard, well over a hundred police vehicles—both marked and unmarked and from various agencies around the state—clogged the streets. Directly across from the promenade, two SFFD fire trucks had extended their aerial ladders in the shape of an X, and the crews had suspended the largest American flag that I'd ever seen from the massive, steel arms.

The jakeys knew how to show their respects; I gave them that.

Since Matt's phone call, I'd learned Dave had been murdered by the driver of a getaway vehicle that was fleeing the scene of a bank robbery, four days prior. Dave had unknowingly walked up on the crime as it was ending and attempted to stop the trio of suspects on foot, as they pulled away in their vehicle. Per witness accounts, the suspects purposely drove onto the sidewalk and crushed Dave between the getaway car's passenger side and the brick wall of a nearby camera store. Dave had only been at his new station, South of Market or "SoMa" Station, for two days. Shortly after my shooting, the last time I saw Dave, his name had come up on a transfer list out of Southeast. He had finally made it downtown to the good land where food was plentiful, projects were rare and women were attractive—down to the one part of San Francisco that didn't mind seeing the police now and then. Dave Costello: an Irish man walking a beat in downtown SF, a perfect match turned cruel fate.

In an impressive display of organizational cramming, a trio of helicopters buzzed overhead, seconds after an unknown member of the SFPD's command staff signaled to our respective platoon leaders to have their men and women, "Present arms!"

We saluted in unison, standing in statuesque silence, our shoulders soon burning and brows furling. For five minutes, I didn't hear one cough or sneeze; I didn't hear one siren or passing car; I didn't hear one customized stereo system or cellular phone ring. I just heard the muted sobs of Dave's widow and whispered consolations from the family members who surrounded her.

Over the last twenty-four hours, I had been to the viewing and the vigil, awkwardly mumbling my way through the Catholic prayers and trying not to make eye contact with those around me—except for Matt. Now Matt and I stood in a platoon with the rest of our academy classmates, Dave's classmates, as was common SFPD funeral procedure.

I kept it together through the two prior ceremonies; I didn't cry. I didn't sob, nor did my knees tremble or my expression change. Though the image danced in my head, I didn't emulate the distraught Italian mothers from gangster movies and throw myself on the coffin or try to pick Dave's lifeless, wax-like body up and hold his heavily made-up head to my breast. Matt and I had sat next to each other on the bus rides to the various services. We walked up to the coffin together during the viewing and we isolated ourselves from the rest of the cops during the down times between events. We played the roles that we thought expected of us: stoic and strong soldiers in the never-ending war against societal chaos. I thought we did marginally well.

But then those goddamn bagpipes started. Specifically, Captain Wong from Narcotics started to play the Great Irish Warpipes, the ones King Richard II outlawed in 1366 because they were thought to make Irishmen prone to acts of insurrection; the Irish version of the Scottish Great Highland Pipes. It could have been worse; some copper could have been playing the Uileann Pipes and I might have just died of grief right there on the spot. Lucky for me, you've got to sit down to play those and there weren't any wheelchair bound pipers about.

Just prior to when I began to bite my lower lip and felt the strength leaving my legs, I thought, *Captain fucking WONG plays the pipes? Are you kidding me?*

Yet, the momentary diversion didn't stop the flood and as Dave's coffin passed by and the pipes wailed a perfect "Amazing Grace," I wept. As my right hand was still up in a salute, tears streaked down my face and down the front my wool uniform. I stood there, sobbing for Dave, poor goddamn Dave; poor blessed Dave.

I cried for Dave the hero.

The coffin bearers slowly began to ascend the stairs of the cathedral and "Amazing Grace" turned to "Danny Boy." For the first time since Tessa left, I cried her out of my head, along with the whiskey and the shameful thoughts of self-annihilation I'd had. I cried away Jameson Ratchet and the murderous preoccupation I constructed in the absence of his death by my hand.

Evil may have killed me, but nagging, ongoing doubt most assuredly would.

President Carter said, *"It is a crisis of confidence. It is a crisis that strikes at the very heart and soul and spirit of our national will. We can see this crisis in the growing doubt about the meaning of our own lives and in the loss of a unity of purpose for our nation."*

He may as well have been addressing the jumbled mess of bickering assholes that comprised the citizenry in my head.

A fiber in the quilted ranks around me, I was as generations of officers before; I was the rank and file. Everybody present wearing a gun on his or her hip had been affected by the job in their own way. I could see it in their eyes. The job had eaten a part of them and they all had given up something to keep doing it. Most sacrificed something small; some gave something they thought huge, like marriage. Some gave something ultimate, like Dave.

They had made it this far; so had I.

We all may not have been best friends, but we would all die for one another because it was the right thing to do; we would die for our worst detractor or our most vocal critic. We would die for federally insured money. We would die at the hands of armed gang members who only sought to kill other armed gang members. We would die at the hands of diabolical madmen without warning or explanation and quickly be forgotten by everyone but ourselves. The history of fallen brothers and sisters was maintained by tradition and sacrifice.

Once inside the cathedral, when the priest began to speak, he talked about the willingness of strangers, cops, to give their lives for the public and one another. He said, "If that isn't love, I don't know what is."

At the conclusion of the ceremony, one by one the entire room filed by Dave's flag-draped coffin. The pipers played again as those in uniform gave a last, final salute to their beloved brother. My turn came and I stopped by my dead friend's side, in front of the mayor and the police commissioners and the chief—the people with the good seats who didn't even know the fallen man in front of them.

I cried; I gave a salute; I kissed my open hand and gently set it down upon the flag.

This is the life I have chosen, I thought.

Enough pity.

Right face.

Forward march.

CHAPTER 23

"The law is reason free from passion."
—Aristotle

If We the People have our collective way and technology cooperates, one day the job of American policing will turned over to robots. Lawmakers and lobbyists, activists and agitators, voters and politicians will usher in a new era of law enforcement: an era free of error.

This will occur because one day another group of unknown race men in blue will be caught on videotape beating an unknown race parolee—who just led the officers on a prolonged car chase—with their batons. The beating will go on for an unreasonable and inexplicable amount of time. It doesn't and won't matter how many repeated failures in life the parolee made to get to that point, or how many times he's been in and out of prison . . . leaving a trail of victims behind him. Police violence isn't supposed to be about revenge, anger or fear; it is to be a means to an end. Every move the officer makes is supposed to lead to the suspect getting handcuffed.

Punishment is not our purpose. The lesson is not ours to teach. That burden lies with the lawmakers, the voters, the District Attorney's Offices, and the judges and juries. It doesn't matter that if criminals actually faced consequences for their actions, if it worked in the interest of justice a little more often, the temptation to punch some asshole in the face for beating up an old woman and stealing her purse might decrease significantly.

Sometime soon—and probably over and over again—some cop who managed to slip through the cracks of the hiring process will use his authority to force sex on a prostitute or manipulate citizens into bribery for his own financial gain. Some bully with a badge/star/shield . . . whatever will abuse the powers given to him by the people and disgrace the oath he took. Bad apples always pop up. I think astronomically less so in modern law enforcement than in the general population. But, as previously stated, it is big news when that screw-up finally gets brought to light.

Knowing or otherwise, some officer will fuck up *big time* and ruin something for the rest of his coworkers.

And, with every new incident, rare though it may be, logic will dictate that removing humans from the equation would be the most effective fix. The lowest bidder will produce an affordable android with basic artificial intelligence and extensive programming algorithms, mapping out the proper verbal or physical response to any enforcement situation or investigation. A system of downloadable updates, like patches for flawed computer games, will keep the unit up to speed.

Program #4431—"Ma'am, you have been the victim of a rape. I need you to come with me to the hospital so forensic tests and DNA swabs can be performed on your mouth, vagina and anus. Then I will take you to speak to a counselor so that you may emote."

Program #205—"Sir, you will either put the weapon down or I will be forced to discharge an electrical arc into your body, which will incapacitate you. You have three seconds."

Program #357—"Ma'am, I must maintain the integrity of the crime scene. Get back or I will be forced to discharge an electrical arc into your body, which will incapacitate you. I understand that the victim is your son. The law states you must get back. You have three seconds."

It'll be a perfect, well-oiled machine of a process. A committee of activists, politicians, scientists, reformed criminals, community members from all cultures and creeds, and professors—experts on police practices—will convene to program the units via fair, democratic process. And then they'll be sent out on patrol.

We'll have flawless tools of policing devoid of prejudice, passion, depression, elation, humor, grief, love or independent thought—an ideal solution to an age old problem. No more scandals; no more accidents; no more mistakes, human qualities far better suited for jobs in which lives don't hang in the balance.

An army of armed, intelligent robots to dictate our comings and goings, our dos and don'ts. What could possibly go wrong?

CHAPTER 24

> *"If you prick us, do we not bleed? If you tickle us, do we not laugh? If you poison us, do we not die? And if you wrong us, shall we not revenge?"*
>
> —William Shakespeare, *Merchant of Venice*

Dave had been buried for seven days and my administrative leave—a mandatory period of paid time off work in the aftermath of any officer-involved shooting—was over. In one of those days off, I'd gone to a follow-up appointment with my doctor in regard to my busted nose.

The doctor made the mistake of asking me, "So, other than the nose, how have you been?"

In a rare moment of candor, I told him what had been going through my head as of late, though I significantly watered down the parts wherein I tried to kill myself, so I didn't wind up in a psych ward and out of the job forever. I confessed that I'd been drinking "a bit" and Dr. Ross scolded me as he drew blood to check my liver enzymes for abnormality.

"Dougie, you don't look too good," the doc told me.

An hour later, I walked out of the medical office complex with a prescription for an antidepressant in a dosage strong enough to make the world's final, starving elephant feel pretty at peace with his race's extinction.

I'd been taking the pills for three days. They helped me sleep blissful, dreamless seven hour segments without interruption. They quieted my mind; it's not that I didn't think about Dave or Tessa, I just didn't care.

Serenity, thy name is: pharmacology.

Matt and I were at work, rolling around the Excelsior District at about 1800 hours, just before the coming of early fall evening's colorful dusk. The moon was materializing above and the first few illuminated stars cast their groggy gazes down to the earth below. The sky was a mix of purple, blue and ochre, one of those nights when San Franciscans flocked to ocean-side restaurants and bars to applaud as the sun set.

While patrolling a particularly rough section of Mission Street, I saw two light-skinned Arab guys— Lebanese, I surmised—dressed all "gangsta" and wearing mirrored sunglasses despite the late hour. They were obviously loitering in front of a corner liquor store, looking nervous as shit. One of the guys, the fatter one with the tight ponytail terminating slicked back hair, was holding a backpack. Both of the guys kept glancing from side to side as if searching for something or someone.

As Matt and I rolled by, the two men both froze and regarded our car with wide-eyed interest. They abruptly turned to walk up Brazil Street toward London Street away from us, but then slowed in a futile attempt to look casual.

Nothing going on here, Officer.

I told Matt, who was driving—naturally—to spin around the block so we could take another look at the guys. I noted, "But play it cool."

Matt cruised down Mission Street and made a left onto Excelsior, out of sight. Once we were behind the building line, Matt jammed on the gas—naturally—and sent our car rocketing forward toward London. Peeling around the corner onto London, Matt continued to blaze toward the two men's last location.

"Slow down, dude. We're gonna be on them in a minute," I told Matt.

"Worry not, my friend," he said.

"You sound like Yoda," I said back. He laughed.

Matt decelerated like we were reverting back to sub-light engines after exiting maximum warp and turned onto Brazil. I saw the two guys at the end of the block, now standing back in front of the liquor store. Again, they were looking back and forth, side to side and shuffling their feet against the filthy pavement below. They were obviously apprehensive about something.

"What do you think?" I asked Matt. "Is it reasonable to walk away from some shady liquor store when the cops show up and then go back when said cops have gone?"

"I'm thinking: no."

"Then let's go introduce ourselves."

I had barely gotten the word "go" out when Matt skid our car to a halt after a brief engine rev of about 4000

RPM, directly next to the two men. Matt had positioned the car in a bus zone facing the wrong way. A group of pedestrians bolted across the sidewalk. Matt and I both threw our doors open and alighted from the car. The two men turned suddenly, saw our vehicle and began to back away from it, as if getting ready to bolt. The big guy dropped the bag onto the sidewalk.

"Don't even think about it, dude!" I ordered.

"Stop," Matt announced, pointing his finger forward in a warning, menacing manner, "both of you."

They froze. This wasn't the projects; there was nowhere to run.

"Turn around and put your hands behind your heads," I instructed.

"For what?" the big guy asked.

"Because I'm gonna check you for a weapon, that's what. You already walked away from us once and were going to do it again. You want to play coy with me, whatever. Just do as you're told."

I knew I was coming on a little strong but the guy didn't argue.

Matt and I patted the two men down, cursory searches for weapons only. I didn't find anything and neither did Matt. We had the two guys sit on the curb and asked for their identifications. Our detainees didn't have those either, in accordance with common criminal— or wannabe criminal—procedure. As Matt asked the smaller guy his name and birthday in order to run him for warrants, a parole record or probation hit, I walked over to the backpack and picked it up.

"Hey," I said to the bigger guy. "Is this yours?"

"No, nigga," he said. I had quickly grown to hate that people used the "n-word" as slang, especially when they weren't even black. But it amused me to think of the reception these two men might get upon using that word in the wrong crowd. "That shit ain't mine."

Pre-Prozac Dougie Cohen would have said, *"I ain't your fucking 'nigga', asshole."* But rested, medicated me said, "Good, then you won't mind if I see what's in it, will you?"

I unzipped the bag.

The big guy started to stand up.

"SIT DOWN," Matt stated, authoritatively.

I smiled at the guy and peeked into the backpack, immediately finding a snub-nosed revolver and, at first glance, a bunch of weed packaged for sale. I zipped the bag back up and put it over my shoulder, nodding at Matt. Matt stopped speaking into his radio and told the big guy, "Stand up."

Though he answered with a stream of colorful language, the suspect complied and Matt cuffed him up. I did the same to the smaller jackass and we walked the two men to our car.

Finally, as if an afterthought, the big guy remembered to ask the obligatory: "What am I being arrested for?"

"For your gun and your drugs, dumbass," I replied.

"That shit ain't mine, nigga," he protested.

"I hope you throw that word around with the black deputies at county intake," Matt said.

"Yeah, they'll love you, tough guy," I added.

Back at the station, I got a chance to search the bag in a more thorough manner. In addition to the loaded .38 caliber Smith and Wesson revolver, we found about an ounce of weed, about twenty grams of cocaine that was buried in the bag's smaller pocket, a digital scale and repackaging materials: i.e. more little baggies imprinted with adorable little pictures of skulls or dice or pot leafs or snowflakes. The *piece de resistance* was the presence of the smaller guy's city college binder bearing his name in big block letters on the exterior, indicia linking him to the crime and fuel to book him as well.

All in all a nice little pinch: gun, dope packaged for resale and two bodies to go with it.

"What punishment do you think the fine San Francisco criminal justice system will give these two upstanding citizens?" Matt asked as he filled out a narcotic evidence envelope.

"A book of gift certificates to the Olive Garden and a souvenir coin," I deadpanned. I hadn't been drunk since before the funeral and my wit was starting to come back to its normal status.

I got a list of charges together and Matt began to book the evidence and prepare arrest cards for the two custodies.

"You want to go get some food while I book these guys in?" Matt inquired.

"Yeah, totally. Are burritos all right?"

"Sure, there's something new." If given the option, I always chose to eat Mexican food. "Need cash?" Matt asked, digging his hands into his pocket.

"No, dude, you deserve a free meal."

I took Matt's order and walked out the door just before the night watch's lineup/roll-call/muster/whatever and drove to the closest taqueria, one which I affectionately referred to as "El Line-o" due to its popularity.

Matt wanted whatever I was getting plus: "two churros . . . and some flan." Matt, still rail thin, could eat anything in any quantity and never fatten for it. It was a good thing too because sweets were to him what whiskey, up until very recently, was to me.

I entered the taqueria and took my place in line; the crowd was relatively light and my turn to order came up soon. One of the several petite Mexican women behind the counter asked me what I wanted. As I told her, a white guy in his early twenties, who was dressed like a skateboarder, and about 5'10" with an average build, walked past me. He was heading from the bathroom to his seat. As he passed he said, "I smell bacon." I could tell he was drunk.

I ignored the comment, as I had learned early in my career that it was the best course of action in such a situation.

"Don't let anybody goad you into a fight if you can avoid it," Dean used to say. "People who pick fights with uniformed police officers are already pathetic enough. They don't need you to teach them a lesson . . . unless, of course, you have to teach the guy a lesson. Know what I mean?"

I finished giving my order and stood at the counter recalling Dean's words as I waited for the food. As I waited, in my peripheral vision, I saw the drunken skater walk over to his table where a friend was already seated. He proceeded to make an exaggerated effort of chomping on his burrito. In between bites, he continued to loudly talk half to his friend and half to the other occupants of the restaurant.

"Fucking pigs," he said. "Fucking burn them all. That's what I say."

I took a deep breath. It annoyed me that I was letting such uninspired insults get to me, but they were. Perhaps we needed to up my dosage.

"Hey . . . HEY," he called to his familiar looking tablemate, a punk rocker who was obviously ignoring his intoxicated comrade. "Did you see that news story about the cop who got run over?"

The other kid didn't answer but the guy went on. My ears started to get hot.

"Yeah, well, some fucking pig got crushed by a car and now it's all over the paper . . . like we give a shit. They let those dudes go, man."

My face started turning red. I repeated Dean's instructions in my head, over and over. Obviously, some vestiges of my more feral personality traits had only been somewhat contained. Luckily, my food was ready. As I paid a thought occurred to me, a dilemma.

I knew I had two distinct and differing options available to me. I could:

1. Take my food and walk out the front door, leaving the public to believe I was lazy and didn't want to do my job by dealing with the drunken loudmouth

who was ruining their dining experience. Conversely, this action could also cause other members of the public to think, "Wow, what a mellow cop? Are all San Francisco cops that way? I'm gonna move here." Unfortunately, an annex of this crowd would likely take that as carte blanche to mock uniformed police officers whenever, wherever they could. Baton, pepper spray and firearm usage would likely skyrocket thereafter and we would all be one step closer to the reign of Officer Robot and his pals.

2. Confront the man and arrest him for being drunk in public, likely after a struggle and a call for backup. (I was suddenly, acutely aware that I didn't have any handcuffs left. Both pairs were in the booking room on one of our custodies, one at the little guy's wrists and the other one attaching him to the bench.) This action would either cause the surrounding citizens entertainment and joy or further cater to their notions that the San Francisco Police Department was one step below the Gestapo in tyrannical rule.

The dilemma was significant. I decided to play the middle ground and appeal to the punk rocker friend's humanity. Upon further facial scrutiny, I thought I may have met him at a concert before but I wasn't sure. He looked like a friend of Tessa's that I met the night we saw The Deadbeats UK, but that was a long time ago and my memory of the night had faded. Regardless, I doubted that he would recognize me in uniform if it was the same guy.

I approached the man, walking right past the drunk who was staring daggers into my head.

"Excuse me, Sir. I can't help but notice that your friend is a little intoxicated and obviously looking for trouble."

The drunk began to spout colorful insults about fellow persons of my profession, involving the words "faggots" and "bitches."

Classy.

I continued to speak, "Anyways, do me a favor and take care of him. If my psychic abilities tell me anything, it's that his evening may end poorly."

"Okay, Officer. I'll take care of him. Thanks for not just dragging him off to jail."

"Like he fucking could," the drunk chimed.

"Not a problem," I said to both of them.

"His brother got killed by a cop in Texas so he hates cops," the punk rock kid explained, oblivious to how ridiculous that sounded.

"Was the cop black? Does he hate them too?" I didn't bother waiting for the answer and walked out the door toward my car.

I almost started to feel like I may have abated the problem when I heard the familiar, though muffled, punk rocker's voice announce, "Don't do it!" I quickly put the bag of food down on the concrete and spun to face the door.

Oh boy. Here we go, I thought.

Upon executing a one-eighty, I saw the angry inebriate barreling out the front door of the *taqueria* toward me. As he charged forward, he brought his hands up in front of him like he might have known how to use them and grunted, "Motherfucker, I can say whatever I—".

At least, that's all he got out.

As usual, I'd left my baton in the car so the brakes on the rest of Jerkoff's statement manifested themselves in the following combination: left jab, overhand right, left shovel-hook. As he reeled back, I yelled, "You're under arrest," like a good little cadet. I shoved the stunned man to the ground, and came down on top of him, kneeling on his chest.

As I reached back for handcuffs that weren't there, I looked over my shoulder and saw the guy's friend running out of the restaurant toward us. I wasn't sure what he intended on doing: coming to his idiot buddy's rescue or merely watching. I regarded him sternly and called for help on my radio.

"Henry-sixteen-david has a resister at Monterey and Congo," I said, as cool as I could, channeling Tom.

I didn't hear the answer if there was one because the "resister" below me reached up and started clawing at my crotch, trying to push me off by the balls. I shifted my weight and position up his body to trap his arm, and saw the former tablemate start to take a step toward us.

"STAY BACK!" I ordered. I grabbed the drunk's arm that was not currently searching for my nuts and did a modified wrist lock on it. With my teeth clenched I said, just audibly enough, "I will rip your goddamn hand off if you don't quit grabbing my dick." I knelt forward on him with my full weight and, surprisingly, he stopped.

Crouched down on top of another formerly-struggling human being, holding him in place and waiting for The Calvary to arrive, I reviewed the years past and what in me had changed. I had grown from green cadet to experienced street cop, from youthful aspirations to near damnation and back again.

I wondered if I made the right decision in choosing police work as a profession; I wondered if I had chosen the path best suited for my abilities. I asked myself if this was the apex of whatever governing supernatural force—"God" for lack of a better word—had chosen for me? Maybe I could have been a doctor or a college professor, something exceptional. I knew that my parents probably would have liked to see me do something wherein my soul would not be sullied, wherein my spirit would not glower.

Then I remembered Dave and how special he was and I thought: *What about this isn't exceptional? What about him wasn't special?*

With the slow countdown in my blood and liver, was there really a point in perseveration?

I grinned a little and chuckled at how my mind wandered in such a situation.

Delightful distraction, thy name is: serotonin reuptake inhibitor.

I looked down at the man below me who was previously laughing at the fact that one of my brothers, my good friends, died protecting the society that enabled him to act like such an asshole.

I thought, *I may not be able to shoot straight, run at superhuman speeds or have bite-proof appendages, but I can, at least, as has been demonstrated and witnessed by the occupants of a crowded urban Mexican food joint* . . . And I said this part out loud, directly to the passive body under my knees, "I can still kick your ass."

Tessa wouldn't have approved of those thoughts; it didn't matter to me anymore.

Ah, catharsis, thy name is: Prozac.

Thirty seconds after my call for assistance, the first patrol car showed up and handcuffed Genius for me. To facilitate this process, I stood up and my new arrestee wasn't just passive, he was unconscious. His skin was ashen and he was taking deep, snoring breaths. It occurred to me that I'd been kneeling on the man's neck and occluding his carotid artery.

Oops, I thought. And, for a moment, I felt something unfamiliar: guilt.

I heard his friend request, "Can you roll him over?"

Good call.

The familiar man must have thought that his fallen comrade was going to puke from all the booze, but I knew differently. I knew that, hopefully, oxygenated blood was beginning to re-perfuse his brain and that he wouldn't stop breathing. And I knew that if I hadn't gotten up when I did, if backup hadn't arrived when it did, that I would have killed the guy.

I felt ill because of what could have happened. I felt relieved that I didn't take a life. Sure, it would have been an accident, but he didn't deserve to die. There's nothing that a man can say that makes him deserving of death. And there's little that a man can do to justify the same.

Getting smacked around a bit though, that's another story, I thought.

Silly as it may have been and though I knew better than to believe in spirits or angels, I thought that maybe Dave was looking out for me that night. I could hear his voice in my head quoting *Blazing Saddles* again:

"You've got to remember that these are just simple farmers. These are people of the land; the common clay of the New West. You know . . . morons."

"Davey, I hardly knew ye," I said, under my breath.

"What was that?" the punk kid asked.

"Don't worry about it," I answered.

"Officer, uh, what's going to happen to my brilliant friend over there?"

"I'm just gonna take him in for a four hour dry-out," I said. "Then he'll be let go with a citation."

"Oh good . . . I'm sorry for this. I shouldn't have let him get so fucked up. He's just been really depressed and stuff, lately."

"Well, I've got a little experience here that I won't go into, but it's not your call to make whether or not your buddy acts like an idiot. You can't be expected to stand by with somebody while they wreck themselves. Sometimes people change for the better, sometimes not."

Cue the after school special, I thought. *Inform the troops that the Dougie Cohen Memorandum of Mental Understanding has been finalized.*

I continued, "He'll call you when he's out of jail, in a few hours."

I started to turn and walk away when he asked one last question: "Hey, didn't you used to go out with that girl, what was her name . . . oh yeah, *Tessa*. I think we met at a show once. Didn't you used to go out with Tessa? She was hot!"

I smiled.

He went on, "I knew you looked familiar, wow. Are you still with her?"

I chuckled and told him, "No, you've got the wrong man." I walked over to the bag of food and picked it up. Matt and I still had a bunch of work to do and I knew he was hungry, just like I was.

I wouldn't want Speedy McSpeedspeed to go into hypoglycemic shock.

Just after recovering our dinners, I glanced at the front page story of the *San Francisco Times* through the dull plastic window of a newspaper box. The title: "Slain Officer May Have Violated Procedure, Times Investigates."

I didn't bother to read any more than that, I just shook my head and kept walking.

If one desires, one can second guess any tragedy; one can pick apart anything that doesn't turn out well. When doctors fuck up, they have "Morbidity and Mortality" conferences over pastries and coffee. When presidents screw the pooch, cabinet members are sacrificed on the pressroom's altar, their severed head portraits displayed for public shame in the little graphic windows next to a news anchor's head. When celebrities make mistakes, they check into rehab for a week, publicly apologize for whatever it was, and resume raking in millions and millions of dollars—not even counting the book royalties.

Our nation's longest war—that between lawlessness and order, pandemonium and pattern—has played out in the streets of our cities, towns and counties right in front of our eyes and for all to see. Our society's disgraceful acts and moments of incomprehensible heroism are matters of public record. Like the plight of soldiers overseas, elected officials, and our local sports teams, We the People second guess and lend armchair expertise to matters of law enforcement that we often know little about: such is the American Way.

And painful though it is to hear and read when it concerns what I do, and how I do it, I understand the necessity of scrutiny; I get paid to scrutinize. I'll change with the prevailing winds. I'll evolve, for as long as I'm able.

Until some asshole, or a relapse of some asshole's disease, takes me from this earth.

Those of us who took the oath to protect and serve will continue to fight and sometimes die, even though certain members the citizenry profess our perceived shortcomings and advocate our destruction.

We're used to it.

Twenty-four-seven, three-sixty-five: john-forty-two-david is still responding to knock on that apartment's door.

From behind me, the young hipster asked, "Really, man? I could have sworn that was you. Tessa's boyfriend looked a lot like you."

I walked back to the patrol car and said, "I'm just a cop."

The End